# BY THE WAY,
# I LOVE YOU

# BY THE WAY, I LOVE YOU

## SUSAN BETH MILLER

Boyle
&
Dalton

Book Design & Production:
Boyle & Dalton
www.BoyleandDalton.com

Song lyrics in Chapter 14 from "Lola" by Chris Smither.

Paperback ISBN: 978-1-63337-848-3
E-book ISBN: 978-1-63337-849-0

Printed in the United States of America
1 3 5 7 9 10 8 6 4 2

*In memory of Jeffrey*

# Part I

# Chapter 1

The door sticks, but I push through. When it swings closed, I get a weird feeling that no one could find me here behind this scratched gray metal. Oversized windows look out onto the courtyard. I want them open, even though it's an uber-gloomy day of bloated clouds that look like they want to spill snow in September. I hang my weight from the pull-cords so I can get the two-ton metal blinds to climb to the top. I have to lower and lift them two more times to get them right. I hate this darkness. It spikes a panicky feeling that I sweep away. Who feels like that when they've just arrived at college to have the time of their life?

Frankly, this room sucks. I imagine telling my high school friend Janey that its decorating theme is dust bunnies. I want to hear her great laugh. Her head bounces with happiness, and she looks at you like you're just the person to share the moment with.

The room has two skimpy beds against the side walls with their heads near the big window, a couple of desks and badly abused wooden dressers, and a postage stamp closet for each person, located close to the door. Everything's the right size for Alice after she nibbled a magic mushroom and shrank. The desk chairs have their backs to each other. There's a lonely feel to that, but at least no one will bother me if I'm studying or examining the scratches in the hospital-green wall paint. The furniture is lined up like train cars. I'm no designer, but even I could improve on this arrangement. I forgot to mention the scuffed, beige nightstand at the head of each bed, and the long-armed lamp screwed to the wall so neither I nor the mystery person soon to arrive will steal it.

I got a letter telling me my roommate is Ivori Ferguson. *Ivori* is more interesting than *Leslie,* for sure, though I have no clue how to pronounce it. Since I'm here first I have dibs on the beds, but I can't see any advantage one has over the other; it's pretty much eeny, meeny, miney, mo. So what do I do? *Go home,* passes through my head, but I shake that away, hard.

Home isn't exactly heaven. My dad is always working and has no discernible sense of humor. He's over-earnest; that's how I'd describe him. Home's neither a fun nor a happening place. And Dad is angry with me most of the time. Did I mention that? And you're not noticing any representatives from home here with me now.

I drift off into pondering the dreariness of hospital green. I think the institution affects the color, not the other way around. So any color you used would get ruined by the place. It's like when you know a dreadful person named Charlotte. The name is tainted ever after.

The door opens, and a mother and daughter wash in on a wave of giggles. So this is it. The roommate reveal. I take a breath.

"Oh, lovely," the woman says. "You must be Leslie. We've been so eager to meet you."

"Yeah," says the girl, but it's the mom who's flashing the enthusiasm.

"Yeah, hi," I say. "Nice to meet you, too." That line is for the presumed mother. They're looking around. The girl looks dazed.

"Hey, by the way, which bed do you want?" I'm trying to sound casual. A relaxed, go-with-the-flow individual. That's me.

"Oh," the mother says. "It's so nice of you to give us the choice." She glances between the beds, rapid as radar. I don't know what she sees that I can't, because she pronounces with certainty, "We'll take this one," as she points to the bed on the north side of the room.

She really does say, "we," not "Ivori," so I wonder if she's planning on moving in, too. The more the merrier. *Maybe she'll pick up the dust bunnies for us*, I think, but then I'm going, *Oh, shit*, because they're African American, and that's probably a racist asshole kind of thought, so I stuff it in the bin with other thoughts I've whooshed away.

I take another look at the beds. Maybe Ivori's mother spotted a grotesque sag in the mattress—the one that's mine now. Something seems unfair. They are a team, and I'm just me. Sure, my dad offered to come with me, but I suspected he was just honoring some parental code of child launching. Ivori's mom seems like she can't think of any place more heavenly to be. My own mother—how would she have been? I don't know.

I park my butt on my southside bed. I'd like to disappear and allow the jolly duo to enjoy each other, but I don't have anywhere to go. At the end of the hall, there's a common area with a scattering of chairs, but if the mom leaves and sees me idly seated there, she'll think I didn't want to hang with them. So I'm just here on the bed, taking up space like a Galapagos tortoise.

Finally, the mother says to Ivori, "Well, I should go and let you girls get acquainted." *Thank god.*

She gets her sweater and coat on, then winds on a mile-long scarf and goes with an unspoken *ta-ta.* I'm hoping Ivori will say *thank god* herself so I'll know her mom is a bit much for her and that she's glad to be on her own, but instead she's eyeing the door as if she's longing for her mother to sail back through. *Oh, fuck, a mama's girl.*

"How do you say your name?" I ask her.

"*e-VOR-e.*" She marks the syllable in the air with her index finger. Accent on the middle.

Lucky I asked. And lucky me to have a roommate with a name I have to practice in my head.

"Have you unpacked your stuff?" she asks me.

I shake my head.

"I hope I didn't bring too much," she says, focusing on her two red suitcases. They sit by the end of her bed like geographical features—Martian mountains in our otherwise bland room. They look expensive. I wonder if her family is wealthy, or maybe they just thought she merited something exceptional for going off to college. My graduation gift from my dad was money, plus that predictable Dr. Seuss book *Oh, the Places You'll Go!* A little lame.

"We've only got one dresser and a small closet each," Ivori says, her brow tightening.

"I didn't bring much."

"Where do you live? I forget." She seems restless, as if she's not sure whether she should unpack or run after her mom.

"Not far. In Saline, a nothing town near here. So I can get things if I need to."

She nods. "You're lucky. I'm from Cleveland. My mom's at the hotel now, but I'll see her later. You can come to dinner with us if you want. If you don't have any plans."

Plans. That's a joke. But *dinner* together. I'm not sure I want to go out with the tight twosome. That picture of Ivori peering at the door longingly is still in my mind. It is making me a little nauseous, to tell you the truth. I could yearn from now to forever, and no mother would walk through the door.

Ivori starts hanging her things in the closet. Something about her is awkward in our small space. Twice she bumps into the corner of her bed. She must have seen me watching her, because she says, "Macular pucker."

"Huh?"

"It's a retinal condition. It just affects one eye, but it screws up my depth perception. And balance."

"Sounds strange."

"A wrinkly membrane's growing over the center of my retina. Everything I see through that eye looks like it goes up- and downhill. Straight lines are wavy. Sucks for reading."

I realize I've puckered my lips in confusion and then stop because she might think I'm mocking her condition. I don't know what to say. I'm not used to people my age having conditions. "Does it bother you?"

"I have to be careful if I go out at night so I don't trip or fall down the stairs." She laughs as if she's tumbled down more than a few.

"We'll have to give you a curfew," I say with a grunt laugh. I notice I made a "we" out of her and me. *Is this where it begins?* I'm imagining life stretched out across a future where Ivori and I are friends. A bubble of excitement rises through me.

"It's bad," she says, "because I'm a night person. Are you a night person or a morning person?" She seems to be waking up as she's talking.

"Um...more of a midday person."

"I like to go out. Party."

I nod but am nervous, as if there is something I need to escape. I feel aware of my unkempt, vaguely brown hair. Do I look like someone you could go out and party with or someone you'd want to bail on?

She looks at me as if she's just now seen me. Her eyes hold mine. "We'll have fun."

"Do you like your name?" The question blurts out of me. "Y'know. Because it's different." I poke myself after speaking. How stupid to ask her that.

"Yeah, I do."

"You can tell me if I say something rude. My dad's usually the one to tell me, but since he's not here."

She clouds over. "My dad does some finance thing. Business. I don't see much of him."

She looks at me like she's waiting for something more and I think, *she knows*—about my mother. I give her a hard look until she drops her eyes. That shriveling stare makes me feel like my old self, and I say, "I'm going to check this place out. Find the mess hall and all that."

She grunts disapprovingly. "It's not a mess hall. You're not in the army."

I nod and I'm out the door, feeling the sting of her correction. Maybe she wanted to go exploring with me, but I feel like being on my own.

There's a turnstile at the entrance to the dining hall, and a perky girl is standing there doing something official. She sees me looking over from afar. "You can go in if you've got your meal card. And if you're hungry," she jokes, "because you can eat all you want."

I'm plenty hungry, and I'm ready to push through the metal contraption when the expression on Ivori's face materializes in front of my eyes. She was snippy in her mess hall retort. I caught a wilted look. She expected me to be pleased to go to dinner with her and her mom; instead, I'm up on my wheels and rolling out. Really, I want to go home. I don't know what I'm doing here. I don't know how to have a roommate and be considerate. I turn away from the girl whose smile is like a daylily sprung open, whose job it is to make everyone thrilled that they've come to eat in this generous cafeteria.

I dawdle my way back to my room, half hoping the food train has already pulled out and I'll be left alone to contemplate my social deficits. But Ivori is there, angling an arm through the sleeve of a cherry-red sweater. "Nice sweater," I say, but her face is firm; she won't be won over so easily. "You go out yet?"

She shakes her head.

"Could I still go?"

"You want to?"

I nod. I've turned on the light of happiness in her face. I'm not eager to go, but okay, I undid some of the damage. Maybe there's hope for me.

Mrs. Ferguson takes us to the Earle, which is fancy, but I don't stand out too badly. We're at a rectangular table where I'm sitting across from them. Suddenly I'm starving, and the pasta and chicken taste amazing, so I don't have to fake being happy. I'm afraid Mrs. Ferguson may look at me and think, *My, this girl is piggy*. But Mrs. Ferguson has a healthy appetite of her own, and Ivori, too.

Mrs. F. is asking me a lot of questions about my hometown and my school interests, but she's steering clear of the mother situation. Since I'm feeling well-fed and more congenial, I finally say, "My mother died from cancer a couple years ago." Mrs. F. is highly sympathetic, and Ivori, too, but thank god they don't act like I'm the first person in the universe ever to lose a parent. The conversation moves on from my mother.

"I'm an opera singer," Mrs. Ferguson tells me. "I travel quite a bit."

Ivori is leaning closer to her mother; I think she might put her head on her mom's shoulder, as if she'd like to go along when her mother is gallivanting from opera house to opera house.

Who on earth is an *opera singer?* I know nothing about opera, but I ask her about foreign cities she's visited and which ones she likes. As she's talking about Vienna and Bucharest, I'm getting enthused to see those places. Ivori looks like she's heard about old cities all her life and finds them yawn-worthy and she'd just like her mom to stay home and chill in our room. I'll need a crowbar to pry them apart, and I get irritable and imagine myself in hand-cuffs as a crowbar-wielding, crazed freshman. Mrs. Ferguson keeps up her conversation with me, but glances repeatedly at Ivori, as if to say, "I'm really with *you*, my love, but I'm being polite to your roommate." My feet circle below the table—one clockwise and the other counterclockwise so that they meet in the middle and bump each other.

Luckily, we have to leave because Mrs. Ferguson has an early flight to some opera venue the next morning. Mentioning her departure, she and Ivori exchange a D-minor sonata of glances. They are two fingers covered in super glue trying to pull apart, and I'm about ready to jump up and overturn the table from all this affection. I can't wait to be in my pajamas in bed, facing the wall.

In bed that night, I go to recheck my class schedule for the third time, but I can't find my phone. I start to panic. It has to be here somewhere. Except it's not. "Shit."

"What?" Ivori says.

I look over at her. "I can't find my phone. I looked everywhere. I don't have it."

"You're positive?"

"A hundred percent."

"Shit. Where could it be?" She's looking up from her papers now.

"The restaurant? I think my backpack was open and I might have kicked it over."

"The restaurant's closed by now. Maybe call your dad."

"Uh, not an option."

"He's not dead too, is he?" She asks in a tone of quiet terror, as if she'll have no idea what to say if both my parents are dead.

"He's alive, but he's not exactly president of the Leslie fan club at the moment."

"Still, couldn't he help?"

I shrug my shoulders. "Don't worry about it. I'll handle it."

"You know what," she says. "I'll call my mom. She loves solving problems. She'll figure out how to reach the owner of the restaurant, even though it's closed, and have them get out of bed and Uber it to the dorm or something random like that."

"Thanks, but I'll just go over there and get it tomorrow."

Ivori frowns. "You don't have a car. And you have classes."

"I'm not helpless," I say, and suddenly feel awash in irritation. I want to say, *Just leave me the fuck alone*, or another of the fine phrases that has taken me off my dad's most-favorite-people list.

"Whatever," Ivori says. She clutches her book with both hands and yawns.

I'm left marinating in my awareness that I can't stand to have people help me. I get that her feelings are hurt, but I am like that wall our stupid once-president wanted to build: I'm not allowing any alien goodwill to trespass here.

I lie in bed, sure now that there's a lump in my mattress under my right rib cage, or maybe the lump is in my breast, which is an even scarier thought. I'm trying to figure out how I'll get my phone, irked by the image of Mrs. Ferguson flying to the rescue. I wonder if my own mom would have done that. Some days, I can barely remember her, except for random video clips that pop into my brain.

I hardly thought about college before I came here. Other kids talked about it incessantly, aggravating me. I figured I'd just show up. When I did think about it for a minute or two, I imagined being a different person. Starting over. A blank slate. But here I am. Same old Leslie in a new, lumpy bed. Without a phone.

# Chapter 2

With no phone, I'm left to find my classes using the paper campus map that blares *freshman*. The US history class is decent, but the psychopathology teacher annoys me. It's obvious he loves putting people into little compartments, checking off their symptoms or pathological traits. I guess he doesn't have any of those weirdo traits himself so he can be smug. I see him scrutinizing the class, wondering, *Which of you fit into which of my boxes?* I'm tempted to stare him down. I am exceptionally good at that. It usually makes people think twice about messing with me. All morning, I am preoccupied because I need my phone. My hands don't know what to do with nothing to hold. I try not to wiggle my fingers in the air. I flex my toes instead. I remember that the restaurant is the Earle but don't know how to get back there. I could get a Lyft, but I don't have my phone to call one.

To get to the biology building for my noon Botany 101 class, I have to walk across the Diag in the center of campus. A bunch of kids are just hanging out there, and others hurry through like me, books or laptops clutched to their chests. I'm sure none of them are stupid enough to be walking around without their phone, wondering how they will reunite with it.

Suddenly, I see myself in my denim jacket, fast-stepping across the Diag, and I think, *You're in college.* I'm torn between feeling giddy-excited and panicking because I don't have a clue what I'm doing. I try to hang onto that first feeling. I only slightly know exactly one human on this campus and her mother is an opera singer and possibly somewhat pretentious. The freak-out feelings are surging, but I manage to spot the brick building with white side columns that is the bio building. It is such an odd assemblage of architectural elements that I feel well put-together in comparison. *Just go sit and listen to the teacher,* I advise myself. *Pretend he's a meditation app.* That much I know how to do.

The instructor is a young, very pale and serious man named Mr. Matz. He has barely brown hair, faint eyebrows, and a soft voice. Everything about him is mild. He brings to mind those white button mushrooms you buy refrigerated at the grocery.

He starts out with some basics about plant parts. I think he wants us to establish a vocabulary so he can talk later about sepals and tepals and such and not have to define everything. I see right away how much of a plant's concern is reproduction. Some of them have landing strips painted on their blossoms so a bee or moth can find the pollen and do the plant's bidding. He claims that some even know what time a bee will visit, so lift up their anthers; I may have to google that to believe it. I wonder if all this plant erotica ever embarrasses a shy guy like Mr. Matz.

After the lecture, all one hundred of us stand, our shoved chairs creating a subdued roar. We are plants unfolding from within a seed and reaching up for some photosynthesis. As I put on my jacket, I spot a kid I recognize across the room and startle. Thanh. I didn't really *know* him in high school; he is just this kid who was in some of my classes. Sometimes I'd notice him because he'd say something funny that you could barely hear, but if you did hear you might spout a laugh. Since he isn't a total stranger like everyone else in the universe, I drift over to him. I don't decide to. I just do it, like a cloud slides across the moon.

"Hi," I say. "I think I know you. From Saline High. Right?"

Weird. He hardly knows me, but he is a wall-to-wall smile. *Jesus*, I think. *I'm not the reincarnation of your dead grandmother. I just know you from our lame high school.*

"You're Leslie."

Shit. He knows my name. He didn't even say it with a question in his voice.

"I heard you were coming to U of M, too," he says. "There are five of us."

I picture myself in a room with all those high school kids and start to sweat. The last thing I need is a high school reunion. "Well, anyway," I say. "Just thought I'd say hello—not be rude or whatever—since I semi-know you."

"We should get Starbucks or bubble tea or something. Compare notes. Hey, do you like this class? I'm a botany nerd, so it's just what I love. So do you want to go somewhere, catch up?"

"To tell you the truth, I have to go back to the dorm and take a nap. These dorm beds aren't the greatest." Sometimes I wonder about how easily I lie. But I'm hoping he isn't going to become like cling wrap or something, just because I said hi and we went to our bullshit high school together. I sigh this incredibly deep sigh, pulling up air from my toes and huffing it all out.

"I've got a car," he says. "We could drive someplace."

A car. *Epiphany*. "Hey, there's a restaurant. I actually left something there. It's kind of fancy, but I guess we could get coffee there." I feel around in my back jeans pocket for my map and in the vain hope my phone has materialized. The map's in tatters, and my mind starts jamming on "I Fall to Pieces"—a hyper-dramatic old song—and it is so loud in my head that I half-wonder if Thanh can hear it. *Don't be a lunatic,* I tell myself. That is my form of personal reassurance, in case you can't tell. I don't actually need the map, because he of course has a phone with GPS, unlike some people.

I am as impressed with Thanh's car as if he had a rocket ship. Nobody my age has a car. Thanh sees me examining its insides and says, "It's kind of weird to have a car, but it's important to my parents. Immigrants made good, that kind of thing."

"Where are they from?"

"Here. But my grandparents are from Vietnam."

At the Earle, the hostess seems excited to be the agent of a person-device reunification. She hands me my phone in its worn purple case, and the endorphins flowing through me make me a little bit grateful, if not friendly, to Thanh. I get black coffee and he gets a latte. "So, you get off on botany?" I ask him.

He tells me he googled all the nature preserves and parks in Ann Arbor before he came. He is excited that there are so many. He wants to explore every one. "This afternoon, I'm going to Bird Hills."

"I don't know anything about birds, but I'm into butterflies." I once decorated a hoodie with fabric paint, and it cartwheels into my mind. I wrote *See you later, pollinator* on it, because I was upset about what is happening to monarchs. My mother was sick then. She was getting ready to die.

I am afraid Thanh can tell I am a million miles away. He puts his elbows on the table and leans in and says, "You should go with me to the park."

Some mental quicksand has oozed up all around me. It makes me fear my own company, so I say, "Yeah, I'll go. Only for a while because I have a shitload of homework already."

Back in the car, I'm thinking about some crappy things happening in this country that make it seem less than desirable and ask, "Why'd your grandparents come here?" I know about the Vietnam War, but not enough to support a conversation.

"My grandfather was a translator for the Americans in the war. Afterwards, the army got him and my grandmother out of the country, though some other relatives had to escape in small boats. I'll tell you sometime how he got to be a translator. You said you were taking psychology, right?"

"Yeah. Though not loving it."

"It's a psychological story."

"Then tell me."

"Everyone expected him to be a fisherman like his parents, but whenever he got in a boat, he'd throw up. Finally, his parents agreed to let him go to guide school and learn English, which is what he wanted all along. His family was sure he'd fail as a guide because of the motion sickness. How could he go in a bus or boat? But once he started school, the motion sickness vanished. He told me that God gave him motion sickness so he could follow his dream. That always made him laugh. In the war, though, there were opportunities for translators, and he'd learned English by then, so the Americans hired him."

"He told you all that?"

"We spent a lot of time together."

I barely know my father's parents. I never knew my mother's parents at all. I have no idea why. My Swiss cheese family, full of holes.


Not many birds are in evidence at Bird Hills, but there are plenty of hills. We trek up and down, trying not to get lost on the twisty trails. Thanh knows all the trees just from their bark. We keep stopping for him to point out some botanical fact or another, and I relax and take everything in. I marvel that I'm in college and off in a nature preserve with a guy. My dad gets worried about my antisocial tendencies. Today, he has no idea at all what I'm doing. I wonder if it's the first day in my life that that's true. Then I remember the summer I went to sleepaway camp. I have a box somewhere with letters from that summer. I never look at them, though.

Thanh shows me a small tree just off the side of the trail. A skinny nothing, not full-grown. He runs his hand up its light gray bark and says, "Musclewood. Feel it. It has long ridges like muscles. Once you know it, you can't mistake it. *Carpinus caroliniana.*"

I start to make a joke about it being scrawny for a muscle tree, but he loves the tree so I don't diss it. He turns and points to another tree, this one with ragged, peeling bark. "They're relatives," he says. "Hornbeam and hop-hornbeam—a.k.a. ironwood. Which do you like more?"

"That's presumptuous."

"I love everything here."

It's hard not to absorb some of Thanh's happy energy. "So, if I were growing here and had roots in the soil, I guess you would love me?" Where in heck that came from, I couldn't tell you. Luckily, we are outside in the chilly air, and he can't see me blushing.

"I would." He is looking right at me with his black coffee eyes.

I get this impulse to kiss him quickly on the lips. I feel like turning him on, showing him what I can do with a hit-and-run kiss. I keep my mouth shut though. I've kissed about three boys in my seventeen years, and just at parties. Enough to know it's no big deal.

I have my head tucked down, but he can see something on my face. "What?" he asks me, his eyes big.

I want to kiss this cute guy all over. No more playing. But for some reason, that makes me mad. "Nothing," I say. I feel guilty, though, for messing with his brain.

He takes me home. In the car in front of my dorm, he gets quiet for a while, then says, "Leslie, I remember when your mom died. We all felt bad for you." I nod. He adds, "You seemed pretty lost for a while."

I don't like people spotting my vulnerabilities. *Undressed* is the word that comes to me, and it's an unfortunate one because it's interwoven with literal nakedness. I'm half-undone by this nerdy, sweet plant geek. I'm mocking myself, too. Just pay me a blink of attention and I'll fall at your feet. Just gift me the name of a few undernourished tree specimens. He looks at me with an I-want-to-kiss-you gaze that whooshes me out of his car.

I climb the stairs and walk down the hall to my room. It is weird not to know if the room will be empty or if Ivori will be there. Nor do I know which condition I prefer.

The room is a cubicle of empty air. I need a nap, and the bed is issuing a siren call. I lie down there and sigh for a minute about the homework I need to do tonight and about what I briefly wanted to do to Thanh's well-constructed body, which is much more muscular than the trees he loves. Then I fall asleep in a curl.

# Chapter 3

Drum music comes through my earphones and fills me up 100 percent. The number 100 hangs in the air, then flips over so it is 001, and then changes to 000. It floats in front of me like a Frisbee, frozen in flight. The zeroes scare me, but I think I know how to play the drums and that uplifts me. I am banging away confidently on the tight skins, keeping the rhythm going. I flip the sticks in the air and catch them a hundred times like a juggler. Then I *am* the flipping sticks, and I'm upside down in the air among 100s and 000s.

The scene changes, and I am a train, and I hear the sound a train makes hurtling over the tracks. I see a dark tunnel ahead, and I'm scared but going so fast I instantly barrel inside the tunnel where the sound reverberates. The tunnel goes on forever, and my fear surges, and then I'm the sound itself, and I'm the vibrations of the tracks. The world seems like it might break apart from violent shaking, and it's too much for me. I wake up. "Woah, shit," I say into the hazy light. I'm grateful I'm awake. I try to shake off the dream and settle the vibrations inside me. I lie there in what my high-school English teacher called "the gloaming," but I call "the glooming."

My psychology professor, Dr. Drenim, has a bristly mustache that he likes to comb with his finger, which is repulsive and makes me think of running a flea comb through a dog. This morning, he assigned us to analyze one of our dreams like we're Freud. What is he up to? All I know is that I'm not eager for him to see inside my head—we may as well pin tags on our foreheads with red letters highlighting our mental conditions. I think of that professor reading my dream and I am creeped out. *Fuck your privacy,* is apparently his attitude. I guess I'll be inventing a dream. See if he can spot a fake. If he does, I'll be a sociopath in his book.

Ivori walks in. She sheds her laptop, backpack, and phone onto her bed as if she's been hiking up a mountain all day.

I'm sitting cross-legged on my bed, and I slide my eyes toward her. "Beat?"

"You have dinner yet?"

"Sleeping. Having weird dreams."

"Because you're in a new place."

"I'm supposed to do a dream analysis for my psych class, but I'm going to make mine up. Why should Dr. Drenim know what I'm dreaming?"

"I'll help you. I'm creative."

Snarkily, I think, *You would be—daughter of an opera singer.* But I don't know what I'm doing with this assignment, so maybe I could benefit from creative input.

She brightens. "My art class is so fabulous. I have a million things I want to make."

I give her a cross-eyed look. Her mind is brimming while mine is a desert.

"C'mon," she says. "I'm starved. Let's get out of here." She thinks it's natural we should go to dinner together. She's an energy wave now so I just get up and go with her. Walking down the hall, I'm self-conscious about the expressions coming and going on my face as we run into people I don't know. I paste on *stern,* my default expression.

We fill up our plates. Since it costs the same whatever you eat, I get roasted chicken legs, a baked potato with six things to go inside it, a roll, a salad of corn and beans, a green salad with croutons, and creamy coleslaw, plus a few other miscellaneous things. Ivori apparently knows where she wants to sit, so I follow her to a table near a wall that's all windows. There's only a wisp of western light left, but there's a salmon-colored streak sandwiched like lunch meat between two dark gray clouds, and it's pretty.

"Look," I say. I figure Ivori the art student might like it.

"Totally," she says, but her focus is on her mountain of food. I wonder if her mother would approve of her sucking up food like a vacuum cleaner. Even though she seems like she's paying no attention, between bites she says, "Let's do your dream."

I sigh. "A dream can be anything, right? So you can't exactly do a bad job making one up."

She nods emphatically between mouthfuls of a dinner roll packed with butter and honey. I should have put honey on mine.

"I took a walk in the woods today with this kid, Thanh, who I know—slightly—from high school. Maybe a woodsy dream."

"Good place to start. Put in some sex, though. Keep your prof entertained. You'll get an A for arousal." She laughs.

"Maybe plant sex. We were in the woods. Thanh is into all things nature."

Ivori nods. "I can see it. Two giant vines are intertwining as they grow. Then they start to grow together up an enormous tree."

29

"They should be poison ivy," I say. "To give a sinister note."

"If it were my dream, I'd make them poison *ivori*, but that probably wouldn't work for yours."

"Hmm. It could work. You're my roommate."

She looks at me. "It will sound like you have a horror movie roommate."

I shrug. "It's only a dream." In a dream paper, you don't have to resolve anything. No proving a thesis, just lay some ideas and images out there and the rest is up to the reader. How can you get a bad grade?

"I'm willing to sacrifice myself," she says. "But if we run into your Professor Dream on campus—"

"Drenim."

"You can introduce me as 'Jet' or something, so he won't connect me with the dream."

I laugh. "I'll keep that in mind."

"We've got it," she says, "a dream masterpiece." She hasn't made it to her desserts yet but puts down her fork long enough to high-five me.

We stuff our faces in silence for a while. The next time she gives her fork a rest, she asks, "Who's Thanh?"

"Just a guy from high school."

"You two hook up?"

I'm possibly blushing. "I barely know him."

She shrugs. "Is he cute?"

"He's all right. He's into botany."

"Cool. Nothing wrong with plants. And as we explored in your dream, plants have sex, too."

"There weren't any monarchs in the woods," I say, frowning.

"Even though it's migration time."

"Apropos of what?" Ivori says.

I shrug.

For a couple days after that, I'm not in the mood to talk with Ivori. I'm taking a break from sociability. On Monday, I listen to seventies music on my oversized squishy headphones, then do a whole lot of reading for English and history and learn some plant parts for Mr. Matz. Dr. Dream has moved on to themes embedded in dreams. Every example he gives is about someone lost to the dreamer. A boyfriend they broke up with or, of course, a dead parent. Those seem to be everywhere you turn in psychology. I'm relieved he won't get much out of my dream if he turns his nosy eye—LOL—on it. I made it up, and it isn't even a solo effort. It's written by committee.

# Chapter 4

A week of classes rolls by. The weather is damp and colorless. Fallen leaves paper the ground, each one hosting its own puddle. They stick to my shoes, so I track them into the dorm. A homey feeling about this place comes and goes. Ivori and I have bursts of esprit but days, too, when we are like strangers or she feels like an irritant in my space, and not one that will give rise to a pearl. This afternoon, classes done, I'm not eager to go back to the green chamber. Thanh keeps texting me. I text him back, but so far I haven't agreed to meet up. I disappeared into the throng after our last class, before he could catch up with me. I get that I'm running away—from this guy, from Ivori—but can't seem to help it. I try to put on the brakes and wheel around, face the people in this new world, but something makes me squirrelly.

When Ivori pushes through the door, I am in a headstand pose against the wall. It's an emergency measure for a collapsing mood. She's a drowned dog sputtering with complaint, cold and sopping. I keep my feet against the wall as she offloads her stuff onto her bed.

"What are you doing?" she asks.

"Nothing," I say from upside-down land.

"You're being strange."

I drop down harder than I want, clapping my feet against the floor. "Thank you."

"Not a compliment."

"I'm taking it as one." I return to my bed and sit in the center, my back holding the stiffness from the headstand.

"Okay," she says. "Take it as one. But I don't get you."

I wish I could vaporize. I hear the question in what she's said. I should explain myself, but I have no idea what to say. So I keep quiet and hope she'll drop it or segue into something friendly. I wish she'd say something so funny I can't help but laugh. Instead, she says, "My mother says to just be nice to you even when you're going off the rails. She thinks you might be lonely." She softens now. Her voice cradles a question. "Because you lost your mother."

I mutter, "Your mother is nosy," but don't look up from my lap. She's telling me about her mother, and I should tell her about mine. She's halfway asking and not in a rude way. But I wouldn't know what to say. The memories I have aren't the best.

I see my father looking at me with tragic pity, as if I'm a sandcastle too close to the water. He says, *Your mother is very sick.* There's a rumble of faraway thunder like when you're reading and you don't know you've heard anything until someone sitting next to you asks, "Did you hear that?"

*Your mother is ill, Leslie.*

Ivori is waiting still. Watching me. I look down and see my breasts like soft hills under my tee shirt. The left one is bigger than the right. There is a beauty mark between them, and it is hard to say if it is closer to the right or the left. I've studied it closely—its colors, its edges, its diameter, its symmetry—because I read that beauty marks can turn to cancer. I measured it to see if it was dangerously large and shined a light on it to see if it had jagged edges or blotchy colors.

Once, I measured the distance from my lip to my nose because I read in a magazine what the ideal measurements should be, and I panicked since my distance was long. I will have to live my whole life with this body, I thought, and my lips will never be any closer to my nose than they are now. I kept bouncing off the future and wondering if I would feel safe there. And now I don't.

Ivori says, "My mother is a Christian. She believes in giving people the benefit of the doubt."

I hope Ivori can't see I'm shaken up. "Apparently I require that."

"You do. It would be nice if you would have a conversation with me sometime."

"What do you want to talk about?" I'm trying to sound sarcastic, but my voice is shrinking into nothing.

"I don't know." She throws up her hands like she's about to give a downbeat to an orchestra. "Lightning bugs? Underwear? The Big Bang? Anything."

"I'm sorry, but I have homework to do." I'm showing her my sharp edges. I can't help it. It's the only place I can go. To hide. If I don't go there, I'll burst into tears and be a melted ice cube on the floor.

"You always have homework to do. You're the world's best-prepared student."

Tuesday afternoon, we're both studying—lying on our beds on our stomachs with our feet up in the air. There's a knock on the door, and Ivori opens it and glances at me. It's Thanh. I give him a *what the fuck* look because I didn't give him permission to come to my dorm room. At the same time, something in me is enormously glad to see his warm face.

He looks one hundred percent embarrassed. "What?" I say, poking at him.

"I brought you a botany ID book that I thought might help with the homework. I got it when I was learning plants, and it helped me out. A lot."

That's a lame reason to stop by uninvited, but I take the book from him. I glance around and see Ivori giving me this knowing look, so I mouth to her, *What?*

"I should go," Thanh says. "I just wanted to drop that off. Wasn't planning to stay or anything."

After he leaves, Ivori says, "Thanh's so cute. Have you slept with him yet?"

"You're out of your mind," I tell her. "We're not even friends."

"So what? He seems nice. It would be fun." She lifts her eyebrows like the Zilwaukee Bridge.

I shrug. I can't think of anything cutting to say. I don't know if it would be fun to sleep with him. Maybe it would be awful. Can I say that to her? I haven't ever slept with a boy. Ivori apparently has. Maybe quite a few of them, from the way she's talking. I'm confused and stay silent until she goes back to her books. I feel cold just looking out the window and wish I had that old black hoodie I decorated. I must have brought it. Right? I dig through my dresser. No hoodie. I feel Ivori's eyes on me again, questioning me. She had the weirdest expression on her face when she was talking about all that fun I could have, so I don't know what's up with her. She sounded wistful, or is *wishful* the word? Either one works. It's five o'clock. My dad gets home from work at five. I grab my phone and order an Uber.

"I have to go home and get something," I say to Ivori. Maybe I'll never come back.

"Lucky you," she says. "Home's just an Uber away." Tension crackles in her voice. I recall her and her mom braided together like the vines in our faux dream. I hope she isn't going to cry.

"Leslie. Good god. What a surprise. You should have called. What if I wasn't here?"

I hear twenty things in what my dad is saying. He's not glad to see me. I shocked him. I shrug and say, "I have a key. If you weren't here, I'd use it."

"Yeah, but…"

"I know, you want to see me."

Even though he nods, I don't believe it. I don't think my dad forgives me for the past.

"I just need to get my butterfly hoodie. Okay? Because it's getting cold."

"I remember that hoodie." He has a glazed expression, as if he's looking back through a time machine into ancient history. "Well, come in. Do you want some dinner, Les? I could rustle something up. Maybe a meatball sandwich?"

I shake my head. "I'll eat in the dorm. It's paid for, you know."

He laughs. "Well, yeah. Who do you think pays for it?"

A predictable Dad statement. I'm not falling for it.

"Well, go get your hoodie then, if that's what you're after."

I go into my old room and start rustling around in my pine dresser. Suddenly, all that's here in this house is my mother and what happened to her. And I'm sure my father hates me because I wasn't kind to her when she was sick. Maybe not *ever*, though my memories from earlier are like islands in a sea of fog.

He told me she was sick, so the next time she came to my door, I squinted and gave her a hard look-over. *Nothing.* My dad can be a drama queen, so I figured that was the point of the sickness story. Probably his way of saying, *Be nicer to your mother, Leslie.* And yeah, she was bugging me around that time, and I was ragging on her some. But I was a teenager. What did they want from me?

But she was actually sick. She called for me one night. I didn't want to go see her in her bed. It was a hospital room in there. The stale smell and clutter. But she called and called, so I had to go. I went and stood at the door, my face a gray wall. "What?" I asked her.

"I just wanted to see you."

"Okay. You've seen me."

When I was back in my room, I replayed how she'd straightened her nightgown because it was twisted and tight around her knees. She combed back her hair with the spread fingers of both hands and tugged at the shoulder straps of her nightgown as if every minor thing was making her uncomfortable and she needed a nurse to straighten her out in the bed. But she got settled and patted her breast affectionately.

She'd attended to that same body, that same frizzy hair that curled over her forehead, for all the years of her life. She knew how her breasts fell against her chest and maybe—who knows—how they'd sagged more over time. She knew if one was bigger than the other like mine and if there was a beauty mark that had turned to cancer in between. And she knew whether she liked having them and liked being a woman—which I don't.

When I first saw that my right breast was bigger, I freaked out and wanted to ask her, *Is that normal? Is it because I'm right-handed?* But I didn't ask. My mother had a way of drifting off to a faraway place. She looked contented there, wearing a little Mona Lisa smile, like she was floating on a raft on a warm day with a delicious iced lemonade in her hand. I didn't want to pull her out of that place with a question and see the smile blink off and a look of tension replace it. So I looked up the thing about breasts. As it turns out, there is a bias toward the opposite side—a bigger left breast for a right-handed person. So I deviate from the norm. And my mother? Was she like that, too, which would make me less weird?

That same week I learned about her cancer was the week I read about monarch butterflies. They were crashing. Millions were dying or not reproducing because there is no milkweed, and they need that plant. Someone posted a picture of a monarch with half its wing eaten away. Probably it didn't have enough energy to get away from what was chasing it. It looked pitiful.

The next week, I saw Mom weeding the garden. It was July, and the air felt like it could birth a thunderstorm any minute. She was wearing a blue-and-pink skirt and a wide-brimmed straw hat. She looked like a mother in a picture book.

"What are you doing?" I punched her with my words.

"I'm weeding the garden."

"That's milkweed you're pulling. Don't you know that? Monarchs *need* milkweed."

"Do they need this particular plant, honey? There's a whole patch by the garage and another clump in the backyard. It's squeezing out the lovely phlox here. Have you smelled them, Les? They're heavenly. And the hydrangeas are blooming. So gorgeous."

"They need *every* plant. They don't have nearly enough."

I could see her wanting to sigh because I was being so difficult, but she didn't. "All right, then. I will leave it if you feel so strongly about it."

"It's not about how I *feel*. It's about reality and all the stupid people who don't care."

She stood up slowly, uncramping herself because she'd been kneeling for a long time. She looked like an old lady with arthritis. "I guess that would include me," she said with a tiny sad laugh.

I wanted to say, *Guess so*, but I kept that to myself. Also, *You're supposed to be sick, so what are you doing out in the garden on your hands and knees?* I shut that up, too. I imagined lightning slicing up the sky, the rain falling in sheets.

I spot the lettering on the half-buried hoodie and dig it out. It still looks good. Not too worn. Having it gives me comfort. It's a touchstone, I guess. It was the next morning, after the milkweed incident, that I'd had the idea for the sweatshirt. I sketched the butterfly on a big piece of paper. Then I drew it on the back of the hoodie with pale blue tailor's chalk before I painted it with orange fabric paint. I let the black show through where I wanted the dark lines of the monarch to be. In orangey-red I wrote above the butterfly, *See you later, pollinator.* I thought that was very clever, though it's possible I saw it on some website or ad and filched it.

A few kids in a summer-school class I was taking gave me compliments. Not just the nerdy kids like *moi*—other kids, too. Everyone liked it. I bet Thanh was one of those kids and feeling sorry for me. Which I hate.

After that, I started painting butterflies on big pieces of brown wrapping paper. All kinds and colors, not just monarchs. I got totally into it and stayed up night after night, painting them in every size. My idea was to cover my entire room—ceiling and all—in a wallpaper of butterflies. I saw a YouTube of a migration of painted-lady butterflies—an endless river of them, so fucking beautiful. I wanted my room to be like that. Just the opposite of the dying monarchs, it would be butterflies everywhere you looked, as if you were set down in the middle of their migration, or you were one of them floating and flapping through the air, not a stupid human stuck in one place.

I was taping them on the walls when he started yelling for me. How was I supposed to hear when my back was to the door, and I was on the tips of my toes on a wobbly chair taping a sunshine-yellow butterfly to the ceiling? Not to mention that the crinkling of the paper was right up against my ears like waves crashing. Later, my father said, "We were calling you." He had that we're-so-disappointed-in-you look on his face, white as a winter sky. "Don't you realize your mother is sick? I wish you could spend a little time with her."

"I'm kind of busy right now."

"Some things are important enough that you do them even if you're busy." He glanced upstairs to where she was, and that's when the blackness really walloped me. I practically flew out of the house. It was summer and warm and bright out, and I needed to hear that door slam behind me. I needed to inhale the outdoor air.

He's downstairs now, probably waiting for me. I don't like imagining his anger. I was floating on an inner tube in a water park lazy river once, and they had to stop the whole river to rescue this girl who got caught in an eddy. They flipped a switch and turned off the river. I wish I had a switch to turn off his anger. I gather up my bits of courage and stick them together to make something solid enough to get me down the stairs, then I walk into the living room with the hoodie over my arm.

My dad is hanging around as if he's in a stranger's house and doesn't know where to sit. I wish he'd settle down and become someone you could talk to, someone who has nothing else to do and wants to talk with you because you're his daughter.

"You sure you don't want something to eat before you go?" he says.

It pisses me off the way he has to emphasize *before you go,* as if he can't wait to get rid of me. "You don't have to be so obvious."

"What are you talking about, Leslie? I'm lost."

"Oh, nothing, Dad. It's just that you're always angry with me. It's glaring."

"Really? I am? I wasn't aware."

"C'mon Dad. Let's not be so phony baloney. You're restless as all get out." This isn't the conversation I had in mind. I'm heading right into an argument. Need to turn off that river. Regroup. Just ask him about things. How they were with my mom. Just talk.

He's tapping the top of his head with his open palm in a weird way. "Well, truth be told, Leslie, I am expecting some company. It's a woman. I'm doing a little dating. Nothing serious, honey."

Oh my god. I was working just to manage one sluggish branch of the river and now the current has pulled me toward the Class-V rapids. "What? Fuck. You're dating? How long has it even been since Mom died? And you don't even say a word about this. Great. Just great."

"I wish I had said something. I should have, but I fell into this. It's nothing serious. I've been a little lonely, losing your mom, and now you're off at school. I barely talk to you, and you're of course making your own friends. New friends. As you should."

If I wasn't already flattened, those words would have struck me down. I think of Ivori and how she couldn't even look at me when I was leaving today. That's how great a job I'm doing making friends. I drop my pack and pull off my denim jacket, then pull on the hoodie.

"You probably don't even miss Mom," I say.

"I don't know why you'd say that. I miss her every day."

"For two minutes, I guess." I feel half-panicked because this new person might show up any minute. I need to get out of there.

"Hey, I remember when you made that hoodie," he says. I hear him trying to reboot the conversation. He's affecting an upbeat tone, but I'm sure he's thinking of me painting and taping things in my room instead of spending time with Mom.

"Not like you offered to help."

His face folds up. "Why do you have to make everything so negative?" He is practically shouting.

I shrug. "It's who I am." I add, "live with it," like I'm twelve, and go out the door. I'll call an Uber from out of sight in case the mystery woman appears. Probably a bitch or a diva I definitely don't want to meet.

The Uber driver is an older guy with black curls that belong on a baby, not an old dude. He's got me behind a plexiglass shield as if we were still deep in Covid, or maybe he's afraid his passengers are going to shoot him. I don't want to talk to him anyway. I'm stewing about my dad's secret woman. He's been hiding her from me. Thanh loves Latin names and told me about a plant named *obscura* something. Something about lungs. *Pulmonaria obscura.* That was it. I tried to guess the obscura part. Hidden, unclear. Dark, Thanh corrected. Dad's *donna obscura.*

I can't wait to get to my room now and lie on that crappy bed and close my eyes.

# Chapter 5

This week, we have a visiting lecturer in psychopathology. This guy's different from the regular instructor. Dr. Drenim—*Dr. Dream,* per Ivy—puts people into closed boxes; this other professor thinks everyone's a box to open, and what's inside is as exciting as a kid's Christmas gift. He tells us our memories of early life are packed with meaning. I hope they're not like a jack-in-the-box where everything can burst out to smack you in the face. Thank God, he doesn't have us tell the whole class our private memories. He's respectful that way.

I wander back to my dorm around noon, dredging for memories. I'm at a house with other little kids. I knock on one of the bedroom doors. Then I'm pounding, because some kids are in there with the door shut, and I want to get in, to play with them. My mom shakes her head and says, "Have some pride, Leslie. Don't try to go where you're not wanted," and woah—I stop banging. Why did I instantly stop? My shrink self says that she stated, as a fact, the thing I wanted to escape. I was longing for them to fling open that door and say, "Oh, Leslie's here, how great, we want Leslie to come in and play with us." But my mom was saying, "They have all the people they want in there. If they wanted you, you'd be inside already." I stopped as if that door was burning hot. Why would my mom say that? Paint that picture of people who don't want me? I have an answer in mind, but I don't like it. I don't even want to think it. I'm so deep in my thoughts that I walk right past my dorm, barely aware of the October chill, then I turn back and press 'eject' on that memory.


At lunch with Ivori, I evaluate everything we're eating then speculate about who might have prepared it—a skinny guy with green frog-skin who sweats into the soup, an anorexic girl who can't stand to eat what she cooks, an old lady whose gray curls are escaping her hair net. I feel Ivori getting exasperated with me, but I won't lay off. She turns her attention to our neighbors, Karen and Junie. She told me they're too Abercrombie for her, but I guess they're less annoying than me. For some reason, I want to double down on my pestering, so I start to goad her about her name being weird.

We usually race each other up to our room, but today we trudge like people crossing the Arctic wilderness. She says in an uber sarcastic tone, "You're even more disagreeable than usual today."

She's ahead of me so she can't see me shrug. I mutter, "What of it?"

"You need psychoanalysis. My mother had it, and she said it gave her insight into her dark corners."

I'm not in the mood for Ivori's mother to nosedive into our conversation. And Ivori sometimes could use a little psychological polishing herself. Every time I turn around, she and Mrs. Ferguson are gabbing on the phone. Not for just a minute, but for half the evening, until I am vaguely nauseous from listening. One night, I seriously thought of sneaking away Ivori's iPhone, maybe running it down the hall to the bathroom and giving it an ocean burial in one of the toilets.

This room is a prison. My ancient blue quilt gets thinner and more fragile every day from me sitting constantly on my bed. My dad suggested I get a new one, but there'll be no one to tell me which of them is shit fabric. My mother knew that stuff, but I'm ignorant. I'll just keep this one, which might still last a long time. Maybe forever.

Ivori says her mother has dark corners. That's halfway interesting. Two small slant-roofed rooms are on either side of our attic, musty and dark and piled with boxes. That's where my mom's stuff all landed. Along with some other antiquated things. When I was young, I'd open the dusty boxes. Once I found a fantastic straw hat. Varnished miniature fruit sat on top. I snuck a mirror up there so I could see how I looked under all those glossy cherries and bananas.

Ivori looks up curiously from her reading—I guess she heard me laugh—but I ignore her and slip back into my memory. I was pretty sure a witch lived in one of the slanted rooms. I liked to go in there though, to see if I could be brave. I can see Ivori's mom sitting on a wooden crate in that closet wearing a deep-plum-colored hat pulled from a battered box. The box and hat seem bruised, but she is radiant. She's quietly looking at me, and I'm looking at her thinking, *What are your dark corners?* I don't suppose she had a mother she dissed when she was dying, and that bad action metamorphosed into a rotten spot in her soul.

Ivori looks at me again. "How was that visit with your dad?" She was unconscious when I got back from that trip.

"Ah. Shitty. He's got a girlfriend. Can you believe that?"

"Fuck. Really?"

"Yeah. I had to get out of there. She was on her way over."

"Do you know anything about her?" Ivori's interest is intense and encourages me to talk.

I shake my head. "I named her Donna Obscura. Thanh's into Latin nomenclature."

"Like Shakespeare's dark lady."

"Who's that?"

"Shakespeare had a lover and wrote all these intense sonnets about her. His dark lady. She was Black and beautiful. Her being Black is kind of obvious if you read the poems."

"Interesting. I don't care if my dad's woman is Black, but she better not be beautiful. For my mom's sake."

"I get it. Men suck generally, you know."

"I thought you wanted me to sleep with Thanh."

"Yeah, maybe, but that's just sex." She adds, "I might have been named for one of those sonnets."

"You're joking."

"It's about piano playing. Shakespeare is envying the piano keys because his lover's fingers are running all over them. Like she's making love to the keys and they're responding. It's pretty awkward."

"That sounds perverted. How is it about *you*?"

"It's a Venn diagram of things my mom goes crazy for. Shakespeare. Music. Piano. You could end up with a name like Ivori."

"Oh. I get it. Like 'ivories'?"

"Yeah. But she wanted to give it an African twist—more exotic, maybe. Plus it's our heritage, and of course ivory is from Africa."

"But what about the fact that ivory means 'white'? Ya know—I mean, I hate to point it out, but it doesn't exactly go with the dark lady idea."

"She says she wanted to claim something, or reclaim it, to say that this thing she loves—her music—isn't just for White people. My mom's intellectual like that. Political. She's into statements."

"It's a little weird, but yeah, I like it. I like weird."

"That's because you are weird." She isn't mean about it this time—more like intimate.

"If it were me, I wouldn't dwell on the making-love-to-a-piano aspect of my identity." I start laughing, as does Ivori. "Which sonnet is it?"

"One twenty-eight. Wait. I'm going to read it to you." She dances her fingers over her laptop keyboard as she googles the sonnet. "Here you go." She stands up, sucks in her breath, and lifts her chest ridiculously, so I'm giggling again but trying to listen as she begins her recitation:

"How oft, when thou, my music, music play'st,
Upon that blessed wood whose motion sounds
With thy sweet fingers when thou gently sway'st
The wiry concord that mine ear confounds,
Do I envy those jacks that nimble leap,
To kiss the tender inward of thy hand,
Whilst my poor lips, which should that harvest reap,
At the wood's boldness by thee blushing stand!"

I stand up and interrupt her. "Hand it over. I'll read the next part." I try to match Ivori's dramatic reading.

"To be so tickled, they would change their state
And situation with those dancing chips,
O'er whom thy fingers walk with gentle gait,
Making dead wood more bless'd than living lips.
Since saucy jacks so happy are in this,
Give them thy fingers, me thy lips to kiss.

"The End." I hand the laptop back to her and say, "I might have to call you Saucy Jacks. Or maybe just Jacks."

"You asshole. Just don't call me 'that blessed wood.'"

Ivori tries to read some more for school, but her book must be boring because she slouches toward sleep in the yellow light from her reading lamp. I'm feeling lonely thinking about my dad and that woman. I'm not ready to be the only one conscious here. I cough noisily and straddle my desk chair to face her.

"So, hey, what dark corners does your mother have?"

She stiffens. I expect her to tell me I'm not wanted in that private room, but she says, "Some bad stuff happened to her when she was young. I'm not sure she wants me to tell anyone." She says *anyone*, not *you, Leslie, oddball new roommate*, so I'm not offended. She pauses, recalculating like a GPS. "I guess it's okay. She knows you, and she likes young women to 'listen up.' Learn to watch out for ourselves and all that."

"Okay."

"She was at a frat party with a lot of extremely wasted guys. She hated the vibe, and some guy offered to walk her home. He acted like he wanted to look out for her, since it was after dark. *Stupid. Stupid. Stupid.* That's Mom faulting herself and warning me. Anyway, the fucking idiot forced her up against the first wall he could find in a dark corner. He raped her. That's about what I know. It left some scars."

I don't ask for details. I am busy imagining how I would get a gun and splatter the guy across that same wall. "I guess she handled it. Me, I'd kill the dude."

"She's had other bad things happen in her life. That isn't the only one." Despite that teaser, Ivori is done talking. An inert cobra now sits on her bed digesting a swallowed hog. Her eyes are glowering. "So, now you know," she says.

Yes, and I'm pretty sure she's holding that against me. It hits me how Ivori's mom has dark corners, but someone dragged her *into* a dark corner. So getting forced into a place makes that place a part of you? I could be a famous psychologist who everyone visits for my acute vision. I would see everyone's secrets—even the ones they can't detect themselves.

Ivori is serious now about sleep. She is holding her flannel nightgown aloft. It envelops her head and she lowers it smoothly like a curtain, then finds a cozy spot between her covers. She turns onto her side and tangles her cover around her legs and hips. There's my mother, lying like a crescent moon in their big bed. She's reaching down to straighten her nightgown where it circles her knees, but she's weak and it's an effort. Her eyes are closed. She's thinking my father should come and help her. Was she thinking about me? That she would miss me? Or that I should come and help her? Every time it comes to me, the scene is different. Nothing stays in place. I want her to want my company, to feel sad she's going to lose me. But I can't find that. I can barely find any memory at all. They slip in and out of focus. I'll see just me refusing to visit her, then I picture her feeling shitty and glad

I'm not banging on her door. Maybe it was just my dad who nagged me to go spend time with her, but she was happy that I wasn't too much of a nuisance.

I guess I tried her patience a time or two toward the end, but she was always well-mannered. I wish she had lost her temper and told me once that she hated me. Then she could have told me she loved me, and it would have meant something. I can't stand the middling, namby-pamby stuff.

I think of the boxes still up in the attic and see the dark lady going through them, trying things on, intensely curious about my mom. She could stuff a pretty sweater in her bag and take it home. I need to go through my mom's things. I never wanted to, but now I do. People put all kinds of things in their pockets. Like notes they write themselves about what's on their mind, what they're worrying about, or who they want to remember to talk to about something important.

Ivori is sound asleep now and peaceful as a floating cloud. I get my backpack and find my wallet. I love this wallet. It's yellow vegan leather printed with hummingbirds. I pull out all the cards—charge cards and gift cards and buy-ten-get-one-free cards—and at the bottom of the bunch is my mother's driver's license. I took it from the last purse she used, a sky-blue Baggallini she loved. I could tell by the way she ran her fingertips over it and fussed over putting all her little things inside, arranging and rearranging her comb and her wallet and her credit-card thingamajig. In the photo, my mother looks pretty and healthy. There's something light and cheerful about her face. She is like a butterfly that's happy it's out in the air. Maybe she was excited about getting her new license. Who knows?

Sprawling from Ivori's nightgown drawer is a soft black

sweater. Angora or something. Her mother breezed in from Cleveland with it last week. She whipped it out of a Saks shopping bag—ta-da!—confident of its quality and beauty. Ivori didn't even try it on. Mrs. F. had a rehearsal and rushed off after consulting her chunky gold watch. Ivori tossed the sweater to the foot of her bed and went back to her chemistry. Later, she stuck it in the drawer, not even folded.

I see how deep Ivori has dived into dreamland and pad softly to the open drawer in my fuzzy socks. I'm a cat burglar. Light on my feet. The sweater is soft in my hands. Luxurious. It has a collar with a scalloped edge. Its oversized buttons are wrapped in the same knitted fabric as the sweater. I glance at Ivori and slip the sweater onto one arm, then the other, and go to the half-length mirror we share. I look good. I feel good, too, and get lost in that feeling. I don't see Ivori sit up until I turn back around.

I'm hugely embarrassed. "Oh," I sputter. "Sorry, sorry, sorry. You didn't model it and I was curious what it looked like. I'm a jerk."

She interrupts me with a shrug. "I'm used to it," she says. "My little cousins try on my stuff all the time."

I nod. I'm gliding on a river of gratitude for her not skewering me. I fold the sweater and lay it in the drawer, not tendriling out like an octopus this time.

# Chapter 6

On Saturday morning, when I am still in bed, Ivori informs me, "I'm going to a party tonight."

I don't open my eyes but say, "What party?"

"I don't know yet."

"That sounds like a great party."

"Don't worry. It will be."

I'm uneasy all day that Ivori might invite me to the party and also that she won't. I'm not sure which is worse. She apparently has echolocation for parties. She tracks one down and says, "You should come with me. You're going to get a permanent crease in your forehead from staring at books all day."

"No thanks."

"That's ridiculous. It's a party. You should come."

"I get that it's a party. That's why I'm not going."

"What are you going to wear?" She goes to my dresser and pulls open the top drawer. I can't complain, and she knows it, because of my sweater larceny. She pulls out a cobalt-blue T-shirt with a V-neck. "Tight. I can tell. Perfect for a party."

"No."

"Put it on."

I am a zombie. I lack independent will. I pull on the T-shirt.

It's cling wrap. I can't breathe. I wear it anyway.

At nine o'clock, we are on the sidewalk in front of South Quad, walking south hurriedly.

"Where are we going?"

"A frat party."

I brake hard. "I'm going home. I don't drink."

Ivori motions forward with her head. "It doesn't matter."

I'm thinking of Mrs. Ferguson and her frat boy assailant. Why would Ivori take us to a frat house, of all places? She is moving like water down a hill. Running into danger, I think. She walks ahead of me, and I see she is not navigating a straight line. "Did you pre-game?" I ask her. "You're wobbling on those heels."

"My macular pucker."

"I'd hate to see you when you're drunk. You better not get wasted."

Now we are on Washtenaw. The frat house is in sight. Ivori pauses. I wonder if she's waking up to where she's dragging us, but she looks me over and nods approval. "You look pretty decent in that shirt. I have good taste—got it from my mother."

I wish I knew what I got from mine, but *not now, not now, not now.*

An atomic blast of music greets us in an expansive lobby. There must be forty people. The light is blessedly feeble. No one notices us come in.

"This looks awful," I whine.

"Give it a chance." She grabs my wrist and pulls me to an array of end-to-end metal tables. It resembles the point of entry where you'd be forced to hand over your valuables before entering prison. The tables are spread with lame airplane snacks. Peanuts and twisted pretzels. I could get those pain-free at the dorm snack bar. My eyes whip right and left. People are shouting to each other as if they're talking inside a hurricane. In a back corner past the endless tables, four or five bare mattresses are dumped on the floor with bedsheets suspended over them, open parachutes floating. My consumption of crappy TV tells me they're there to pull down onto the mattresses in case people have an urgent need for privacy while making out. I would pull them over me to hide. I flash on an image of me and my mom playing "tent" under my bedsheets when I was little. A nice safe space. The thought relaxes me a bit. I hope to escape this place before anything gross happens on the mattresses.

Ivori grabs a red plastic cup full of something alcoholic. I imagine her wobble devolving into a full-on tilt. A grinning, shaggy-haired White guy starts chatting us up. No doubt his eyes are on Ivori. She's wearing a short skirt and a red tee as tight as mine. The dozen bangles on her wrist make her a tambourine section. I notice her flinch when he reaches out a hand to touch her arm. Her face tightens into an angry question mark. Soon she's smiling again, but I can't tell how genuine her bubbly laughter is. I'm not sure whether she's here to flirt with these guys or hunt one down for slaughter. Maybe she's got a gun up under her skirt and is planning to avenge her mom.

I see a bench at the edge of the room, growing out of the wall like the shelf fungus Thanh ID'd for me. I think I'll go sit there and be an official wallflower. I poke Ivori in the side and point to where I'm going. She frowns but then shrugs. Is her face frantic or fierce? I can't read her tonight, and she's scaring me a little. Dr. Dream said people replay traumas, even across generations. I go to my shelf and sit down, but plan to keep an eye on her from afar. I am relieved to check out of this party and shut my eyes. My ears are still captive but at least I can pause what I see. I'm peacefully absent—letting the music blur and soften—when I feel the air beside me alter. I open my eyes and slide them left like abacus beads without turning my head.

A person is sitting there. I can't say whether it's a guy or a girl. Lipstick. One small, tasteful gold hoop earring. Tight capri pants. Lilac fingernail polish. But a guy's broad shoulders. A model's high, flaring cheekbones. Short hair, except long on top and swept to the side, opposite its natural flow. A tsunami of dyed platinum. Probably a guy. Whoever it is is dolled up for this lame party.

"Hey, hi," he says.

"Hey, hi," I say back, then pinch myself for mocking him.

He blinks hard as if he's flattening my affront with his eyelids so he can carry on. "I hate parties," he says. "You look like you do, too. So I'm seeking refuge with you."

He puts on a faux fur stole he's been carrying. I'm fascinated by his fashion. I can't help trying to place him in the male bin or the female one. "What's your name?"

"Arwyn. Previously Erwin, but you probably don't need to know that."

I nod. "Leslie." I realize I'm the one with the gender-ambiguous name and semi laugh.

He cocks his head, and I see him thinking of asking what the laugh's about but concluding that it's private. I like him for that. I wouldn't want to jam onto a bench with a nosy person. Still, we're crowded.

"Should we go outside?" he asks. "It's delightfully warm out."

He seems safe and I'm relaxing. "What are your pronouns?" I ask.

He shrugs. "He, him—at the moment I'm cis-adjacent."

"Whatever that is," I say but smile so he hopefully won't take offense.

"My thought exactly."

I stand up and lead us toward the exit. Every step lightens the air. I ought to tell Ivori I'm going out. She's still by the snack tables with the guy who looks like the mushroom Thanh called 'shaggy mane,' a.k.a. *Coprinus*-something, which frankly means 'fed by shit.' I totally don't get why she wanted to come to this party after what happened to her mom, but whatever. That's her minefield. I have my own to negotiate. I go ahead and shout, since that's the communication mode here. "Hey, Jacks. Come over here." She zigzags my way. "We're going outside." She doesn't question the unidentified person at my side. "You're okay," I say. "Wobbliness level two."

There's a bench outside, but it's in the klieg lights, where a thousand gnats circle, not knowing it's October. I walk back to the frat house and lean against the cool brick in deep shadow. It's peaceful. Arwyn rests against the wall beside me. "Two peas in a pod," he says. "Are you cold? You can share my stole. It's faux so you don't have to worry that I've engaged in animal cruelty."

"I can tell."

"Oh." His face falls.

"I didn't mean it that way. It's nice. I just can tell the difference."

He sighs. "My feelings are easily hurt. Don't worry though. I'm not delicate or anything. I recover."

I laugh. It's wonderful to be out of that place.

"I'll be right back," Arwyn says. He's gone in a flash, and I instantly miss his company. The wait seems long, but finally he emerges from the double-height door with two plastic champagne glasses. "Not sure what it is. Something bubbly. Fake champagne."

I'm surprisingly happy he's brought me this silly glass of fizz. "Why did you even come to this party?" I ask him.

"You first."

"Easy. My roommate tortured me into it. Ivori."

"Oh. Lovely name. Why did I have to be Erwin?"

"So why did you come? It's so vile."

"Guys in my dorm were talking about it. They said it was open to the public. But why come? I suppose I'm lonely. I just got to campus. Don't know a soul. Do you, Leslie?"

"One guy from my school. Thanh. I know him slightly. And Ivori, kind of. I didn't, but now I do."

"Lucky you. And Thanh. What kind of name is that?"

"Vietnamese."

"You lead an exotic life. You have racial and ethnic diversity in your itty-bitty circle."

I look at him and feel surprisingly safe. "Well, you have gender variety."

He holds out his hands and examines his nails in the moonlight. "I'm a package deal. You get multiple for the price of one."

Ivori wanders out through the door and I can see I've fallen down on the job. Her wobbliness factor has skyrocketed. "Uh-oh."

"A bit too much to drink," Arwyn says. He has a tolerant mom voice. Consoling but concerned.

"It's also her pucker," I say. "She sees the world through a wrinkled cloth."

"Another on your list of exoticisms."

"Iv," I say from our grotto. "I'm taking you home." This is the moment I've been waiting for. My chance to escape the dreadful party. But I'm sad to go, because of Arwyn. God, what has become of me?

"Ivori, this is Arwyn," I say. I open my hand toward Iv. "Ivori."

"Pleased."

Ivori belches.

"Oh, nice," I say.

Arwyn pulls out his phone, and the bright screen light cuts through the soft darkness. "Wait," he says. "New contact. Your phone number—please. Then I'll know a human on this enormo campus." I give him my number. "I'm going to call you. Be forewarned. It's the price you pay for being my new and only friend."

I laugh. I wonder if it's possible to get angry at Arwyn. He seems too kind to head-butt, even a little. I'm feeling stupid, though, about half the things I've said to him.

Ivori belches again and lifts an arm to point to the far edge of the spacious lawn. Several guys are gathered around a small fire in a barrel. The fire is growing exponentially as they feed objects into it. We wander over, transfixed by the flames. The fire is head-high now and sparking. Embers shoot into the air, travel a short way, then blacken.

"It's like my life," Ivori says. She's loud, even though we've left the bedlam inside. Zero modulation.

"Your life is a dumpster fire?" I ask.

"No. More like shooting stars. They flame out."

"Too far from the mother ship," Arwyn says.

Ivori looks at him with intense curiosity. "What do you mean?"

"They flame out when they're too far from the fire. They're in cold, deep space, distant from the central heat source. The mother ship. They lose their will to live."

"Wow," Ivori says. "You are profound."

"You are drunk," I say.

She gives me a helpless look. "Yeah. But. What he said. Too far from the mother ship."

Oh. I get it. Mrs. Ferguson off touring Timbuktu. "I better take her home," I say to Arwyn. I'm feeling almost buoyant with a new friend and new responsibility, and typically commanding Ivori mushed by intoxication.

We walk down Washtenaw. I stay in the lead and watch for drunk drivers until we get to a decent sidewalk. "Are you missing your mother?" I ask Ivori.

She looks at me wide-eyed, the way she looked at Arwyn. As if I'm Einstein discovering the natural laws of the universe. "That queer guy was nice," she says.

"Arwyn."

"What was *your* mother like?" she asks.

She's never asked me that before. Not directly. No one has. I panic and shrug my shoulders. "I don't know."

Ivori's too drunk to ask more questions, and I'm relieved. Because I don't know. I really don't. I feel blank and kind of sick when I think about her. Between the butterflies and the funeral was nothingness. Not even space because space is *something*—you can say *how much* space there is. In my memory, one thing smacks up against the other. Months must have passed, but they are gone. Like when you switch off a bright light and it doesn't leave any trace. You just have darkness.

I remember being at the graveyard. I still feel the itchy wool cranberry-and-brown tartan skirt I wore in the early winter cold and the black sweater that didn't match. I stood there like a hangnail alongside my father and a little behind him. He turned to me when it was time to throw dirt on the grave, and I wanted to disappear because that icy shovel in my hands might make me pass out from horror.

Ivori stumbles over a curb and whacks her face hard against the front window of a barber shop on the way down. We're both freaked out, but only one of us is yowling like an insane cat.

"Shit, Ivori, quiet down. Tell me if you're okay or not?"

She's shaking her head like she wants it to fly off her neck. My heart has taken off at a dead run. I'm supposed to be keeping her safe. Now she's yelling and crying all at once. Ten people hanging around the bars and party stores stare at us, but no one is coming over.

Finally a young semi-Asian, semi-Thanh-look-alike guy comes over. I wonder if he's an escapee from that frat party. He gives Ivori a goofy smile and says, "Hey, you all right? I can grab under your arms and pick you up if you want."

Ivori is screeching again.

"Don't touch her," I bark. "I can handle this. Just give us some space." This is probably the last time he offers to help someone who's fallen on the ground. But he keeps hanging around, at the edge of our drama.

"What's wrong? *Words,* Ivori. Stop yelling if you can."

She gapes her mouth wide. I don't see any blood or gashed tongue. Then she rubs her finger over a bottom tooth, close to the front. "I broke my tooth."

"Does it hurt?"

"No. But it's jagged. I'll have to go to the dentist."

I sigh. "It's okay, Iv. They can fix anything now. You'll be perfect again."

"No. No. It's not that."

I'm picturing Mrs. Ferguson alarmed, then severe with me for my screw-up. *What kind of roommate are you? What kind of friend?* And my dad's in there, too, because he hasn't finished being disappointed with me for the last ten things I fumbled. He's apparently not even speaking with me, though that may be because he's too busy with his new woman. Which reminds me that I need to go over there and make sure she isn't rifling through what's left of my mom's possessions. I have so much homework I'm behind on, too. I'm going in six directions, but better just get this wasted woman home without any more accidents.

You'd think that Good Samaritan kid would have wandered off by now, but he's still in worried watching mode. As we're walking off, I nod to him—my reluctant thanks—and he jumps forward and hands me a scrap of paper with his number on it and his name, Fletcher.

"Let me know how she is."

I resist some snark about his gentlemanly conduct. "Sure. Thanks."

"Cute," Ivori says, after we get some distance.

"What? I thought you were busy dying."

We finally make it home. I help Ivori evaluate her tooth, a bicuspid. It's just chipped. We change and get in bed. I feel like we've traversed the worst of things, but Ivori can't stop sighing and whimpering and wriggling around on top of her covers. I don't have a lot of experience with drunk people, so wonder if these are side effects until she says, with little sound of intoxication, "You don't understand."

Now *I* sigh because I'm not really up for being critiqued by Ivori when my dad and also Mrs. Ferguson are chasing me around in my head with baseball bats. "What's wrong with you?" There's a broken-glass edge to my voice that people have when they ask that. It's not a question but a statement suggesting, 'You're a freak.' I tell myself to quit being an asshole and say, "I mean it." I'm trying to sound understanding. "What's wrong?"

She's face down, nodding her head in and out of the quilt like an excavating machine. I imagine fluffy white batting rising from the bed surface. Cotton candy.

"You wouldn't want to sit up?" I suggest.

She swings her body into a sitting position with her legs over the edge of the bed, but she keeps her head down.

"So?" My voice lifts. I'm anxious. This could be something terrible.

"'The dentist." She's flat. I am supposed to guess at her meaning.

"You don't like the dentist?"

"Hate." A squall has taken up residence in her voice. "I can't stand going there."

Ivori's right. I don't understand. Is she phobic? I get an idea. "Your dentist at home hit on you?"

She shakes me off. Sharp and annoyed. "Nothing like that."

"So. What? You're scaring me."

She shrugs. "I don't get it either. I just *hate, hate, hate* going there."

Dr. Dream and his catalogue of common phobias run through my head. "The pain? The shots?"

"I told you, I don't get it. It might not be that rational." She looks up and nearly jabs me with her eyes. I think she's mustering some courage. She's going to tell me something.

I drag over my desk chair and straddle it, holding on to the chair back. "Okay. Go."

"I get this creeped out feeling when a dentist starts studying my teeth. Makes me open wide and all that." She shakes her head as if there's an image that needs dislodging.

"That's weird." I'm not harsh. Just matter-of-fact. Interested, like that visiting psych prof who approaches everyone with an engaged furrow of the brow.

"I get angry," she says. "Like *fucking leave me alone* furious. I want to stand up and knock over every one of the guy's glaring instruments and tear out of there. One time I actually did that—ran out—and squatted in the hall. Couldn't stop crying. The nurse came out and tried to reassure me it wouldn't be too painful. Put her arm around me. I started laughing hysterically and couldn't stop because I was so embarrassed."

"You did that? Wow. So, what is it?" My budding psychologist skills are failing me.

"I told you. *I. Don't. Know.*" She's starting to yell again, but it's not personal.

"Okay, here's the deal. Think about sitting there in the dentist's chair, with all those gleaming implements staring at you and the dentist is walking over in a white coat. Now just see where your mind wanders. Let it go wherever it wants."

"What are you now? A shrink?"

I'm a little excited, as if I'm going on an exotic trip. But I'm firm. "Just try it, E.V."

She sucks in air and pushes it out in a hard *pff* like she's going to birth a baby. She closes her eyes, and a minute slowly passes. "You'll think I'm crazy."

"After this evening, it's possible that I already think that. You don't have much to lose."

She smiles. I see her feistiness stirring. "Fuck you," she says. "And I'm not an electric vehicle."

I feel a little better. My excitement's been shoulder to shoulder with my fear. "People get scared of oddball things," I say. I'm thinking about Dr. Dream and his theories. I admit that he has some interesting ideas.

"You're not going to get it. It's not something you'd understand."

Ouch. "Because…?"

"You're White."

Ugh. That. I scour the room with my eyes as if I could exit through a crack in the wall. "I'm aware."

Ivori takes another big breath and huffs it out. She's definitely come to life. She's a flattened vinyl Halloween ghost picked up off the cold ground and inflated.

"It's fucking slavery," she says.

"Huh?"

"I told you you wouldn't understand."

"Way to give a person half a chance."

"All those pictures I saw, my whole damn life. Black people standing on the fucking auction block with chains around their wrists and ankles and horrid White men making them open their mouths and show their teeth. The slavers want to see if they're good stock. God forbid they spend their money to get a human with crooked teeth."

I'm shocked. Of course, I've heard about these things before, but I never thought of Ivori seeing herself in those pictures.

"The whole thing is so disgusting. I can barely stand it."

"You think of that when you go to the dentist?"

"No. I don't think of it. I *feel* it. When they put their hands on me. I get antsy. I get mad and restless, like, 'Why don't you get your goddamn hands off me? Stop looking at me.' Then if he keeps squinting and looking in there and he's breathing his sour breath on me, I just get furious and want to put a knee in his chest and get out of there."

"Your dentist is a White guy?"

"Old White dude."

"No way he'd understand." I'm saying what I think she's thinking. Meanwhile, I'm feeling my way into that scene until I halfway get that feeling, *Leave me the fuck alone.* And then there's Ivori's mother and what that slimy guy did to her. That's lurking, too.

"And that guy who assaulted your mom was White?"

She is too emotional to say anything.

"I don't know what to say. All White guys are dicks. Maybe you should go to a Black dentist."

She nods. "Most of this country is White, in case you haven't noticed."

That might not be true, but I'm not going to argue with her at this moment.

She's back on her belly, talking into her quilt. "I gotta think. Leave me alone. But thanks."

Luckily, a chip in a tooth isn't an emergency. It isn't even visible. So she doesn't have to rush off to the dentist tonight or even next week. Her phone is at the foot of her bed, half-tucked into a fold in her rumpled quilt. Why's she not calling her mom? I could press 'redial' and it would go straight to her mother. And when Mrs. Ferguson answers, what would I say? Maybe just "la, la, la,"—y'know, a little opera singing.

My dad calls me a few days after the frat party. I'm in a bad mood because I'm struggling with a US History short essay. When I hear his voice, I see the girlfriend—or a flip-book of my hundred images of her. That makes me want to hang up on him *tout de suite.*

"I'm just checking in," he says. "Since we didn't end on the best note the other day."

"Yeah," I say. "I'm alright. Just too much homework. And Ivori chipped a tooth."

"Oh. How'd that happen?"

I'm not going into the gory details of her intoxication and pucker. "She kind of tripped. She's okay. She just doesn't like dentists."

Dad makes a big guffaw out of that, as if it's a funny statement because no one, not a single soul on earth, likes dentists, and aren't we all in that same boat. Ha ha ha.

I try to laugh along a little and not be too obnoxious, but my heart isn't in it. Then I just spit out, "Well, how's the dating going?"

"Oh. Isn't it nice of you to ask, Leslie. It's going well. I'm enjoying myself, and I have a little diversion. You know me, how I get caught up in my work sometimes and practically forget to eat."

"Yeah, well I better get a little caught up on mine or I'm going to get an F on an assignment. But oh, yeah, I was going to say, I'm gonna come over and go through some of Mom's things in the attic."

"Great. That's such a good idea."

"They're still there, right? You didn't, like, give everything away, or let anybody else paw through it."

He makes some indecipherable noises that I don't interrogate. When I hang up, I remember I was supposed to text Ivori's would-be rescuer, Fletcher whoever, so I do that and tell him she just chipped a tooth. He texts back and says, *that's a relief.* Then two minutes later, I get a second text saying, *Do you want to get coffee sometime?*

What kind of catfishing is this? I don't answer.

# Chapter 7

Thanh and I start sitting next to each other in Botany. Today we have distance between our desks, but we're two particles inside one atom. We're in our own small universe apart from the hundred others in the room. My charge pushes off from his, but we don't get far from each other. He smiles his nerdy smile at me after inhaling more plant parts and processes and says, "Isn't this stuff cool?" and it seems a little cooler when I see it through Thanh's excitement, so I nod and say, "Yeah, sort of." Pretty much every time I see him, he asks me to check out some park or another. Ann Arbor appears to have a never-ending supply of them, a fact that makes Thanh high. Mostly I say, "Nah, not today," and I see his soufflé collapse. But he's quick to revive, as if he's thinking, "But wait, there's tomorrow. Maybe she'll go with me tomorrow." What's his thing about hanging out with me? I'm semi-mean, in my own estimation. Much of the time—especially after listening to Dr. Dream—I don't even feel normal. Most people would say that normal is a low bar.

But Thanh persists. Today he's set his sights on Delhi Park, which he shows me on a map as he points out that it has an actual river running through it. It's wild to have a river here in the city, and lately I'm like a snail crammed into too small a shell. Too much sitting in tight desks in class or curling up on my bed with homework. Wild sounds good.

"Yeah. Okay," I say. His grin looks like it could shoot past his ears, wrap around the world, and tie in a bow on the other side, somewhere near Vietnam. I'm about to make one of those slap-down comments, but I stop myself. Dr. Dream would say I'm revealing my insecurities. Can't deal with joy, or whatever. I see how joy is like knocking on that kids-room door insisting, *Let me in.* It acknowledges that you like what the other person is offering and that you might just want more of it. That might be a ridiculous analysis, but possibly good enough for a future Dr. Dream paper if I can hold onto it.

We walk to Thanh's car, the fact of which still seems unfathomable, as does his parking space, a square of private property his father rents for him behind an all-night party store up on the Geddes hill. I've never been to Thanh's dorm and don't want to go there, but I've been to his parking space. The quality of the space speaks to how hard they are to come by. It backs to some ancient battered metal garbage cans in a short and somewhat creepy alley that's lit by one extra-large bulb in a crooked metal shade. And there's a lot of crap on the ground. Cigarette butts, rolling papers, condom wrappers, a few orange peels for a touch of wholesomeness.

"I know it's a train wreck," Thanh says. "I'm sure my dad is imagining something higher-class—well-swept cement, at least, with one or two stains and a streetlamp. I'm not telling him."

At Delhi Park, we stand at the edge of the river watching the surface twist and bubble over the rocks. The Huron is a real river, not a stream, and it calms me. How odd that you can be walking on ordinary dry land, then the earth surprises you by offering up this great ribbon of deep water, something entirely different that moves past you, carrying its own life forms. I can feel myself floating on the water, just moving along at an easy pace, looking up at the clouds.

My mind turns philosophical and reimagines the river as life running past. Ceaseless and rapid. My peaceful feeling fades as I think of my mother. Today, I can hardly remember her, and I feel a little panicky, as if something I need is flowing down that one-way river, and I know for certain that nothing that floats past will ever return. I want her to jump out of that river, proclaiming, "I'm not leaving my Leslie behind," but she just keeps going until I snag on a thought that's bothered me before, the idea that she didn't love me all that much, not like Mrs. Ferguson, who'd stop the river with force of willpower if it was whisking her away from Ivori.

Thanh is studying the plants along the riverbank, so he's walked away from me. His head is down and lost in his consideration of the vegetation. I'm relieved when he stops wandering and comes to a rest right beside me. His hand swings over and touches my hand. A mistake, I'm sure. He's probably embarrassed, so I don't look at him and make it worse. But shit, something is unleashed in me, because Thanh does have the most beautiful skin and his almond eyes are pretty, too. Jesus. What the fuck. I just needed someone to stand beside me, not to make me crazy.

"Let's go," I say to him, and his face collapses like a punched dough. I think of describing that to him, with a laugh, but I stop. I just stop, and don't go forward or back.

"Okay," he says hesitantly, and then we are back in his car moving over the asphalt.

He's driving slowly, and I think again of the river. I imagine myself in a stream of migrating butterflies high above the ground. "Why aren't there any butterflies at that park?" I ask him. "I saw milkweed, but there were no monarchs."

"It's October, Leslie," he says, and he sounds impatient. "They're gone, okay. They've moved on."

"I have to go someplace."

"Now?"

"No, just sometime. I have to go home. My dad's house. Go through some old stuff."

"Stuff?"

"Stuff that was my mom's. That my dad might not be taking care of."

"Sure. Your mom's stuff. That's important. I can give you a ride if you want. Drop you off. Or go with you even. Y'know, moral support."

I feel like telling him I don't need that, but stifle the impulse, in part because it's a lie.

"I remember when your mom died," he says. "It was awful." Thanh's voice is gently tiptoeing, but I don't want to hear it anyway. Did everyone in the whole school know? "You got kind of weird around that time, but it was understandable."

We've come to another one of the thousand roads I don't want to go down, so I get quiet and put on a faraway look so Thanh will just take me home and drop me off. I imagine opening those boxes, and things come flying out. Not sweaters and skirts. More like memories and feelings. And voices. Little snippets of sound I can't place. Or stories that make no sense to me.

I have one memory from when she was in chemo. Leaves

were piling on the ground, just like now, and I was on the city bus. This scruffy, flabby guy was bustling up and down the aisle and between the seats picking up plastic junk-food wrappers and container lids, etcetera. He was comical, though semi-gross, bent over with his butt hanging out. He and I were the only passengers.

Finally, I couldn't keep from asking the driver, "What is that guy doing?"

The driver chuckled. "Your guess is as good as mine." He rolled his eyes.

"I'm going to ask him," I said. Or something like that—it was a long time ago.

"Be my guest," the driver told me. He gave a laugh like a cough, meaning *good luck with that.*

So I said to the pants-down guy, "What the heck are you doing?" and the guy—barely stopping—looked all umbrage-y and said, "Don't you know about plastic? It's poisoning the world."

"Yeah, sure, but what's with the bus cleanup?"

"Haven't you heard of recycling?"

"Yeah, of course, everyone has. But why are you doing it on the bus?"

He looked like he was exploding. "It's my terrain, my assign-ment—my *universe.*"

I looked at the bus driver—who had his eyebrows raised so high they could brush the ceiling—and I shrugged. I heard my dad telling me, "Leslie, sometimes you need to mind your own business. *Please.* Don't get involved." Those were his words of wis-dom. They usually made me mad, but for once, I decided I better listen, even though my dad was just talking in my head.

I told that story to my mother. After the bus ride, I wrapped it up and put it in my backpack and took it home to her. She was deep into her chemo by then, and not much made her smile, but that story got her laughing so hard she couldn't breathe. I looked at her laughing and happy and there was something I wanted to say to her, but I didn't know what, and I guess I didn't try to figure it out. Now I see that I was the plastics guy—all determination and no sense of humor—though at least my butt wasn't hanging out of my pants. Maybe I wanted to apologize, just a little.

It's too late now for apologies, but back in my room, in the thin light, I pretend I'm together with my mom. I try to tell her about things I regret. I could have been a lot nicer. I can't get to where she forgives me. I just can't picture it that well.

Ivori comes in excited and in motion. She's pacing around talking about the things she's started to construct in the art studio. She's lit up inside like a jack-o-lantern while I'm still darkened by my mother worries.

I have a dream that night. I'm writing with a white pen on a white surface. Ivori comes in and I tell her, "This is a whiteboard." She makes a face and leaves. Then she comes back and hands me a broken old laptop. I say, "Oh, it's a motherboard." I wake up and think for a while about a blackboard or bulletin board—like they have on detective shows—where I could hang all the pieces of my mother puzzle. All the suspects and victims. The solid leads and weak possibilities. I don't have the time. But I might do it one of these days.

My mom and my mean, ungrateful self won't stop pestering me about my deficiencies. For distraction, I think of that kid who tried to help Ivori, who wanted to get coffee. I think of Thanh, too, and how I feel better when he's around, but I'm not sure I like his having all that power in my life. In my dumb head. So I just text that random guy. Fletcher.

I'm texting mindlessly. "Uh. Not the name I would have guessed. You look like a guy I know whose parents are Vietnamese."

He texts me a headshot of himself and says, "A reminder." Weird thing to do, but his pic is pretty Hollywood. Ivori noticed his good looks, even in her compromised state. "Mom's Korean," he adds.

That's enough for me. "Gotta go," I say.

# Chapter 8

A small miracle. I made it through the first semester without failing any classes. Thanh moved out of his dorm into an apartment his parents are renting or maybe buying for him. He keeps bugging me to come see it.

"It's nice," he tells me. "Not like my parking space."

One afternoon, I'm sick of studying and I hurt my shoulder, which feels pretty achy and makes me irritable, so I relent and call Thanh. "Okay I'm coming over. Assuming you want company."

"For sure." He sounds all excited.

Thanh's place is on the second floor. When I get to his door, I push it. It's open, and I get a look at his living room before he knows I'm there. The room is picked up and decorated with small items, each one cool-looking in its own way. There are a couple intricate clocks and some lacquer boxes that might be from Vietnam.

Thanh comes in and smiles at me. "Hey, you're here. How are you?"

"I messed up my shoulder, possibly from leaning on it all the time when I'm studying on my bed. Or maybe it's from lugging books."

"I told you I'd carry that heavy bio book."

"Oh, right. What is this, the 1950s?"

Thanh stutters for a minute, then says, "My aunt is a masseuse." More stuttering. "She taught me how to do some things. I could massage your shoulder; relax the muscles, maybe find trigger points." He points me to the sofa. It's a disgusting brown. Some kind of nubby material. The only thing in this apartment that's edging toward ugly. If you were nervous, you could sit and pick off all the little fluffballs like with a sweater that's pilled in the wash. I'm not crazy about sitting on this sofa, but okay, I do.

"Could you sit cross-legged? So your back is to me?"

I feel comfortable with my legs crossed, up on the sofa. He puts his hands near my neck, so his fingers are on my collar bones and his palms on top of my shoulders. The pressure is totally even from one hand to the next, as if he had an instrument to check. I'm just now realizing that I've invited Thanh to put his hands on me, and I'm not so sure I'm down with that. But I'm not going to make a fool of myself by saying, "I changed my mind. I didn't know you were going to *touch* me."

He kneads my shoulders, and then he starts on the muscles all down my back and along my sides. I'd redirect him, since this is coloring a little outside the lines, but it feels too good. Finally I say, "My shoulder is what's stiff."

He removes his hands from my waist, fast, and lifts them to my shoulders. He massages the back of my neck with his thumbs, then goes back to the starting line. He finds some sore spots that hurt and also feel good when they're pressed. He has big hands, and a couple fingers slide down to where the skin is softer, by the edge of my bra, the touch clearly by accident. I don't think Thanh knows a thing about girl anatomy. He's an expert on plant parts, but the human stuff, not so much. On that I'm confident. Still, I'm not risking his hands meandering down by my breasts again, maybe inside my bra, so I say, "Yeah, thanks. I appreciate it."

"How does your shoulder feel now?" he asks, but I think he wants to say, "Wasn't that a damn good massage? Did you notice how skilled I am?"

I keep it cool and say, "Pretty good. A little better. Thanks." I'm formal, as if he is hired help, but Thanh seems satisfied. It doesn't take much to please him.

I'm standing now, because I've had enough of that tufted sofa with all its little knobs.

Ivori texts and asks, *Where are you? Are you coming home for dinner?*

*Yes to dinner. Visiting Thanh,* I write. She'll probably approve of the visit, though you never know with Ivori.

"I gotta go," I tell Thanh. "I've got to study some more."

"We could study together."

"Another time." I pick up this tiny carving on his bureau and turn it in my hand. It's a miniature horse, curled up as if it was made to fit in an egg.

"It's a netsuke," he says. "It's Japanese. Made from ivory."

"That's illegal," I practically shout. "And besides, it's evil." I'm confused. Thanh seems like the last person to want to mutilate an elephant.

"It was my grandfather's. Made before people thought about what they're doing when they use ivory. I've got some others in my bedroom. He gave me his whole collection. I can show you."

I hear myself yelling at my mother over pulling out her milkweed. Suddenly I feel like she's been gone for a century. I tell

Thanh, "That's okay. Not today," and I run my hand all over the little horse before I set it down. I have to admit, it's beautiful.

That guy Fletcher has been texting me from time to time. When I get back from Thanh's, I text him back and say hi. He wants to come visit me. I don't feel like studying and my head is haunted by Thanh's weird sofa and his beautiful ivory horse, so I just say yes. What the fuck. Ivori's out at one of her enthralling art classes, though she'll be home for dinner.

He comes over in half an hour and oh, yeah, he *is* cute. What Thanh would look like crossed with Jungkook. I suddenly feel sorry for Thanh because he's definitely not *this* guy, and I bet he'd like to be.

He takes one of the desk chairs and spins it around in a quick, one-handed motion so he can straddle it. I sit on my bed because that's about it for options. He asks about Ivori's state of health. I try to answer, but my head is a minefield of thoughts to avoid. Like the whole slavery overtone in the dental visit, and the fact that I'm sitting with this random gorgeous guy.

He reaches over and grabs my hand, flips it palm side up, and examines it. "Long heart line."

"And that means?"

"I have no idea. A long lifeline is good though. That much I know."

We talk for a while, his eyes finding me again and again, feeding my amazement. We talk about nothing, and more nothing, until he says, "Let me see that hand again." I put it out for him, though I have no clue what he's looking at. Truthfully, I don't think he has any idea, either. I notice my shoulder's okay. Thanh fixed it. Then Fletcher kind of uses my hand and arm to make a quick spin and butt transfer onto my bed so he's sitting beside me, cheek to cheek. He draws my hand behind him as if we're slow dancing and pastes it there. Then he glances into my eyes and starts to kiss me. Shit. What is happening here? I have a split-second to decide. But a person can't decide anything in half a second. Already his lips are on mine and I know right away he's a *très bon* kisser. Not that I've had much experience. Fuck. This shouldn't be happening. I've led Thanh to think I have no use for men whatsoever. But I'm letting this guy, Fletcher somebody, who I don't know, manhandle me. My body is an idiot and has already decided what it wants. He has one paw under my shirt now. *Phew.* I'm not having sex for the first time in my life with a sketchy Don Juan whose full name I don't know even though he is astonishingly good-looking. He bends me over onto the bed. Gently. Oh my God. Maybe I will. Because of this body. But it's noisy suddenly. Noise in the hall. Clumpy feet I recognize. Shit. Ivori pushes through the door. I bolt upright but she's staring at me, looking like she's going to drop her books. Fletcher jumps to his feet like in a movie and looks hugely nervous. Says, "Hey. I'm glad you're okay. That was a bad accident." He puts out his hand. "Fletcher." Same hand that was fondling my boob so spectacularly. God, I half-wish Ivori hadn't interrupted. My body wholly wishes it.

Ivori ignores the hand. Then Fletcher is gone. I'm not even sure how that happened, but I am alone with Ivori.

She is oozing annoyance.

"What?"

"You're too much. You won't go near a guy who actually likes you—remember Thanh?—then you're ready to put out for some random guy you met in an alley.

"Alley?" I wonder what's become of her sex-positive energy but I'm so embarrassed that I'm desperate to change the subject. I just shrug. I'm short on words and my body is still mourning his departure.

She starts muttering about a "random cute guy." I let her dither, then start to la la la about the RCG, trying to make a melody and a sort-of joke. But it falls flat. She's not amusable. She finally wanders down to the bathroom. Thank goodness.

Thanh would like to be where Fletcher was this afternoon, but it's true, poor guy, I keep him at arm's length. Literally. Sometimes I feel powerful giving him nothing but nos. He gets to be the kid banging on the door. I get to be the one inside laughing, saying, *No way are you coming in.* Once again, it's evident that I'm not that nice a person. Ivori is as confusing as I am. What happened to delighting in Shakespeare's erotic sonnets? Now it's Ivori the prude passing judgement. As if I'm a traitor to the female race. She has her own dark corners and I have no light to shine there.

I could use some maternal advice but that's in short supply unless I want to hit up Mrs. Ferguson, whose daughter now hates me. Mrs. F. has been lurking in my mind with her eyebrows crossed ever since I let Ivori practically knock herself out wobbling home from the frat party. Fuck all that guilt. I turn back to Fletcher and my body revisits the happy state of his hands all over me, driving me a little crazy. I try to get him into one box and keep Thanh with his delicate ivory horse in a separate one. That's not entirely easy.

# Chapter 9

On Halloween, Arwyn, Ivori, and I made piles of masks from foamboard and construction paper, under Ivori's artistic tutelage. I conjured up gory things, and Arwyn restrained us from perverse excesses.

Now it's getting close to Thanksgiving, but I still have a drawer full of masks. I pick out a predatory insect face, then I call Thanh and take him up on his offer of a ride home so I can look through some of my mom's things. I've been dreading this, but I keep bumping into it in my mind. I'll turn away for a while, but then I round a corner and there it is again, staring at me. It's haunting me—that's my lame Halloween joke. Thanh says he'll drop me off and go to a coffee shop he found in Saline. A barista made a not-too-subtle racist comment at his usual Starbucks, so he's no longer a fan.

I could just use my key but I want to greet my dad masked.

"Jeez, Leslie, what are you, a praying mantis? That's awful."

"C'mon dad. Sense of humor."

"At least I knew you were coming this time. You're going to go through what's in the attic? I don't suppose you want help up there?"

"Nah. I'm good."

Our attic is long and skinny like a train; small rooms on either side have steeply sloping walls and deep corners. The side rooms are where the witch lived. That made them scary but kind of wonderful.

I pull a couple large flat boxes out of one side room and bring them out to the center space. Holy moly. These are *my* things. From when I was a kid. It's weird they're here with her stuff, like I'm dead, too, which gives me the creeps. I lift up some summer tees and there's—wow. That hat. The one I loved. Almost like I remember. Stiff woven straw that's varnished so it gleams, and on top are the shellacked miniature pears and grapes. Cherries. Very far-out. Fantastically gaudy. I remember being so happy when I got to try it on. I felt incredibly fancy. I set it on my head now and laugh. It's way too small. Still, I wish I had a mirror. I grab my phone and call Thanh. He answers right away.

"Are you at the coffee shop?"

"No. Walking around. I'm looking for a park. Why?"

"You wanna come over here?"

"Really?"

"Yeah. Just come over. You can look through some of this stuff with me."

"Sure. Your dad won't mind?"

"Why would he care? Just come."

Thanh rings the bell five minutes later. I race down the stairs. My dad is in the living room, next to the front hall, but I get to the door before him.

My dad has become an enormous, gaping mouth. God, why should he be so surprised?

"This is my friend, Thanh," I say with a semi-frowny face while my dad nods fifteen times. Thanh starts to go into polite, meet-a-parent mode, which frankly annoys me, so I hurry to the staircase and gesture *come on* with an impatient hand.

In the attic, Thanh grimaces at me.

"What?"

"You could have let me say hello to your dad."

"He doesn't care. It's bullshit stuff anyway."

"It's polite, Leslie."

"Forget about that. Look at these things I found." I pick up the hat and my heart starts to ping pong around in my chest. I didn't expect that and don't know what it's about. "From when I was a kid."

Thanh takes the hat and runs his fingers over the little fruits the way I did with his netsuke. "Those are so sweet."

"Huh. I wouldn't take a bite."

"No. Sweet like things from your childhood can be."

"Joking."

"What's in the other boxes?"

"Mostly my mom's things, I guess. I want to go through them. I don't want my dad's girlfriend mauling everything, maybe helping herself."

"Would she do that?" Thanh sounds shocked and deeply disapproving. I love him for that.

"I haven't met her. Yet."

We go through a couple boxes. There's nothing I want to take with me or even think about wearing. It's nondescript stuff in solid, neutral colors. Not a single dancing-teddy-bear print or an eye-popping plaid.

My dad is calling. I feel like ignoring him. I glance at Thanh, who's also listening. "He can never leave me alone. Just a minute."

I run down the first flight of stairs, and my dad is on the landing. "There's someone I want you to meet, Leslie."

I step back. "Who?"

"Jean. The woman I've been seeing. You brought your friend by so I figured it would be okay if I had Jean drop by."

"Uh. Huh. Huh." I'm stuttering. I desperately want to refuse, but I'm also effing curious. I follow him down. A lamb to the slaughter.

She's sitting upright on our sofa, her hands folded on her lap. She looks eager and nervous. She has short dark hair, a long skirt, and a summery top. Out of season. She looks kind of dated herself. I wonder if she's going to stand up. Wouldn't that be the polite thing to do? But she appears glued to the sofa.

"Leslie, this is my chemist, Jean." He points his opened hand toward her. That is such a lame introduction. I start to feel sorry for her. She should be named Jane because she is plain. My mom was so much prettier. I guess I'm relieved. I want to say to my dad, "Can't you *see* her?" Meaning, can't he see that she's not to the standard of my mom. But I know that's beyond shallow.

"Nice to meet you," I say. Like a human. "A chemist. Cool." I'm done now. A person couldn't get much more polite than me. I assess that Jean the chemist is struggling to speak. I feel an impulse to help her out. Leslie, queen of social skills. "Do you work at the university?"

"Oh. Yes," she says, relieved, I think, that I've provided content.

"She's a full professor," my dad chimes in. "How about that? Impressive. Maybe she'll go easy on you if you have to take her class."

Jean frowns. My dad has tramped too close to a suggestion of academic impropriety, and he is chuckling about it. I should feel intimidated by Jean. She's a professor. Yet I feel like I have the upper hand here, maybe because she's trying to date my dad and he's so pitiful.

"Hey, I better go back up. I left my friend up in the attic." I think of unnerving her by saying we're sorting through my mom's things, but I zip it up. This woman doesn't seem like she's floating on cloud nine; she doesn't need to be knocked down to earth with a thud.

Thanh is immersed in his phone when I get back. Probably studying sedges and hedges again.

"You wouldn't believe it. My dad's girlfriend came over. I was called down to meet her."

"Woah."

I shrug. "Not a big deal. She was, like, *basic*. In a sciency way. Straightforward. Practical. Like baking soda."

"I get it. Sort of. Though I thought you'd be more upset."

It's possible I *am* upset. My heart is racing, and my mind is jumpy.

I slip back into the side room, and he stands at the door as if he's too large to fit inside no matter how many shrinking mushrooms he eats. Some of my mother's nicer clothes are hanging on a metal rack at the back of the room. There's a stretchy lime-green dress covered in open netting. I remember it. I thought the netting was cool. I remember putting it up to my face to see if the world became honeycombed. Again, my heart starts leading a percussion section. Here's a blue dress that's silky and bright. The color is beautiful. I don't recognize this one at all. I imagine her all dressed up and preparing to go out. Away. Somewhere I don't know a thing about. There's a brown fuzzy suit. Fuzzy Wuzzy. I knew a nursery rhyme. It ends, "Fuzzy Wuzzy wasn't fuzzy, was he." It's not a question; it's an assertion about a sad bear that has no hair. Poor Fuzzy. Not much of a life.

I need to dress up in something opposite of Plain Jean. I pull from its hanger an unfamiliar rose-pink sweater with crocheted flowers sewn all over it, little turquoise cups with a red ball inside. I thought my mom was beautiful. Maybe in this, or some other outfit. Poor Jean. A baked potato without any toppings.

Thanh's watching. He's hunched at the door in the dusty light. I hold the sweater out toward him. "This is hideous," I say, abruptly finished with it. Thanh's head is tilted sideways to accommodate the slanting ceiling. I suddenly remember my mom in this sweater, and I'm gulping air.

"Put it on," he says, laughing.

I back him up into the main room where the light is better. I pull on the ridiculous sweater and see Mrs. Ferguson bunching her lips, trying to think of something diplomatic to say. The wool is itchy on my arms. Where would she have worn this? In the garden in the fall? It smells of perfume. Au de toilette. Jean Naté. Things come back. I see her at the door. Going out. Excited. Bubbly. Her smile nervous but happy, a quick departure. Did she kiss my cheek?

"I like it," Thanh says.

"You're crazy."

"You look...*decorated* in it."

"*You* put something on."

Would my dad like someone trying on his stuff? So what?

He's probably mad at me already. About something. Maybe the praying mantis mask. Or I wasn't perfect with his new girlfriend, who's likely still down there, creepily. I lead Thanh into the other small room where my father's clothes hang on a wooden bar against the wall, deep in the shadows. He comes out wearing a black suit jacket—a nice one, like a guy might buy for a wedding—and a loosely knotted tie. Electric blue.

I'm shocked by how handsome he looks. I've only seen him in jeans and shirts. Or a hoodie. Here comes Fletcher. RCG. I barely remember his face, but my body remembers him. Thanh looks even better than Fletcher did, if possible. I feel a little frantic. "Now switch," I say, to get back to nonsense. I pull off the pink sweater and thrust it at him, duck back into the room that has my mother's stuff. I come out holding a puffy, lemon-colored hat my mom possibly knit herself. I remember that she wore it when it was super cold out. It's so soft and the color is the prettiest you could imagine. I want to press it to my nose and search for her smell, but Thanh is watching and I toss it at him. He puts it on like a beret along with the sweater. So much for elegance.

Thanh returns to my father's rack and gets me suit pants and a rust-brown tie. I try to lift a leg to put the pants on, but I lose my balance. He catches my arm with one hand, then holds on tightly to steady me. I think for a second of Ivori and wonder if she's worried about where I disappeared to. The pants puddle on the ground. I snort and put the tie around my neck but don't know how to knot it. I can't stop laughing. Thanh is laughing too. He squints at me fumbling with the tie. "I can do that," he says, but doesn't make a move.

"Do it, then."

He steps forward, and his concentrating face is close to mine, though his eyes are looking down at the tie. Here comes Fletcher again.

He finishes and steps back. "Good evening, Mr. Jones," he says to me, still very close. "You look splendid in your attire."

I look at him in his sweater and yellow hat and the giggles reclaim me. "You look *un peu* odd in yours."

He sets aside the hat on the sofa. "I have a question for you, sir." He's aiming for a French accent but doesn't have a clue. Now he is just breathing and speechless.

"Very well. Ask your question, Mrs. Jones. Madame."

I think he's going to ask about the cut of my suit or something ridiculous. Instead, he says shyly, "Since it is playtime."

"Yes?"

"Since it is playtime, may I kiss you, sir?"

I'm a captive of the giggles now. They grab hold of me and carry me away somewhere. The truth is, I want to kiss him. I get myself to stop giggling. "Perhaps, madame," I say softly. "But only if the hour is between"—I pick up my phone and take a long, stalling breath—"one and one-fifteen, eastern daylight time."

Now his energy is quiet. More settled. "I'm in luck, then." He puts one hand on the side of my face and kisses me—for at least three seconds. I am melting even faster than with Fletcher. I didn't know his lips could be so pillowy. I didn't know he knew how to kiss like that. He should have warned me. I start to get angry, like I do, but the feeling can't get up on its feet. Even so, I glance at my phone. "I'm very sorry madame but your hat has fallen on the floor and your time is about to expire."

He steps away from me. "Never mind. I am already perfectly happy."

I want to say something clever to recover from nearly collapsing but I have nothing. I take off the suit and lay it on the
sofa, but Thanh's lips have taken over my mind. I hear my father
calling me from below. For once I'm relieved at his butting in
and run down the two flights of stairs. Thanh follows me down,
though he stops on the stairs when he's half a flight above us.

"What? What?" I pound my dad. "Is the house on fire?"

"I just wanted to see you. Next thing you know, you'll be
leaving, and I'll barely have laid eyes on you."

"What about your friend?"

"Jean had to go. To her office."

I lead Thanh into the living room and plop myself in the
biggest, most comfortable armchair. Thanh takes the end of the
sofa. My dad sits in an armchair, so now we're a triangle.

"Did you make any progress up there?" my dad asks.

I'm afraid I might get the giggles again, so I bite my lip and
scowl.

"Okay. None of my business. I'm just glad you stopped by.
You can do that any time you like."

"I guess I know that," I say. "It's my house."

My dad looks flummoxed. "I'm glad you feel that way, Leslie.
I just didn't know if you still did."

"We were in the same biology class," I say, apropos of nothing. "Me and Thanh. We should go now. Hey, good to see you,
Dad." I pop a kiss on his cheek and then we are out on the street
as if we teleported.

In the car, I say to Thanh, "I guess now you can see what I
mean about my dad. He's seriously on his own planet."

"Seems like he just wants to spend time with you."

The giggles and silliness are gone. Fury flashes through me. "You're delusional," I tell him. "Half the time he's angry with me." I wish I could take back that kiss. I feel like shoving Thanh and getting out of the car, but it's moving.

He shrugs. "You can't upset me today." But he's lying because I have upset him, just like I wanted to. Something is wrong with me. I'm yearning in six different directions. All I can think of is crawling under my covers and pressing 'pause' on my entire mind.

The next day, Thanh wants to go on another of his park adventures before class. I'm off kilter still, like someone flattened by a wave who gets hit by another one before they are standing. But I agree to go with him to Marshall Park. As we're climbing a hill that directs all your attention upward into a seriously impressive forest, I stumble over a rock and fall hard into him. He keeps his balance as I recover mine. I think of Ivori combining her pucker with alcohol and I tell him, "Ivi and I went to a party."

"Last night?" He looks alarmed.

"A couple weeks ago. House party." I keep my eyes on him like Hubble tracking a celestial body.

"Oh." He pauses. "How was that?"

"Um, good, bad. Too much to drink possibly." I add, "And some behavior of questionable judgment flowed from it. Indirectly." I am veering into dangerous water, but it feels inevitable. I don't try to stop it.

"Like what?" His voice is a sky-scraping question mark.

I shrug. "A few random kisses." I say it as if kisses were rose petals scattered by a flower girl. Innocent. Sweet.

Thanh has frozen.

"What's wrong?" I ask, feigning naivete.

"Nothing, It's not my business. I'm fine."

"You're not appearing fine." I think he is angry, but Thanh can't help but be subtle, so it is hard to know.

"Well, why did you tell me?"

"It wasn't anything. Not worth hiding. Just what Ivori calls an RCG."

"Am I supposed to know what that means?"

"Random cute guy. Random meaning no big deal. It doesn't count."

Walking back from class later, he's twenty feet from me, practically off the sidewalk and in the dirt. I know what he's thinking about and try to shock him into normalcy. "You know, get over it. I told you it's not that big a deal. If you want, I'll do the same whatever-it-was with you so you can stop feeling so bad."

"No, thank you. That's a shitty offer."

I shrug. "A shitty offer's better than no offer at all."

"Is it? I don't think so, Leslie. You can be so childish and don't know how to treat people or yourself. Maybe you should see a shrink."

I give him the silent treatment after that. My mind is webbed with sticky memories of how I gave that same treatment to my mom. I think she hated it, too, because she'd shadow me. Waiting, I guess, for me to turn around and say I'm sorry, but I never said that. I half-liked her trailing behind me.

Back in our room, Ivori is napping. I wake her by stomping in. "Thanh says I should see a shrink."

"Well, that wouldn't be the craziest idea I've heard. Why did he?"

I shrug. "Because I somewhat told him about that gorgeous guy Fletcher who I sort of fooled around with."

"Oh. Brilliant." She's disgusted with me. "You obviously were trying to hurt him."

"It was just information," I say. I'm pacing. My head is full of Jean the chemist, prim and frowny on the sofa, sopping up my dad's attention. Plus my mom's old clothes and the memories they exhaled and Thanh's lips, which somehow race my heart and slow my breathing all at once.

# Part II

# Chapter 10

It's the end of April. The air is bursting with sunshine, and we're in a rental house—Ivori, Arwyn, me, and a new guy, Alex. It was a no-brainer for me and Ivori to invite Arwyn, because who doesn't love Arwyn, who said, "I'd be honored." Iv and I took him to see the place, and he spun around in the decrepit kitchen, beaming as if it was a house in Barton Hills, a ritzy area where the Obamas supposedly bought a mansion, though no one's seen them. Arwyn took an orange off the counter and set it on the floor; it rolled a few yards and bonked the outer wall. "This house has character," he said.

"Oh, no. Unwise, girls," Mrs. Ferguson tsked when Ivori posted online to try to get someone for the fourth bedroom, but we blew past her. After a lot of duds, we got an email from Alexander Kuznetsov, whose name Arwyn loved so much that he insisted we had to interview him, though he's twenty-one. By then we were desperate, since we needed help covering the rent. Arwyn especially has a tight budget.

Soon we had a Russian bear hulking at our dorm-room door—tall and hunched and slant-shouldered, so paunchy for a half-young guy that his body is slightly disgusting. Alex is pasty. And his rough skin has a few pimples and a lot of razor bumps.

Someone needs to teach him how to shave. I wonder if he is missing one parent, like half the people I know, or has a father who has fallen down on the job. He came with his mother in tow. Pretty weird. She was looming over him, big though he is.

I sat on my bed, with Arwyn and Ivori on either side of me, so we're lined up in a bed-based interviewing committee. Mrs. Kuznetsov dragged her chair over beside Alex. I'm concerned that this is a worse intimacy derangement than Ivori and her mother.

At the end of Arwyn's show-n-tell of the tactfully curated house photos he took, Mrs. Kuznetsov says, "It will do. If Alexei is content with it."

"Yes, Mother." I can't tell if Alex's submission is the real thing or him mocking her for her maternal dominance.

Ivori is frowning at the edge of my vision. I can see she's thinking, "Wait a minute. Who's judging who, here?" She starts in with a laundry list of questions about what Alex studies (Russian history) and what year he is in school (senior) and does he smoke (a little) or cook (um, no). The answers are all irrelevant, except for the smoking. Arwyn gives a twisted smile and says, "You can do that outside," and he offers Alexander an open-eyed, patient look, as if he's awaiting a nod regarding his counsel. Finally, he gets one, though I think it's half-hearted and don't trust it.

After they leave, we have to consider that we've been looking for weeks and have come up dry.

"Maybe he'll grow on us," I say.

"*Cancer* does that," Ivori says. She adds, "I'm not sharing a bathroom with him."

"I'll share," Arwyn says. I know that's a sacrifice for him because he's fastidious, and Alex's slovenly nature shone through, even though his mother probably supervised his dressing.

Thank goodness for Arwyn. Without him, our house would be a pigsty. It's also possible we might starve. Ivori, Arwyn, and I are taking spring-summer classes. I haven't a clue yet what subjects I'm really interested in, so I'm taking a human biology class with Thanh and a class in essay writing that purports to sharpen the student's ability to put forth a cogent and persuasive argument.

I'm walking back to the house one day, lugging my massive bio book, and I get the feeling the house is emanating some new energy. I see a dark blob pressing against the bottom of the screen door. When I open the door, a skinny medium-sized tea-splotched dog with two cute clumps of black nose-freckles darts out. I'm still holding the door as Arwyn races past to catch up with the dog, who is methodically sniffing the perimeter of the muddy front yard. Arwyn shoots me a look, his eyebrows lifted and yanked together, his mouth contorted, apologizing without words. He bunches the scruff of the dog's collarless neck in his hand and encourages her back to the house with repetition of her name. It's Doris, which is a ridiculous name for a dog. Now she's cataloguing the smells in the living room. Arwyn looks at me plaintively and says, "Leslie, I love you, and please, please, please let me keep Doris."

"Not with that name." I'm deadpan.

"*You* name her. Anything. I don't care." He gives her one last look as Doris, the name he likes. "Well okay, I *do* care, but it's up to you."

The dog is busy pushing her nose along the floor, nostrils puffing. "Nosey?" I ask, knowing Arwyn will hate the name—so unsophisticated, a name a kid would pick.

Arwyn looks stricken. He sighs and studies the dog.

"Nose?" I modify my suggestion.

"K."

"Really? Okay?"

Arwyn shakes his head. "K as in K-N-O-S-E. A little more outré. Not quite so kindergarten. Sorry. You know I love you, Les."

I don't object. "Where did you get her?"

"The poor thing was just wandering. I checked with the Humane Society and looked all over the internet for listings. Nothing. She came to us, Les. And we have a house now, and a yard, right?"

"She's pretty cute if you ignore her boniness." I'm watching her move, her nose mobile and fascinated. Her limbs turn corners smoothly as a stream. Outside, she'd be lightning, running after a ball or stick. I'd like to wander around town with her. Maybe walk her over to meet Thanh, though, oops, he's allergic.

I pat my thigh and she comes to me and lets me rub behind her ears. I thump my chest a couple times with both hands, and she jumps up and lays her paws on my shoulders. "Okay, now get down," I say and bend forward as well as I can with Knose pressed against me and snap my fingers near the floor. She drops down.

"Smart." Arwyn lights with pride. Knose barks sharply, twice. Her ears have taken over from her nose, and her eyes drift as she focuses on the sound above. Alex is trudging eccentric shapes around his room.

Alex is generally upstairs in his room, just across from mine, and it's frankly unsettling that he's that close. Alex is the person that someone imagined when they invented the phrase "crawled out from under a rock." Primitive. Lizardly. At the same time, he's mister deep thinker. As if Dostoyevsky mated with the Creature from the Black Lagoon. A bizarre coupling of Russian intellectual history and a room piled high with old Domino's pizza boxes. His hair is getting longer and longer, as if he's aiming for some kind of Jared Leto. Greasier and greasier is what I notice. He probably likes to see me and Iv squirm and turn up our noses at him. Any time his mother visits, Alex follows her like a cub. Maybe that's why he loves to show me and Ivori that he can muscle us around.

The next morning, Thanh comes by to walk with me to our bio class, even though the route distorts a beeline into a semicircle.

"We got a dog," I tell Thanh.

"I can tell," he says, rubbing his nose a little sheepishly like he doesn't want to spoil the party.

"I forgot," I half-lie to him.

I'm happy today. I don't know if it's the dog or maybe the breezy weather that feels as if it could carry me like a scarf blown high into the sky. Thanh can tell, and he looks at me as if he's hoping he's the cause of my minor delirium. "What?" I ask.

He shakes his head and shrugs. His hand is swinging beside him as he walks, and I think of grabbing it and giving it a little kiss on the back. I'm not sure I like these hit-and-run emotions. They splash odd possibilities in front of my eyes. I glance down at his hand moving metronomically. I try to mix the colors of Thanh's lovely skin on one of Ivori's paint palettes. A little brown ochre. A little lemon yellow. A touch of sap green. I look again to see if I have the color right in my mind. *Perfect.* I still can't decide if I just want him as a friend or if I want to do something with him in the sex category. Luckily, Thanh's a no-pressure person if there ever was one.

He's got wind of something in me that he wants to decipher. "What?" I ask him again, but it's one of those questions that puts up a wall.

"Never mind."

Biology is the Krebs cycle, which is not easy-peasy, so I have to pay attention. I wrinkle my forehead, which seems to improve my intake of complex information, as if all those horizontal wrinkles were vents for sucking stuff in. I am squished in tight against Thanh because the loose chairs in this lecture hall get shoved all over the place, and today we're in a high-density chair-ball. I think I can feel the hair on my arms catching on the hair of his. I want to make a dumb joke to him about cotton candy—which is all sugar—as a source of cellular energy. I remember what it's like to pinch that pink sticky stuff between my fingers and pull off pieces, stuffing my mouth as my mom, my dad, and I wander past spotted cows and gigantic pigs at the state fair. Cotton candy doesn't look like something you could eat—it is more like a sunlit cloud you would just admire. Today, I feel like cotton candy. I feel rosy and fluffy and full of energy, which must come from the Krebs cycle consuming whatever fuel it can find.

I get back to the business of following the long sequence of chemical reactions our elderly no-nonsense instructor is walking us through. I imagine that her intelligence is stored in the tight-wound miniature gray curls set on her scalp in an arrangement that might defy the laws of physics, or at least of design. I have a stack of note cards like a person from a past millennium. I write out the Krebs cycle steps, one stacked over the other in a neat pile that makes the prospect of memorizing them more hopeful. Thanh glances at me, then at my tower of chem reactions. I press my pen down harder and imagine he's taking stock of what level of student I might be. *A,* I want him to think. Maybe *A+*. *Damn, she's smart.* That's what he's thinking.

When I get home, Ivori is in a rotten mood because some guy has been sexting her, but I try not to let her bring me down. I need to keep my focus on my battle with the Krebs cycle. Alex is in his room making soft, scratchy noises. I think he's rebuilding his pizza box monument. Once, I had to knock on his door and tell him to move his car (yeah, he's got one too), and he came out in a short bathrobe, not properly tied. He leaned close to me and lifted his eyebrows, knowing he was freaking me out. When he does emerge from his cave, he has to make a snide remark, usually about what my or Ivori's clothing says about our desperation to meet a hot guy or some such bullshit. Sometimes he offers up an infuriating lecture on Tolstoy or Pushkin, the point of which is to make me feel stupid. I just say, "Fuck, Alex. Can't you get rid of those pizza boxes? You've probably got roaches."

He tells me, "I do have roaches. Lots of them. I'm going to catch a few in a caviar jar so I can bring them in to show you. I think I'll let some go. I'm sure they would have a fine party exploring under your bed."

I want to scream. "Just keep your fucking cockroaches to yourself." I think the Dr. Dream diagnosis for Alex would be sadist. I bet you could tag him with half a dozen others as well.

"Aw, c'mon. Teenie weenie cockroaches crawling over your bed and desk. I think you'll like it."

"I'm calling the health department about your shithole room." It's lucky I know how to swear because otherwise I might explode.

Today, Alex seems to be dragging his pizza box towers from one side of his room to the other. What can a person say about that? I'm not sure you can get someone arrested just for being strange. Ivori has a room full of empty boxes too, so it's a household theme, but hers are for an art project, so they're at least marginally more functional. My only boxes are properly stashed in the closet, where boxes belong. I brought a few things here from home, including a shoebox of old letters. I'm letting them live a lonely life on the top shelf, behind some shoes and other junk.

# Chapter 11

We're in the car. We're going south on State Street. Ivori's driving insanely fast. I keep quiet and let her merge onto I-94 East where her speed will better suit the road. "Who lit you on fire?"

She shrugs. "I keep getting texts from that creep."

Now I get why she was hanging around in front of my bed, shifting back and forth on her feet like a corralled horse. After a minute of rock 'n' roll, she barked, "Let's get out of here."

She wanted to go to the city—which necessitated her reminding me that the city means Detroit, since "Ann Arbor's not a city, in case you didn't know." I sighed, but part of me was excited. I'm thinking music. I'm thinking dark-roast coffee.

I had to remind her that we don't have a car. She pressed me to call and beg Thanh, which I did, hesitantly. He was taking a quiz but, nice guy that he is, he offered up his car.

"Bummer about the sexter."

"I swear he's watching me. Sometimes he knows what I'm wearing. That's spooky, right?"

"Ugh. Yeah. That is."

"My mom would freak. She'd race up here and try to pack

me up and drag me home. And she's touring. Not the right time to unbalance her."

"My dad is good about safety protocols. I think he's speaking to me this week. He's still got Plain Jean, so he's high on life."

"No. Keep him out of it, too."

"Where exactly are we going, Jacks?" I laugh a little because I feel like I've asked her that same question on a dozen occasions. I feel a spike of what I think is love. It's odd to be feeling that sitting here in the dark and chill, speeding to a mysterious place Ivori's set her sights on.

"A club. On Gratiot."

I'm suspicious. "Someplace you've been?"

"Not recently."

"Not ever, you mean."

"I read about it. Sick place."

There aren't a heck of a lot of cars on the street in Detroit, but it's pretty parked-up in front of a place that stands out in the dark due to the magenta-colored neon script on the front.

"Lucky us," Ivori says, because she sees a car pulling out just past the door. She's rocking in her seat as if she's just won the lottery. "This is it. Melody's. They better let us in."

I'm alarmed. "I thought you checked this place out."

"Halfway."

"Fuck. You always trick me into going random places."

"I'd go by myself, but you're forever wanting to mother-hen me. Watch me walk. Etcetera."

"Yeah, like I love that."

She shrugs. I think I hurt her feelings. "I had such a fucked-up day," she says. "Who *is* this pervert who's sexting me?"

"You should have called your mom," I say, but really, I'm glad that for once she didn't.

The entrance is squeezed and dark. A birth canal, but noisy. I can tell from the sounds that it's crowded in there, and I'm strung out between fear and excitement. No one is in the entrance except a guy my dad's age perched on a high stool. He's the person who's supposed to let us in. Or not. I give him a wary look, but Ivori's shimmying and glittering in front of him. Not too outrageous. Just enough. I can see him calculating, *This one would add some sparkle to our little joint here.* It's obvious he knows we're underage. He's got a sober, decision-making countenance.

"Twelve dollars," he says. "Not once. *Twice.*" He must think we're paupers. I hear the music from inside the club. Jazz. Piano. Still indistinct.

The narrow hallway opens into a large room of small tables where every seat appears to be taken. A young woman with a clip-board meets us as we walk in.

"I only have space up on the stage, in front," she says. "Right by the musicians. Is that all right with you?"

Excitement overtakes me. I say, "Sure," without even looking at Ivori, because who wouldn't want to sit close to the musicians? Aren't those the best seats in the house? Maybe there's a catch. Maybe they're five inches from the bathroom door or right where the trombone player dumps the spit from his horn.

The hostess leads the way up over the lip of the stage to a single table up there. There's a trio—piano, bass, and saxophone—and the table is smack behind the piano player and a little to his right, so you can see the keyboard. The hostess hands us leather-bound menus, and Ivori and I are looking at each other, thinking, *Wow, we made it in.* I look around, and we're definitely the youngest people here. The only other really young person is the piano player. He's a skinny Black dude who looks like he's my age. I start to watch the crazy speed of his fingers. All three musicians are great in their own ways, but it's this piano-playing kid that's amazing. He's so close that his flying fingers are magnets to my eyes.

"Are you ordering food?" Ivori asks me.

I nod. I'm not that hungry, but I need to taste something from this place. And we better buy some food and make some money for our server, who's heading our way, or she might be inclined to remark how young we are and get us kicked out.

Here she comes. Tall. Twenty-something. Perfect, non-slouchy posture and wiry hair that's cropped so you can see the full round of her head, a little bulbous on top as if her brain might need extra space. She steps up to the table and cocks her head. "Ladies?"

I order a burger with blue cheese. I can see one at the table a half-step down from us, just off the stage, hot juice oozing from it. And coffee. Ivori nods that she'll have the same burger. "And a coke."

A minute later, waitress Jan is back, not with our food but with a short glass of golden liquid she sets on the table and slides toward Ivori as she jerks her head over her shoulder toward another table. Two men. They're easily twice our age. Decent-looking though. Dressed in suit jackets, like no one I know.

"Are you going to drink that?" I ask Ivori. I think my voice might be shaking, but I can't exactly tell what's in my voice and what's in my head. I'm nervous.

Ivori lifts her brows and pins them there in a scared-excited expression that accompanies a slow nod. She doesn't say a word. I think she's imagining those guys can hear us, though they're too far away.

"You are?" It's definitely not beer. I'm wondering what the hell it is.

Again, that hesitant nod. Shit, I'm going to have to drive us home. But I'm not going to tell her what to do. I'm a little pissed those men were rude enough to send Ivori a drink and not me. Okay, she's the sexy one, but I'm not a toadstool. I'm also certain they are sleazeballs of some variety, despite their nice clothes, but I'd have to squint more closely to suss out their pathology. Ivori's not even paying attention to them. Her focus is on the caramel-colored drink in front of her.

"Maybe it's a Moscow mule," I say, because it's the one drink I've heard of. She doesn't appear to like the taste, but her sips have a steady, workmanlike rhythm. They're synced with the string bass reverberating behind us. She looks determined. I turn my attention back to the music. The piano player is dishing out all kinds of jazzy glissandos and accelerandos. I wish he'd turn around when he's taking a break because I want to show him some appreciation. I tilt my head his way and whisper, "Nimble jacks," to Ivi.

Jan is on the way with our burgers. I'm suddenly starving, my stomach folded in two. Ivori gets up to use the ladies' room, not even glancing at the guy who sent her the drink. He's probably disappointed, possibly pissed that he wasted his money on a rude juvenile. She's wearing somewhat high and very skinny heels. I'll give her a pass on one point of wobbliness for those, but what

I'm seeing is higher up on the scale. Heels plus real alcohol plus pucker. Oh, man. There's no doubt who's driving home.

When she gets back, we eat and sigh and wipe our chins because the hamburgers are spectacularly delicious and juicy. And I focus on the piano player's beautiful long fingers. I think he uses lotion on those hands. They're his equipment, so he has to take good care of them. I wonder if they're insured. I want to watch and listen and swallow up the music along with the burger. The saxophone player is sweating streams and wiping his face every two seconds. It's not elegant, but his broad sound is mellow. The double bass doesn't have the beauty of the piano or the saxophone, but its deep thrumming is a pedestal for the others' music.

Ivori is barely listening. She's done eating and is still sipping on that drink. I'm not sure where her head is, though I'm guessing it's stuck on the asshole who's been sexting her. Unlike me, she can hear music any day of the week given that her mom's a diva. I think Mrs. Ferguson plays the piano, too, and probably accompanies herself and sings at home and their house swells with music.

I hate to tear myself away from Melody's, but the adorable piano player has finished his two sets and exited the stage, and something in me says we better leave. I have a slightly anxious feeling as if I might lose my mind and follow him back into the dressing room and jump his bones. I think there are women who actually do that sort of thing, so it's not that far-fetched. What if I did that and later came out of my horny trance and discovered he's Thanh. I tell Ivori I'm driving. I'm nervous about taking the highway in the dark, but I'm the better bet of the two of us. And I feel responsible for E.V. After that last accident, I have a complex about not being a good friend, so I want to get this right.

In the car, Ivori has a haunted look, and I assume it's about that sexter. She keeps running her tongue over her chipped tooth, which tells me she's still not managed to make a dentist appointment. While I'm watching the road, she tells me the creep is writing a couple times a day and stating in graphic detail what he'd like to do to her body. "Nothing racist, thank god," she says. "But gross, because who the hell is he? And I swear he sometimes seems like he knows what I'm wearing."

"What exactly does this guy say?"

"I'm the most beautiful woman he's ever seen, and he thinks about me 24/7. He can't get his work done. He wants to make love, or 'do it' with me so bad."

"His work?"

"Yeah. He's probably a trash collector."

"I think that's classist or something, Iv."

"Fuck it. So maybe he's a professor or a banker."

I can't decide if she's making too big a deal out of this and should just delete the texts and not let the jerk get to her. I mean, the guy says he wants to "make love." Do rapists use that language?

Out of the corner of my eye, I see Ivori twist her mouth and shake her head. "I don't know about men."

"I thought you were an enthusiast. You know, 'love to party,' and all."

"Can't a person have mixed feelings? Sex is great, but sometimes men are just so. *Rude*, I guess. Or crude. They don't think we're human. Except for Arwyn, you know. Sweet guys like him. But they're usually queer."

"Thanh's okay, right?"

She nods. "He's one of the good ones." She sighs. "You're lucky."

I admit I'm thinking about the sexiness of the piano kid this evening. I wish I had a clue about these things. "I don't know about sex," I say, tiptoeing. "I don't think I'll even like it." A mother who talked to me during the sex-ed era of middle school might have helped this situation. I could have used that. "I mean, somebody *in* your body. That's a very private space."

I'm looking at the road but can see Ivori looking at me directly, probably thinking how odd I am. "You'll like it. Trust me. I mean, you're the nature girl, not me, but I'm telling you, Mother Nature got that part figured out."

I'm still wishing I had a regular mother somewhere in the picture. I kind of take it personally that she died. As if she'd run away from home. From me.

We get the car back to Thanh's wreck of a parking space. I feel an impulse to knock on his door just to look at him for a minute, but it's two a.m. A few people are wandering the streets—some looking drunk, some homeless, others students like us, I'm guessing. I feel safe with Ivori, and she seems revived and capable of walking. It's pitch dark, but the night is strangely beautiful. Maybe it's the spring air. When we get back to our apartment, I pronounce, "The end to another magnificent Ivori-adventure."

I'm in my room and a stream of questions about my absent mother is flooding my mind. I think of the sketches Ivori has littered all over her bed and night table half the time, and now she's got cardboard pieces and some empty boxes scattered across her floor. Her room is a creative mess of stuff in motion. I remember that motherboard dream, but I didn't do anything about it. An actual board is way too public. Shit. Alex Creep is across the hall. There's an essay I have to write for English by the end of the term in which I argue for and against a thesis. Can you argue a point—cogently and persuasively—about who your mother was and whether she gave a crap about you? Probably I'm just overtired and will forget all this in the morning. Sleep. Unconsciousness. My solution to three-quarters of life's problems.

# Chapter 12

I took the Krebs cycle test and got an A-. It's not an A+ and probably wouldn't impress Thanh, though he'd be polite about it, but I'm celebrating anyway by doing no schoolwork today. It's a beautiful day. Ivori's door is closed—she's sleeping in—so I can't get her to go out with me. I reach for Knose's leash. She does an airborne three-sixty. Spinning is her superpower. I walk her down Geddes to Observatory. She lopes beside me, pulling ahead from time to time. We're beside a cemetery. She wants to go in, and I follow her through the gate. We weave a line among the gray and pink gravestones. I'm not interested in looking at the names, but Knose squats down and pees at the edge of one, and I feel compelled to look and see whose grave she's desecrated. Mary Linn, born 1990 and died 2000. A kid. Why did Knose have to pick that one? I look around. The place is huge and seems devoid of the living. I am glad no one saw.

Now she's pulling me every which way, eager to explore. I probably shouldn't, but I let her off the leash so she can revel in following her nose. Some of the trees are in bloom. My mother would have liked this; the beauty is dramatic, like her dahlia blooms. I have to admit it's nice. One tree looks like an Easter bonnet. Even *I* know it's a magnolia. The petals are like skin:

thick, but with a surface that's delicate. I pick some up from the ground and push my finger over them, hard. The finger leaves a bruised trail, and I drop them and watch how they scatter. I call Knose, but she is following her eponymous equipment and not my voice, and the next time I look at her she is digging a hole to China. She has it dug in a hot minute and is ready to begin another. I look around and see that she's already completed a dozen. I tell myself a lame joke about Knose volunteering as a gravedigger. I'm trying to calm myself down, since she's messing up the grass badly.

My mother's grave comes to mind, which is not so funny. I can't remember if her grave has a gray stone or a pink one, and something about that unsettles me. I have to say Knose's name sixteen times to get her attention. I want to go ASAP, so I click on her leash and yank her at the neck. She doesn't get mad. She just looks up, like she's saying, "Oh, yeah, I remember you," and follows me. I have a strange impulse to photograph her excavation work, so I pull out my phone, wondering what part of me likes to document graveyard defilement. My mind goes all abstract art on me, and I'm not in a graveyard where Mary Linn is buried, where my mother could be. I'm in a Jackson Pollock world, like Ivori's room, where any kind of chaos is art.

I need to sit down cross-legged on a cold stone grave marker to regroup, Knose held close by her leash.

"Hey, little lady," I hear from a ways off.

I mutter, *ugh,* and tighten up. Maybe I should feel threatened, but I don't bother. I've got a protector dog. I just look up at the man who's now standing nearby.

"You come here regularly?" he asks.

*Ugh,* again. He is a big-boned, strong-looking older Black man, maybe fifty. His voice is smooth and bathwater warm, like that saxophone we heard at Melody's. I put him somewhere between a jazz singer and a television grandfather.

I guess I'll play this game, so I ask, "And if I do?"

"No bother. It's a peaceful place. Lots of folks come here to visit someone, or just to spend time. Maybe visit with themselves, if you know what I mean."

"I'm walking my dog."

"Ah. I see. Now that was going to be my next question. 'This old guy is full of questions,' you might be thinking."

"I'm not thinking."

"But it seems you're indicating that pretty dog is yours."

"She belongs to one of my housemates. I walk her."

"So she's under your supervision."

I scan the grass where Knose has been running. It looks like a prairie dog village. I might know where this man is heading, and I tense up, but also want to get this over with.

"You've got a point you're wanting to make? About my dog?" I'm surprised I'm so forward with an older man.

"I think you know my point. I see where your eyes are moving, and see your eyes speak to your brain as well. So I expect you know I'm going to say you're welcome to walk here, but we can't have the dog tearing up the ground. Some folks are particular about how this place looks. It's where their people are buried."

"I know that." I want to say, *I'm not stupid,* but abort that because in fact I'm feeling like an idiot and apparently I've behaved like one. I also want to say, *All these dirty plastic bouquets and ragged ribbons and flags don't speak to particularity in my book,* but I just mutter, "To each his own."

"Exactly," he says. "You've got to respect the other individual."

"Well, where am I supposed to take my dog?" I know it's childish and beyond presumptuous to ask that. For some reason, I like talking to this man. And I get the feeling he's the kind of person who might help you ponder some insignificant problem you've got, like where to walk your dog, who isn't even yours.

And sure enough, he says, "I happen to know a place, not too far down the road from here. I can't say I know who owns the land, but I've walked there and it's a pretty place. Don't tell anyone I sent you because I've got no claim on the land—and I'm probably setting you out to be a trespasser." A wistful look I can't parse crosses his face. "But I doubt anyone will notice you being there. Unlike here, where there's a big old caretaker with a book of rules."

I laugh and wonder if I'll run into him at that mystery place if I should happen to go there. I like it here, though. I like the labyrinth of graves and the stones that invite you to sit down and cool your butt.

"I'm Frank," he says. He's taken a mini pad of paper and a ballpoint pen from his pocket, and he's sketching something. "There you go." He hands me the rectangle of paper he's ripped off, which has a neatly drawn little map.

A laugh bubbles up. "Treasure map?" I used to love all those buried treasure cartoons on TV when I was a kid.

"It just might be," he says. "It's a special place. You'll like it there. Your dog will like it too, I expect." Quietly he adds, keeping his own company now, "I like it." He nods thoughtfully.

"Well, maybe I'll see you there sometime." I feel a pinch of sadness leaving this place and a weird despondency about this man, too, as if I'd known him my entire life instead of ten min-utes, as if I'm Thanh losing his grandfather or something. But oh, shit. Here comes out of my brain an automatic weapon and I'm bang-bang-banging at that sadness. I remember something my dimply psychology TA said about a mindful approach to feelings where you just nod hello to them and don't try to wreak havoc on them—like with a machine gun, for instance. I think of walking down the street and some sketchy person is coming my way on the sidewalk, and I just say a peaceable hello and kind of tip my imaginary hat. Now I'm supposed to raise my hat to this sadness and leave it lying there.

Frank walks off, trusting me to behave, and I'm left with the headstone and with Knose, who's looking up at me with her head tilted, curious what I'm thinking. She's not even contemplating what she needs to bury.

"The damage is already done," I tell her. "You got us kicked out."

A wind rips through and the temperature drops twenty degrees in two minutes. I need to go. My butt is ice cold. I take a look at the stone I've been sitting on and I'm startled to see that the grave is for someone exactly my age. Tabitha James. The stone is inscribed, *We will never stop missing you, our beloved.* I feel a little nauseous—the words are a bit much—but I also feel ashamed of all the holes I let Knose dig, so that Tabitha's gravesite looks like it's lying in a bombed-out village. Tabitha's family will probably come here and feel helpless about all those holes when they're already distraught about the big thing—Tabitha. I guess I have a lousy relationship with the dead. I don't visit my mother's grave, even in my mind. I don't know what words are engraved on the stone or whether it's pink like Tabitha's or gray like some of the others.

Before I go, I push some soil back with my foot into the two or three holes closest to Tabitha and reset the turf where I can. It's a mess, even with the miniature sod toupees. I imagine describing the scene to Thanh, who laughs in that mild, warm-milk way he has, and I feel a little less like a criminal vandal.

When I get home, Arwyn isn't amused with the muddy condition Knose is in, but I'm relieved to see he won't have the heart to say no if I ask to borrow Knose again.

Later in the evening, I stare at the map Frank drew in pretty blue ink. *It's not a treasure map*, I tell myself. *Calm down, you dumbo.* Still, I want to go there ASAP and see why Frank's face got so dreamy when he mentioned the place. It doesn't seem like a place me and Knose can walk to, and it's not like we could take the bus or Uber together unless I dress Knose like Little Red Riding Hood. Thanh's car is sitting there in a thought bubble, and I'm contemplating. Knowing Thanh, he'd want to come along, and that's not my vision. Right now, this is my adventure, not one for sharing.

It's disturbing me too that I can't remember the color of my own mom's headstone. I'm looking for her and she's playing a game of hide and seek. I already looked behind the curtains and under the bed. Where are you? Who are you?

After she died, I found a calendar on her nightstand full of fantastic fish photos. Under the fish were chemotherapy dates written in my mother's pretty, regular handwriting—much nicer than mine, which looks like something a beetle would make wandering over a page. The month she died had a clown fish, but there was nothing amusing about that month. I looked up clown fish online. They have some wild characteristics, like changing from boy to girl in order to become the female powerhouse of a group. I took the calendar off her nightstand and put it under some notebooks in my bedroom. I didn't look at it, but I dreamt a lot that next year about fish, not just clown fish but all kinds of far-out fish and other sea creatures.

I ran across the calendar while packing for college. I walked it to the garbage can, but then I held my breath and paged through it. I noticed how my mother had written down the session number and target number by each chemo date: *#1 (of 10)*, *#2 (of 10)*, etcetera. You could tell she was trying to get herself through an ordeal.

My mom tried to stay upbeat and hopeful. I remember her tense smile when she was stressed out and making an effort not to show it. The hint of pleading annoyed me. Maybe she was begging me not to be so hard on her, but that only made me behave worse. By the time she was writing in the calendar, I think she was appealing to the universe to let her keep on living. Unfortunately, the universe can be as jerky as me and didn't take pity on her either.

I have some letters in my closet. I avoid thinking about them, but there's a whole box Dad gave me when I moved into this house, along with other things that are mine. He must have thought that a real adult with an actual house should be in possession of their things. Or he was kicking me out, possibly making more space for Jean, though she doesn't seem like a person who needs empty closets for her fantastic wardrobe or her museum-quality collectibles. She brings out the snob in me. I'm not proud of that. I don't like this snooty person I become; this disagreeable Leslie belongs with the dislikable one who couldn't give her dying mother the time of day.

I go into my clothes closet and stand a minute, facing into the dark, remembering with a spurt of cheeriness the silly attic dress-up with Mr. and Mrs. Jones. A restless energy is rising through me. I stand on my toes in the velvety dark and feel around for the sick-green cardboard box from Macy's that's behind the others. I trap it between my right and left index fingers and inch it forward. I go sit at the edge of my bed, my nose tickling from the mildew on the lid. Mildew might be in the process of eating up everything in the box and digesting it into nothingness. An urgency switches on in me and I pull up one of the letters like you'd slide a card from a magician's deck. I was at sleepaway camp when she wrote these letters. I had no friends. I wanted to go home, though I didn't want to be such a crybaby that they'd pack me up and ship me home with everyone's eyes pinned on me. They did that with a girl named Beverly who had freckles thick as galaxies.

I looked forward to those letters. *These letters,* because here they are in front of me. I'd lie on my stomach on my bunk at night, reading them with a flashlight, my feet drawing circles in the air. I can't believe they're here on my lap. It's weird the way time swims forward, goes on and on, but your mind jumps ahead and back like it's playing Chutes and Ladders.

I'm not sure I want to open this, but there's the death by mildew to consider, so I do. And what about the motherboard project or the pros-and-cons essay I'm supposed to be writing? How can I answer any questions if I can't even read a letter she wrote? Here's her neat, careful handwriting. *Dearest Lessie,* it says. I guess she wasn't worrying about connotations. But *Dearest*. Woo…don't remember that endearment. It makes my heart flutter. Nervous. Hopeful, I guess, because I'm always looking for affection seeping through.

*Dearest Lessie,*

*How are you sweetheart? I hope you are enjoying camp. Have you made some friends? I hope you have. Things are fine here with me and Dad but of course we miss you. I could have used your help in the garden today! Weeds overran it when I turned my back for half a minute. My poor dahlias are surrounded. But I think I have things under control now. Speaking of untidy, you might have straightened your room a bit before you left, honeybun. A tornado appears to have touched down! But oh well, I just closed the door. It awaits your attention—unless I get charitable and straighten it for you. What sports are you doing dear? Do they have you stay overnight in a tent, Lennie? Toast marshmallows or make s'mores? Well, Dad is calling. He wants to take me out to dinner and I'm happy to have the night off from the kitchen. Enjoy yourself, sweetest.*

*Your loving Mom*

*P.S., remember that time you called me "Momsicle?" That was so funny. And we drew pictures of a popsicle-shaped mom in different flavors. I can't remember if it was your idea or mine to get out the crayons. Such fun, though I remember you made me dreadfully chubby.*

I feel weak. That's weird, right? I want to show Ivori the letter, but I'm embarrassed by the honeybuns and dearests and don't trust I'd get any sympathy from her since she seems annoyed with me of late. I could show Arwyn or Thanh. I might, but I should think about it myself, too, not just run to grab someone else's ear and see what *they* think. I love the honeys. I love the dearests. But are they nice or phony? That's what needles me. If I were Dr. Dream or his wise visiting professor I could tell, but I keep seeing it one way, then twisting it so that I see another side, and the views are as different as the faces of the moon. The letter seems sweet, but I'm the messy one, the tornado, the one whose door needs closing. And she's so tired of that kitchen, and her garden's clogged with weeds. I hope I'm not the weeds that have rampaged her life with nuisance.

I lie down on my bed to consider my obligations. My essay, for one, which needs a thesis. You establish a thesis, then argue for and against it. We can write about anything. So far, no thesis has announced itself to my eagerly awaiting brain. If I write a mother essay it could be, *Thesis: This young woman's mother loved her deeply. Anti-thesis: This young woman's mother didn't love her much at all. Arguments in favor: The mother wrote many letters and called her daughter by loving names. Arguments against: The girl doesn't recall many warm, snuggly moments, many safe and happy feelings. In favor: She recently remembered a silly day of playing tent under the sheets; wasn't that a safe, happy time?*

I'm getting sleepy and get under these sheets, where I try to recall that long-ago time. My mind is turning to fuzz. I have to visit my dad, despite Jean. I might ask him some questions about Mom. I might ask him what to do about Ivori's sexter. He's not the wisest of dads, but he has been around the block a few times, as old people say.

# Chapter 13

I text back and forth with my dad and arrange a visit next weekend. Meanwhile, I'm going to find the land on Frank's map. As always, Thanh's a pushover and I get what I want. I shake off the prickles of conscience and take his car. Frank has me parking in a pullout right beside the road, but I tuck Thanh's car in there behind a line of tall shrubs stiff as palace guards. Thanh could name them, I'm sure.

I walk back from the road and am quickly tangled in thorny plants with canes like the McDonald's golden arches. They grab my clothes, and I'm envious of Knose, who somehow slips through without getting caught. I'm angry now that Frank may have sent me to visit a hideous place with shrubs that molest a person, but okay, there's a little path through this grabby stuff, so I take it—pushing away the canes as I go, swearing when they attack me—until the land opens up into a woods. I remember that Frank's map has an area just near the parking spot that's busily crosshatched, so I guess that's the cane forest that hides the good stuff, like in a kids' book. I wonder why he didn't tell me about all that shit, but maybe he didn't want me to say, *Thanks, but I'll pass.* I breathe deep and feel better as I forgive him and look around.

This place is wet. The ground between the trees is mushy. I've seen pictures of rice paddies like this—cheerful green shoots upright in the water. One part of me is saying, WTF, this place is a wreck, and hell, cold water is starting to seep through my shoes. But another part of me is holding my breath as if there's magic here. Because the parts of it that are green are startling, psychedelic green. Plants high on the joy of growing here, as if there is something delicious in all this water that is flowing past silently, going who knows where. I make a note to wear rubber boots next time I visit. Well, *if* I come back. Because I've got wet, frozen feet now. Knose is soaked from rolling on the ground, but she's in her happy zone. It's been warm lately, and the ground has thawed, so I guess that explains the flood. To the right of this water-logged forest is an actual swamp that has trees with their feet in the water. I hear sounds like fingers running over the teeth of plastic combs, which I think is frogs, but it might be giant bugs I'd rather not imagine.

Curled up baby leaves cover some of the branches. Others are colored with the miniature red or chartreuse flowers that bloom before the leaves come (okay, Thanh told me that). Looking toward the sky, the woods are lacy with colors and texture. Beautiful, actually. Knose *never* looks up. She must be a hound dog because her nose is obsessed with the ground.

"Look up, Knose," I tell her. "You're missing some good stuff." She can tell I am giving her advice, and she gives me that quizzical tilt-head look, but the ground smells are calling her, and she wants to get back to the joy of sniffing. If Thanh were here, he would look up and be in awe of the prettiness. He'd follow my gaze and see what I'm seeing. Still, I don't want him here. Not yet. I walk toward the swamp because it looks interesting over there.

Tons of stuff is unfurling at its edges and erupting in tiny islands in the middle, islands that have their own small trees and bushes growing on them. If I were a conductor, I'd raise my baton and all the leaves in the forest would unfurl at once.

I still don't know a lot about plant ID, but I can at least pick out the lacy ferns. Some wide-leafed plants are beyond green; they need a special word. I take a photo with my phone and use the iNaturalist app Thanh made me download. I ID the plant that spreads for a mile where the land turns to swamp. *Skunk cabbage*, the app says, and it explains that the leaves, when bruised, are stinky. When it comes up through the ground, its chemistry lets it melt the surrounding snow.

Swamps are supposed to be smelly, kind of creepy places, so I don't know what it is about this place, but it's super nice here. Everywhere I step there's something else that has poked up through the leafy ground and is busy doing its plant thing, spreading open a leaf or showing off a flower. I have to watch where I step to not trample on anything. Of course, Knose is just following her sniffer and setting her paws wherever she pleases, but at least she's not tearing up the place. I still feel somewhat bad that I let her do what she did in the cemetery. I try not to think about it, especially Tabitha James and her heartbroken family. Next time I go there, I might leave Knose home. I stop to ID a shrub with miniature chartreuse flowers growing straight from the branches, but my phone is out of range so I can't ID it. I could ask Thanh about this one, but he'll ask me where I saw it. I might have to lie, though I only do that in emergencies. No cell connection is a little scary because no one knows I'm here, but it's cool, too, to be all alone in this place.

Maybe it would be okay for Frank to be here since he gave me the treasure map. If I were to look up and see him standing on one of those mini-islands, he'd seem like a genie materializing. *Presto.*

Back home, I'm tired but excited. I take Knose into my room and rub her dry with a big towel. I hear voices from Arwyn's room. It's Arwyn and Ivori, who's talking loud and fast and sounds upset. Iv's distress is a magnet to me—you'd think I was her mother—and I can't keep from knocking softly on the door. I get a rush of anxiety, like they're talking in secret and won't want me there, but Arwyn opens the door, his eyes wide, and motions me in. Knose pushes ahead, so we both join the group. Arwyn is sitting on his bed and Ivori's on the only chair, so I sit next to Arwyn on the bed while Knose makes herself comfortable on the floor.

"The *guy*," Ivori says in response to my nervously questioning face.

"The sexter," Arwyn clarifies. "I asked Ivori what he wrote—if she didn't mind sharing—so she showed me a couple."

"Here." Ivori thrusts her tablet at me, and my mind flashes to the Mom letter I want Ivori to read.

*You are so beautiful. I am tired of what I've been eating. I want to eat what's between your legs.*

"Gross. Definitely. Ick. Double triple ick." I hand the tablet back.

"But not violent," Arwyn says circumspectly. "Technically, he—let's stipulate we are assuming a *he* here—he is within the range of normal sexual impulse. He's just very inappropriate with respect to where he's communicating those desires. And his language isn't the best."

I keep quiet because Arwyn has journeyed outside the area of my expertise and I'm not eager to advertise that.

"Oh, great," Ivori says. "Arwyn, professor of human sexuality, says this is A-okay."

"Well, he didn't," I say, though I have to admit Arwyn is atypically obtuse. "I mean, context matters."

"It does," Arwyn clarifies. "This is definitely not okay, Iv. I'm just saying, he might be a pathetic dude rather than anyone violent. Probably a horny virgin."

I shrivel at that characterization but tell myself this is not about me. I'm not grossly texting anyone.

"Have you told your mother?" I ask. No snarkiness this time—I hope she can hear that. It wouldn't be a bad idea to tell Mrs. Ferguson.

Ivori is making faces. "I don't like talking to her about this category of thing. Men behaving badly."

"Remember we're assuming," Arwyn clarifies. "On the gender aspect."

"I get it, I get it," Ivori says, impatient with what she probably takes as Arwyn-style political correctness. She gets up to go, holding her tablet between two fingers like a piece of used toilet paper.

I follow Ivori upstairs and into her room. "Are you okay?"

"I made an appointment to go to the dentist," she says. "I didn't even mention that. Among my multiple problems."

"Oh. Brave. Did you get over the slavery thing?"

"No. I'm just dealing with it, okay? Don't be a turd." I flash on the wild green place I visited. The day seems gentle, and I don't need to fight.

"Got it. Instructions received and accepted." I don't want to think about Ivori's sexter now, or her teeth. I'm thinking of going to Frank's land again. I'm going to try walking next time I go, in order to keep Thanh and his car out of it. I might leave Knose home, too, though that would break her heart. I want to be there alone. Just me and the trees.

# Chapter 14

I don't want to ask Thanh for another ride to my dad's after so much recent borrowing. Alex's car is rusting in our driveway, but I won't ask him for anything. I don't even want to imagine what gross action he would try to extort from me. My dad said it's okay to get an Uber when needed, so that's the plan.

I'm nervous about this visit since we're going to "talk," and I'm the one providing the content. I want to ask him some things about my mom and confer about Ivori's sexter. I told him I only had an hour. That way, things won't drag on and get awkward.

When I get there, he is subdued. He isn't cranky or complaining about my facial expressions but doesn't seem thrilled either. He sits me down in the living room. I feel like a guest and accept his offer of something to drink. I could have gone in there myself and turned on the tap, but okay, he brings me some fizzy stuff and I've got a cold, sweaty glass to occupy my hands. Trying to be in grown-up guest mode, I ask, "How are things with you and Jean?"

His face falls a degree from where it was, and I realize he was sad about something before I got here. A jeering person in my head disses me, saying, *Not everything's about you, Leslie.*

Cueing sad music, my dad says, "That didn't work out." I flash on a vague memory of my mom, unhappy with Dad. Some talk about divorce, or maybe I'm misremembering.

I'm not sure I want to say, "How come?" I might not want to know—it could be that there was sexual incompatibility or something way outside my comfort zone.

"I'm not always the most empathetic. So I hear. From women."

"You're nicer than most people, Dad." For once, I feel genuinely protective of him.

"I'm told that 'nice' and 'empathetic' aren't equivalent."

"Hmm." I wouldn't know, not being an expert on niceness.

"I think your mother had the same opinion, at least some of the time."

This is weird. Dad's starting to talk about Mom without my floating any of the embarrassing, time-to-interview-your-father prompts I kept trying to conjure. He somewhat knew what I wanted to talk about, so maybe he's helping me open that door. That's kind of empathetic, isn't it?

I should take advantage of the opening but suddenly I feel the need to interject Ivori's crisis. "Dad, another thing—different topic now. Someone's been sending Ivori creepy texts, very inappropriate and frankly gross, and she's freaked out. I don't know if it's serious and don't know what to do."

"Sexting? That sort of inappropriate?"

I nod.

"I don't like the sound of that. Someone should call the police if it continues. Do you want me to do that? Or should we call Ivori's mother?"

I shake my head, though I feel a flash of relief at the idea of my dad and Mrs. Ferguson sorting this out. "Ivori would hate that. I can call the police. Or get her to do it." Of course, I'm thinking, *Fat chance E.V. is going to make this call.*

"Please do that. Don't forget," Dad says. "You wanted to talk about your mother?"

"Yeah. I guess." That's the best I can do.

His face is furrowing. "Your mother wasn't always happy. No one is, of course. Not all the time. But she seemed to feel she was missing something. She looked to me to fill this need, but honestly, Leslie, I never could figure out just what she wanted."

Too much information. I'm headed for a free fall. I need something to grab hold of. I flash on an image of our family. Ours is the oddball in a photo exhibit of families. "Most families around here have more kids. More than one," I say. "Mom probably wanted more kids." This ground is dangerous, too. Do I really want to know my mom was mourning over not having a son?

Dad shakes his head. "That wasn't it." He pauses for what seems like half an hour. "You know, I think she started looking *elsewhere.*"

"Huh?"

He's looking at his lap now. "Outside the house. The home. From time to time."

It takes me a while to get it. Shock grabs hold of me. "Oh. That. That sucks."

"I didn't want anything like that happening with Jean, so when she seemed discontented, I just told her, 'Let's not continue things.' None of that, 'I need more understanding,' or 'let's go to couples counseling.'" He looks so defeated. I'm starting to wonder who wanted to talk to whom in this conversation.

He's falling apart, so I should be brave. I have to be. "So Mom was having an affair?" I say it out loud. Blurting. Loud. I bring it to life in the air.

"I don't know that for certain, Leslie. Maybe. Or maybe she was just going shopping or taking pictures. She loved to do that, you know. Gardens especially. I just know she was looking for something, and it wasn't here."

"She never took pictures of me."

Dad laughs. "Well, she tried. You always stuck your tongue out. Kept doing it until she had to give up."

She tried. She tried to take my picture. I'm relieved but embarrassed because of the tongue. I don't remember that. Why did I do that? What kind of dumb kid was I?

"Are you sure she didn't want more children, Dad? One isn't a big number."

He sighs, and again there's an enormous pause. "It wasn't that," he says. "Trust me."

My dad has put up an enormous stop sign, and I'm going to heed it. I'm grateful he's shared a lot of this stuff that's seriously unsettling for him, but I've had enough. My body is squirming inside my skin.

"I have to go now, Dad. Studying, you know. I'm behind. I better go."

"There was something she told me about her family…a sister."

"I need to go, Dad. You know. School work and all that. And an essay. I'm getting behind."

"I know, honey."

I fish my phone out of my jacket pocket and call an Uber. Four minutes. I give him a hug before I run out to meet the car.

When I get outside, I'm shaking. I feel strange, as if someone new just left that house. Not the person who went in. I know that's backward; it's my mother who's changed, but it's me, too. I'm different. My mind pulls up a picture of my mom now. She's putting on nice clothes and adding touches like a necklace and cologne. She looks excited, and she pecks me on the cheek as she rushes out the door. I'm confused because I love the feel of her excitement in the air, but she's taking it away with her, in a hurry. I can't shake my shock. My mind hands me a funny song Ivori played for me. An old blues guy singing about Lola, who jilted him. He's a mess and needs reassuring, because he thinks he's disappointed her, so that's why she's leaving. But her reassurance sucks: he doesn't figure. That's what she says. You don't figure in the way I feel. *I don't hate you, it ain't that big a deal. You don't even figure in the way I feel.* Hah, hah. Great reassurance. You're nobody. Nothing. Mom was out of there looking for someone else. I didn't figure. That's my shock. Not funny.

I want to see Frank. I don't know why I don't just forget about him. He gave me the map. I used it and found the land, and now I can go there whenever I want. I don't need him. But I want to see him. Frank's face was filled with loss. I am sad and confused. I want to see him.

I get the Uber guy to drop me at Frank's land to see if I can calm down there. I feel bad being here without Knose. I plan to give her a hamburger when I get home, to improve her day. Without her running around, I can hear the birds and leaves like a tambourine section conducted by the breeze.

Last night, it rained like crazy. Today, the swamp is overflowing with water and spilling over onto what two days ago was probably dry land. I stand in a few inches of water and love the feeling; it's moving all around me in a gentle pool that's going to feed the roots of the plants that were dry and waiting. It seems like a whole world is streaming past. I spot a tiny frog camouflaged among the leaves. I don't know if it's a baby or just a miniature, and whether it's specially patterned to hide in its surroundings. Its toes are transparent like something not born yet and almost too delicate to survive. I go out onto the dry land and startle a few small driftwood-colored frogs with dark masks. They try to out-hop me on the ground. I manage to trap one under my hand, against the ground, then nudge it to step onto my palm for a minute so I can feel how alive with hopping energy it is. It wants to get out of my hand, back to the ground, and I don't keep it long.

It's a wild garden here. How can you not love everything and want to take care of it? Frank told me he comes here, too, and I wonder if he has these feelings. I imagine going to the cemetery and bringing him a bunch of flowers so big it hides my face. I let him guess who's walking his way. I only stay among the trees an hour, until my mind straightens out. As I'm heading back to the road to call an Uber, I see two foxes chase each other down a fallen log only a few yards from me. Who gets to see that sort of thing? For me, it's all brand new and wonderful.

# Chapter 15

It's a cool, still afternoon. My butt has been parked for quite a while on a worn gravestone, though definitely not Tabitha's. I picked an old lady instead. I've left Knose home, for obvious reasons, even though she turned mid-air circles in her excitement to go. It broke my heart a little to leave her, but I reminded myself of the heartbroken people who visit their loved deceased and don't want to see signs that a wild creature is disinterring them.

Sure enough, Frank comes strolling out of the little chapel building at about four in the afternoon. I'm not going to make a ruckus to get his attention. I just sit here and wait and see what happens. His eyes spring right to me and shine. He must know this cemetery so well that he's quick to spot anything new—a seated body sprung up like a giant mushroom, for instance. He gives me a broad, warm smile. He knows me.

"Hey there," he says. "I see you're without your friend."

I nod.

"How are you, my dear?"

"I went to the place."

His face lights. "Did you now?"

"It's pretty cool."

He cocks his head in curiosity.

"How did you know about that place?" I ask him. My question is direct and insists on an answer.

He gets his faraway look and shrugs. "I've always known about it." He's still distant as he says, "All my life. Used to belong to my family."

I am taken aback.

He shrugs. "They lost it. Had it on a land contract and missed a payment."

"Missed one payment?"

Frank shrugs again. "Wasn't right. A lot of things about the situation weren't."

I get up. I'm suddenly uneasy and unsure why I'm here. "Hey. See ya," I say, and start to walk in the direction of the gate. I wonder if I cut him off mid-sentence. But I have to get going. I waited here so long before he popped up. Anyway, I saw him like I intended, told him I went to the spot, and now I've got to go.

"Well, thanks for stopping by, young lady." His words chase after me. I get to the last grouping of gravestones, close to the gate, and check a few names and dates. The year of death on a deep gray stone is my mom's year. I imagine her being right here, in this cemetery Frank tends, directly under this stone, tucked into the ground just beneath me. I wish she'd had someone to tuck her in just before she died. It's dumb, but I imagine her going to a dark place where you'd need some security against terror. Maybe my dad tucked her in. But I don't know. Because now he says she didn't think he was empathetic. Something like that. I should have forgiven her for all the times she floated away like Mona Lisa and remembered the times she might have read me *The*

*Giving Tree* or told it to me by heart before I got a soft kiss on the forehead. The trouble is, I can't remember. Just fragments. If she were here in this place, she'd at least have Frank, who keeps a good eye on his people. I shake out the tight muscles in my legs. This is the end of it. I won't see him again. Why would I? I'm not going to keep showing up at this depressing cemetery. I'm not his family and he's not mine, and my mother isn't even buried here. I'm suddenly furious that his family let that awesome land go. They didn't love it enough. My anger gels into a cold, fuck-you feeling. I'd like to run a nail down the side of someone's car. Leave an ugly scar.

I halfway wish I had Thanh's car to return, because a part of me wants to go to his place and run my fingers over his baby horse netsuke while I get ideas about the muscles in his arms. I am right near the gate and hear Frank far behind me, getting closer.

"I don't suppose you'd want to tell me your name?"

I turn around and toss out, "Leslie," and he slowly nods his chin all the way down to his chest, as if he's taking in the nicest name he ever heard.


I'm home in time for a pathetic dinner of rice and over-steamed veggies—Ivori's production. Afterward, I'm restless. Both Ivori and Arwyn are out. Arwyn must have Knose, because she's not around either. I'm lonely on top of being edgy. I think of looking at more of my mom's letters, but I can't handle that. I've had enough revelations. What was she so unhappy about? I guess I wasn't good enough. My dad feels the same way as me. That's weird. It's both of us. Together, we couldn't fill whatever hole was in her. Still, that one letter—the Momsicle letter—was pretty sweet. At least, I thought so when I read it before. I'm not reading it again. It's still in my backpack.

Impulsively, I call Thanh and ask him how his human bio studying is going. I hope one of the two of us is mastering the digestive tract. Predictably, he asks if I want to come over and study, and predictably, I say no. I add that it's too far to walk, knowing of course that he's going to offer to pick me up, which he does. I make my mind go blank—it doesn't have far to go—and say yes.

When we get into his apartment, the light's a little dim. My mood is so shaky that I need some brightness. I click on the lamp, then pick up the netsuke. I'm squinting at how the sculptor carved all that fine detail. Thanh tells me he's got the whole zodiac of netsukes in the other room. "C'mon," he says, so I follow him.

Of course, the "other room" is his bedroom, which I try not to notice as I examine the twelve amazing little zodiac creatures clustered on a pretty wooden table. He hands me the rabbit. He lays it on my open hand and closes my hand over it, gently. I remember the feel of the tiny, delicate frog. I start to say something, but stop. I want to keep Frank's land secret. I do and I don't. I open my hand and put the rabbit back on the table.

"You can keep it," he says.

I shake my head.

"Borrow it. Return it later."

I have a pants pocket that zips, so I put it in there. "I'll bring it back."

Thanh nods. I think he likes the idea that something of his will be going home with me. That's weird, but I get it. I would have wanted my mom to have a picture of me, or at least a hair ribbon or Happy Meal toy when she went out on those dates. And when she got buried. My mind snags on that, feeling suddenly that I *needed* her to have something of mine in her hand or her pocket when they buried her. I could have asked for that. Given something to my dad to tuck in next to her. But I didn't think of it then. And now it's too late. Even though I still need it, I can't make it happen. Things would be so much better if I could put something beside her that would stay there with her. But I can't. Not ever.

Thanh nods and walks back into the living room, gets us a couple cans of Coke, and sits on the sofa. I sit next to him and say, "I visited my dad. Not today but I did." I know my face is squirmy.

"That's good."

I shrug. "Not so good. He told me some peculiar things about my mom. I'm kind of trying to figure her out. I might even write my essay about her." Then I say, "Hey," as if this thing I've been obsessed over just occurred to me. From my backpack's outer pocket, I pull out the letter. "I found this letter from my mother. She wrote it when I was away at camp." I add, "I read it a couple times, but I can't digest it. Must be lacking the enzymes." Thanh smiles at my digestion joke.

"You want me to read it? Offer supplementary enzymes? Probiotics?"

I nod.

Thanh takes the letter, opens the trifold, and smooths it on his lap as if he were ironing. It takes forever for him to get it flat and an infinity of time for him to get through it. I'm tempted to snatch it back and say, "Forget about it." Or ask if he took a course in slow reading. When he's finally done, he shakes his head, says, "I don't know."

I am embarrassed I've asked. I don't love wide-open, vulnerable spaces, in case you haven't figured that out by now. And I've spent a lot of time there since these recent visits to see my dad.

"Hey, why is she calling you Lennie?"

"What do you mean?"

He points to a spot in the letter. "Lennie."

"I didn't even see that. It's just a mistake."

Thanh doesn't like to be short on answers, and I don't think he wants me giving up on him as a fount of wisdom. He says, "Your mom's endearments aren't ones my family would use. Ours are Vietnamese. Like *Cuc Vang*."

"What's that?"

"Something like 'piece of gold.' But I guess I'd say your mom's affectionate words seem a little much."

Uh-oh. "Fake, you mean?"

"No. Possibly forced. But maybe not, Leslie. I'm not an expert."

"Same thing as fake."

"No. Fake is insincere. Forced is just trying a little too hard. Maybe overcompensating. "

"Yeah. Okay. But neither is good."

"You shouldn't trust me on this. I don't have the best ear for English-language nuance. I can hear that it's bothering you though. That much I get." Thanh puts his arms around me and kisses the top of my head. It's the strangest thing, but I'm hearing, *Little one*. I want to hear it. I whisper it.

"What's that?"

"It might be something my mom called me. It popped into my head."

"It must be hard. To lose her so young."

"It's not the best." I feel myself curling into a pill bug. I mentioned them once to Thanh and he said *Armadillidiidae*. That name gave me a laughing attack. Armadillo gone wild. So I say, "Armadillidiidae."

"You're crazy," he says, but we both start to laugh. Despite that, I'm still worried about all this mom stuff and the letter that's possibly, probably insincere. I might show it to Ivori if she wasn't preoccupied with her sexter and upcoming visit to the dentist. And when she's not distracted, she's immersed in building her cardboard empire. Half the time she's in what she calls a "flow state." I've yet to determine what that means.

After Thanh drives me home, I'm fixating on *little one*. Was that real? It could go in the "pro" essay, if I write it. But only if it's real. I guess I'm glad Thanh didn't try to turn that hug into anything more erogenous. He's sensitive that way, to my mood. And I'm grateful. Sort of. But now I'm left thinking about him half the night. I think about his hand cupping mine around the netsuke. The rabbit! I tossed the pants in the laundry basket and forgot all about the little rabbit. That forgetting stabs me; here I am again, a thoughtless person. That person who couldn't even spend a little time with her dying mother, just because the room smelled like sickness. Or death. I transferred the letter to my bathrobe pocket but forgot the poor little rabbit. I cringe thinking about it going into the washing machine and can't get that thought out of my head. If only I'd put a little rabbit in her pocket when we buried her, or tucked that hoodie in beside her.

I can't sleep. I can tell Ivori's made it home. I hear her busy in her room even though it's close to midnight. She's like an energy field of late, or a minor, unnamed hurricane. Sometimes she's spinning up angry energy because of the sexter or dentist or who knows what else. Sometimes she's a blizzard of creativity—painting, cutting, pasting, pounding things together into forms never before seen by humankind.

I go out into the hall, and it's Alex's door that opens, not Ivori's. There he is in his bathrobe. At least it's decently tied. I want to stare at the knot that's keeping the sides overlapped to eye-laser it shut. Instead, he's staring at me, his eyes sliding up and down like a textbook pervert. I'm not scared of him because I know he's all bullshit. Still, I hate that he's in my way and I snarl at him. I'm not sure if my snarl is audible, but it's definitely visible.

"Aw, Leslie," he says in his sarcastic voice that's dripping with fake honey. "C'mon, now. We're friends, aren't we? You and I, right across the hall. So close. Intimate neighbors."

I actually growl now. It's that or yell, "Shut the fuck up," and tonight something inhibits me from that level of directness.

I knock on Ivori's door. Now I'm pounding for refuge as well as company.

"Oh, no," Alex sighs. "You want to leave me."

Ivori yells to come in and I blast through the door, close it, and put my back to it. "I might kill him," I say.

She's sitting on the floor, legs spread wide with papers and paints between them. She makes a face. "He's too weird. As soon as this lease is up, he's out of here."

"How's the masterpiece going?"

"I'm painting now. Then I'll start assembling." She points to a stack of empty cardboard boxes in the corner. "Building supplies."

I nod and sit down on the floor across from her.

"Where'd you go today?" she asks.

"I visited Thanh."

She raises her eyebrows and gives me one of her pointed, fuck-the-cute-guy looks.

"I wanted to show him something." I go into mouth-twisting mode. "I have these letters from my mother. They're confusing, though. I showed him one."

She's looks up and gives me her attention. "What did he think?"

"He wasn't sure."

"Hand it over."

I pull the letter out of my bathrobe pocket and pass it to her. Her eyes read hungrily.

I watch her brow slowly tightening. "What do you think?"

She shakes her head. I think she's rereading. Again, I am nervously waiting. I feel like I've spent half my life in this state. She sets it on her lap and looks at me. "It's just a regular camp letter, isn't it? Nice but a little nerdy. I could show it to my mom if you're looking for some kind of hidden meaning."

Ivori is tentative, which is not her usual. I am terrified and thrilled by the idea of consulting her mom. I suppose it's not just the letter I want to give her. It's everything. The whole package. The letters, my dad's pathetic story of Mom's misery. My fragments of memory and odd, motherboard dreams. But I say, "Do."

"Okay. She's in Helsinki, but I'll scan it."

"She won't want to read my letter while she's touring."

"Why not? She's stuck in a hotel room half the time. Probably nothing to do but write philosophical thoughts in her journal."

"Another thing. I went to see my dad. He said we have to call the police if the sexter continues."

"Nah-uh."

"I know. I get it. You don't trust the police. But you need to do something. I'll call if you want. Explain the situation. Make a complaint."

Ivori takes some time. She's pondering. "*You* do it. Maybe if a scared White girl calls. You can say he's spying on me and that scares you, too, because we live together."

I nod.

"You were at Thanh's all afternoon and just talked about your mom?"

"I went somewhere else before dinner."

"Where?"

"That cemetery. I told you about the caretaker who sent me to some wild land. Turns out his family used to own it, and they lost it. Didn't sell it. *Lost* it. Some kind of bad contract."

"No surprise in that." Ivori's voice is huffy. "Land contract. That's the way a ton of Black people lost their land. Wasn't any accident, either."

"I don't get it."

"The banks wouldn't loan money to African Americans, so if you wanted some land or a house you had to get a land contract from the owner. But if you missed a single payment, you'd forfeit what you already paid. The property isn't yours until you've made every one of those payments. Years and years of them. And then a depression or some other bad thing would come along. Someone would lose a job and miss one payment. Like magic, the land and all of what you invested goes to the White person. Surprise, surprise, the Black person doesn't come away with a fucking thing. Bunch of bullshit."

She looks like she wants to say something else, but she's mostly sputtering. "Another White dude," I hear, and "professor," but she's not making sense. She's already so pissed at me for what all those shitty White people and their twisted laws did that I'm not putting my total effort into deciphering her.

I'm thinking about Frank and that half-loving, half-sad look on his face when he talked about the land. "I'm glad whoever owns it now doesn't care who visits there," I say to Ivori, apropos of what's in my head, not what's coming out of her mouth.

"Yeah. Generous of them." Between her and Alex, they've cornered the market on sarcasm.

# Chapter 16

When I go to the land these days, I don't walk much: I stand so I can look and listen and not be Bigfoot disturbing the peace. Or I walk a few yards, then sit on a log. When I notice odd things about the plants, I look them up on a plant app, if I have a cell connection. I still don't ask Thanh about what I see because he'll get elated about a private nirvana and want to come. Okay, I did bring him one time for a quick minute, but that's all for now, even though he pesters me about coming back. I'm addicted to this place. I don't want him hungering like I do, so I've got him on a strict diet. Mostly I come here alone.

Today's my seventh visit. Late in the afternoon when the sun is still high, I spot a little cabin deep in the woods. How could I not have seen it? Maybe it's a magic cabin that only materializes when you most need it. I follow a deer trail through the dinner-plate-sized umbrellas I now know are mayapples. A few of them are flattened, their stems broken. Some creature walked on them. I stand at the door a while, then push it with my palm. It creaks and swings—slow and reluctant, horror-movie vibes—and I almost fall over because a man is sitting on a small bed and looks up. Only after my heart's jumped out of my body do I see it's Frank.

"Oh. Shit." You can probably guess whose words those are. He nods, then laughs. "Nice greeting."

"Nice way of scaring a person half to death."

"Not my intention."

"What is this place?"

"Little cabin my family built way back when." He's clutching a damp rag, and I can see he's been tidying up.

"When you owned the land?"

"Not since we lost it, that's for certain. I doubt the current owners would look kindly on that."

I don't like his making fun of me. "But you're trespassing now and cleaning, so I guess you don't care that much about what anyone thinks." Half the place is draped in cobwebs, half is swept clean.

"More factual is that I don't like seeing the place untended." Frank has that weary look that frightens me.

"You look like you're going to cry."

Instead, he laughs in surprise. "I guess a person doesn't know what's printed across their face half the time. Truth is, I was just planning to leave."

He doesn't want me claiming any part of his cabin. It's like me wanting to keep the land from Thanh. I get it. Still, I'm a little hurt. I want him to make space for me, not get up and leave. He stands up, and I see he's stiff. Not exactly a youngster.

"You left your dog home," he says.

"She tramples a lot of plants." I think of the cemetery and feel embarrassed, which makes me irritated. I follow him out into the woods and trail after him. "You don't seem all that happy," I say, nagging him.

"This place can make me sad."

I try the numbskull approach. "I thought you loved it here."

"A little too much is all. Can't help wishing we held on tighter. Didn't know how, though."

I'm asking no more questions. I've got a closetful of funny feelings about this topic. Ivori's inside that closet, too. I lift my hand and shimmy it to catch his eye and let him know my skedaddling intention.

He nods. He's not wasting extra words on me. I've already put enough little paper cuts into our relationship for him to feel the sting.

I'm out of there. It's just been fifteen minutes, but the land has changed for me. It isn't quite so private a place because Frank and I have been there together.

After that awkward visit, I open the door a little, which means that I think of taking Thanh. We're into summer now and all the unfurling is done. The place isn't as wonderfully fresh or wet, but the days are long. They climb into night. The cabin pops in and out of my thoughts, but I don't go there. I picture it being dollhouse-sized, so when Frank appears in my thoughts, he's huge as he sits on the little bed like *The Thinker*, pondering his misery.

On a damp morning late in June, I take Thanh with me. The woods slow us down. They make us meander. Thanh breaks a leaf on a small bush and rubs the cut end with his fingers. He holds the side of his index finger to my nose.

The smell gives me a shock. "Spicy."

Thanh's smile is delighted. "Spicebush. A nice little native."

I tip my head way back and look at the sky. It's clear blue except for a train of floating cotton balls. My head is so far back it's calling for something to rest on, wanting Thanh's shoulder. He's been working out and his shoulders are hard, but probably a comfortable hard. We stroll on. I've learned to notice things. I see every lacy complication of a fern leaf when it's just opening. A green oak leaf by my feet gets my attention with its enormity. It must lack the "Stop! Enough!" gene to regulate growth. I pick it up. The leaf is rough and has a hard little pimple inside its skin. A cyst, I think, but Thanh says it's a *gall*. I ask if it's a cancer that's killing the plant, but no, it's just a bug's little home where it's reproducing, living its own tiny life.

"A life within a life," Thanh says.

I like that. Because too many things are dying in the world, cut off when they're just trying to get going, a lot because of climate change, which scares everyone, me especially. Thanh sees things that still slip past me. He's been taking note all his life while I was off in la-la land with cut-out paper butterflies and didn't know there were any butterflies other than monarchs. His noticing is one of the things I like about Thanh. And I like that he's put up with me even when my eyes are like those butterflies— they've flitted off somewhere and aren't looking at him. Now I do give him a good look, though a quick one.

I think, *What the hell,* and lead him over to the cabin. "Push the door." He does, and it's still open. Frank can't lock it, I realize. He has no key.

I walk in first. Thanh walks around the space, touching his hand to each of its quiet furnishings. "It looks dusted," he says.

I nod, but don't tell him what I know. Some things I still hold close.

Thanh sits on the narrow bed and pats the spot beside him.

I sit next to him, and there we are. Because the bed sags in the middle, we're pushed up against each other like apples in a bag.

"Hansel and Gretel's gingerbread house," I say. I look around and assess the potential for lurking witches.

Thanh sees my eyes running over the place and says, "A lot of mice here." He beams and adds, "They are Beatrix Potter mice." He stretches back across the bed. That irks me. It's my cabin and Frank's. Who asked him to make himself at home. I frown and get up and am out the door.

The next time we're in the woods, Thanh twists through the vegetation until we're at the cabin. I'm annoyed a little but trail after him. He's brought a clean, blue-striped bedspread to sit on.

With a flourish, he spreads it over the mattress. "Because of the mice," he says. My mind flashes to those stupid frat party sheets.

"I thought of a game," he says. He seems spectacularly nervous.

"What?" I am suspicious.

"Umm…a nerdy version of strip poker." He barely has the courage to look at me. "Science questions, maybe botany." He bites his lower lip and looks at me from under his eyelids.

*Botany?* I can imagine whose clothes will be coming off faster. I'm trying to stay in snide mode, not panic mode and ask, "Botany? How fair is that?"

He gets my inference. "Okay, a modification. If I get one wrong, I, you know, take something off." He starts to have a coughing fit but chokes it off. "If you get two wrong, then I guess it can be. You know. Your turn." He's even more nervous, if that's possible. I think he's wondering what low blow I'll deliver next.

I wrinkle all the muscles in my face that are capable of movement. My heart is bouncing in my chest. "Exactly why are we playing this game?"

Thanh looks like an electric cord someone has yanked out of the socket and left dangling. Helpless. Hurt.

"Okay, okay," I say. "Don't explain. Just let me think."

He revives slightly. "I wish you wouldn't try so hard to hurt my feelings," he says. "It's not that great an accomplishment. It's pretty easy to do."

"I'm sorry. I'm an asshole, in case you haven't noticed. You shouldn't hang out with me."

He shrugs. Inhales. "I'm gonna answer your question, though. About why."

Part of me thinks, *No, don't*, but also in that instant I give Thanh a ton of credit for being insanely brave. He is looking at me, steady now and serious, wanting to tell me something. And I am wanting to hide under the bed where the mice hang out.

"Two reasons: One, I come from a conservative family culture, and I know next to nothing about girls. *Women*. It's embarrassing. I want to at least know—close up, not on some website or an accidental glimpse of my mother once a year—what a human female looks like. Up close. Three dimensionally. I know, how weird is that. But it's true."

I'm gulping, trying not to lose it and say something rude. The mean comments line up in my throat like people crowded at the exit door of a bus.

"Two," he says, "you're my friend, and I love you—in a whole variety of ways—and I think you're beautiful. And I like the idea of looking at you with one or two less layers."

"*Fewer* layers," I find it necessary to interject.

"Whatever. It's overwhelmingly nice to me."

I can see he is trying not to look down at his lap in mortification. Meanwhile, my embarrassment is building like floodwaters, and I feel both flattered and small as a pinhead, because Thanh is so much gutsier than me. But I can refrain from being a turd. That much I can manage. I nod a few times and give him a nice little smile that causes me to feel like someone I've never met. He's just looking at me now. Waiting.

I take a deep breath and tell myself, *What the fuck, it's just a body. Same old body I've lived in forever. No big deal.* I see Ivori laughing at me and shaking her head, teasing me for being backward. To calm things down, I get out my phone and start tooling around on PlantNet, then in a while I say, "Okay, what is the name of the tree that has leaves in alternate arrangement? They're pinnately compound. It's nut-bearing and the leaves are glaucous. And sessile." I reel off words. Nevertheless, the mouthful of scientific terms makes me feel calmer. Thanh's face opens in wonderment that I'm playing his game.

"You don't even know what those words mean." He laughs.

"I'm asking the question," I say. "You're answering it."

"I know the answer."

"You're a genius," I say, sarcastic.

"*Genus*," he says, and I ugh at his botany joke. Then he says, "butternut," with perceptible pride, which is rare for Thanh.

I scowl mildly. "I made it too easy. I shouldn't have mentioned the nuts."

I can see he knew he'd suggest this game, so he put some random blue bandana around his neck as a bullshit piece of clothing to remove. I'd been eyeing it all morning, wondering why Thanh got the impulse to be fashion forward. I bet he's been imagining this game for half his life.

He sticks close to the nut trees and gives me black walnut, which, of course, I don't have a clue about. I dip on eastern red juniper, too. What normal person would know these things? Lucky for me I'm wearing a sweater, and that's no big deal to yank off over my head, but I see where this is going.

I give him Kentucky coffee tree, because who's even heard of that, and he hesitates for a minute, so I don't know if he's stumped or is just playing around. When he announces the right answer, I tighten my lips and feel pissed, maybe because of the clothes and maybe because he knows so much more than me. I want to pop him in the arm, and not in a friendly way. Some of the hurting things that whoosh through my mind are pretty bad. *Sadistic.* That's what Dr. Dream would say, squishing me into a box with Alex. Ivori's still got my letter, and her mom must have seen it by now. I'm afraid of what I'll learn, and this meanness is hanging out with that fear.

He sees my discontent and says, "Give me a harder one," so I google the trees of Vietnam and give him *Camellia pleurocarpa*. He dips on that. Finally. He digresses into questions about the species. "Endemic," I say. I'm still mad and worried that I want to hurt someone badly when they've nicked me just a little.

I thought Thanh might have packed on some extra layers, but except for the bandana he's wearing normal stuff. At least we both have shoes and socks to remove, which keeps us on safe terrain. Though they're only shoes, bending down to untie them makes me nervous. It has implications. Next go the socks. I silently repeat my just-a-body mantra, and when I can't get kousa dogwood, I go robotic and unbutton my five shirt buttons, bang-bang-bang-bang-bang, and off goes the shirt, which I toss on the bed as if I am miserably hot and sweaty and can't wait to get rid of the thing.

He takes a deep breath, and I can't see that he ever lets it out. Maybe he should, before he passes out. He's trying not to look at me. *Just look*, I think of shouting. That's what he wanted, wasn't it? I should at least be interesting enough to overcome his stupid modesty. He starts to lose on purpose now—it's obvious—so he has to take his shirt off too. Even though guys can go shirtless, this is the first time I've seen Thanh that way, and *wow*, though I don't say a word. He must be working out, plus his skin is perfect, not freckled like mine, or so pale that it makes you look like you're cold.

He gives me a couple ridiculously easy ones like maple and oak. He's slowing things down. I'm deliberating now whether it's going to be the white bra or the jeans. I decide to go with the bra and keep half my body dressed. Boobs are nothing anyway, though I suppose he'll notice mine are lopsided if he ever gets around to opening his eyes.

The bra is front-closing, so I don't have to reach around. I keep my eyes on Thanh. I'm watching him with laser eyes, but I have a frozen face so there's no way he can see my feelings.

I get my bra off, and my boobs relax a little. Thanh looks like he's going to faint, and I come near to belching a big laugh. It's obvious he wants to touch me from the way his breathing practically stops, but we're not going there. Still, my nipples perk up imagining it. I'm not pleased about that. "Your turn," I say.

He shakes his head. "I can't," he says. "I'm sorry. You're beautiful and I can't do this. Something's not right about it."

Someone just turned off the river. I give him a look that says *suit yourself.* But I feel disappointed. I feel mad. I feel relieved. What a mess.

He hands me my sweater as if it's the folded American flag the corpsmen hand to the widow after her husband is shot down in an airplane.

I can see that the rest of the day is going to be exceptionally weird, following this strippus interruptus, so I tell him I should get back to my house. When we leave the cabin, an electric-pink plastic flag on top of a metal stake catches my eye. It's in the middle of the swamp, bent down so that it brushes the water.

"What is that?" I ask Thanh, as if he has an answer for everything.

"Was it there before?"

I shake my head. It wasn't. I know this place. I flare with anger. "What is that thing doing in the water?"

"There's another one, farther out."

"No way."

He lifts my arm and points it to the spot he's focused on. I see it. A triangle of garish pink, way in the distance. My place is being invaded from every direction. First Frank. Then Thanh. Now whoever stuck those stakes in the ground.

Thanh is watching me carefully as we walk to his car and I know what he's thinking. He's hurt that my mind's not on him and his gorgeous pecs, which it would be if it weren't for those flags. I'm honestly thinking about Mother Nature and how she takes care of all the fragile things on this land, and I can understand why Frank gets that mournful look on his face thinking what his family lost. I wish he were the caretaker, because he wouldn't let anyone stick a plastic party decoration in the earth. But I'm as much of a caretaker as this fairy land has now, so what am I doing letting strangers wade through the water and mark it that way? I'm thinking hard about all that, and, okay, it's true, Thanh's beautiful body keeps sliding into my mind, too. The two things are flipping back and forth like letters on an optician's light box.

Thanh kills the engine in front of my house and says, "Wait." I think he's going to squirrel around and kiss me, because he looks tense, but that's not where he's going. "I have to tell you something."

Nothing good ever follows that intro, so I just hang an "oh" in the air and let it sit.

"The flags," he says. "They usually mean construction."

I give him an I-don't-get-it face.

"Construction," he repeats. "Development. Of the land."

"Development?"

He nods.

"You mean?"

"Yes. Condos or whatever. It's a prime location. It's amazing that patch of green has lasted this long."

"But don't they know what's there? Haven't they seen it?"

"They don't care, Leslie. They don't look at it the way you do. To them, it's just vacant land."

I jump out of the car and run for the house to escape.

I'm on my bed with my face buried in the mattress. Chain saws cutting into the flesh of old trees. Bulldozers that don't care that the land is carpeted in perfect yellow trout lilies with leaves mottled like fish. The more they pulverize, the better. I can't stand it. I think about Frank. He would feel so awful, but what would he do? Nothing. Because his family did nothing when the land was slipping through their fingers. They abandoned it and let this happen. I am drumming up anger at Frank now. And Thanh, what was he doing with that crazy game? Teasing me. Was some dreadful developer out there piercing the ground with metal spikes while we were fooling around like middle schoolers?

I start to think about these Ethiopian monks I saw a TV special about who spend their whole lives guarding the little patches of forest around their temples. Half the country used to be wooded and beautiful, but now it's desert except for the islands the monks protect, where they shoo away people who bring axes and saws and bad intentions toward the animals.

I want to talk to Ivori. I don't like knocking on her door as if we're strangers. I don't feel good barging in, either. My mind travels back to being little. My dad towers over me. The bedroom door is closed, and my mom's in there. *You can knock*, he says, and he clucks as if my hesitation seems silly. *Go on*, he says. *Do you want me to do it?* I shake my head. Then he just twists the knob and walks right in, because it's his room, too. He's a king and doesn't have to knock. Only me. I'm the one who has to ask permission. If I knock and she has five seconds to know I'm coming in, what happens to her face in that time? Her smile is stiff, and I don't trust it. I don't try to climb onto her lap. I'd rather be on my own legs on the ground.

Ivori says, "Come in." She is sitting on the floor pasting cut-outs onto her construction.

I plop onto her bed, suddenly afraid she'll have something to say about my mom's letter. Comments from her mother that I'm not ready to hear. "They want to dig up my land," I say. "Build some stupid thing there."

"Who does?"

"Someone. An owner. Some company that put magenta flags in the water."

She gives me a flat-eyed look. I'm making no sense.

"Frank's family should have held onto that land. They let it slip away."

She's instantly aggravated. "You don't know what you're talking about. They didn't *let* anything happen. It happened *to* them—them and a boatload of other Black people."

"Oh, sorry, I know you've got your political angle on everything."

"You're being a total jerk, but I'll forgive you since you're messed up at the moment."

"I *am* messed up. You've never been there so you don't understand."

I leave and see that Alex's door is open, which is a rarity. He's working at his desk against the far wall. I stare in amazement because the leaning tower of pizza boxes is gone. I'd like to go back and tell Ivori, but I've made myself unwelcome.

Alex hears me and turns around. "Hey, Lessie." He says that to piss me off because it suggests I'm a lesbian. As far as I know,

I'm not, but if I were, I'd hate his nastiness even more. Today, he doesn't get to me. I know he semi-likes me, so maybe that's why his insults bug me less than usual.

"Yeah, yeah," I say. He sweeps his arm in the direction of the vacated pizza box construction site, and I nod. "Yeah, good. Someone finally got to you, I guess."

"*You*, my dear. Your influence is great."

I shrug.

"It's felt around the world," he adds, because he has to ridicule me. It's his joy in life. This is where I usually say, *Asshole*, but I'm so defeated at the moment that I can't get there.

"I'm writing a paper," Alex says like a normal person.

"I need to write one, too. An essay. Mine's not going great."

Alex nods. "Mine's on Catherine the Great."

"Sounds fantastic." I know nothing about his topic, but don't feel like advertising my ignorance.

"Can I ask you something?"

"I guess. As long as you're not going to be obnoxious."

He looks embarrassed and runs his hand along the side of his face. "Does Ivori hate me?"

I'm shocked. My impulse is to laugh and say, "We all hate you, Alex," but my weariness leads me to say, "Hate is a strong word." Like a parent might say to a schoolkid.

Distress joins the embarrassment on Alex's face. "My social skills aren't the best," he says.

I am surprised. He's making progress. I shrug and say, "A little self-awareness isn't a bad thing." I consider letting Alex in on my fury about the land, but it's against my principles to speak with him for more than six seconds. Plus, I don't want Ivori to come out of her room and see me schmoozing with Alex, since her loathing for him is unmitigated.

I am exhausted by this day. Everything about it has thrown me. I crash onto my bed, which feels like a life raft. I wonder what Dr. Dream would say about Alex. I might become a psych professor myself, so I have to understand these things. I'm not sure about becoming an actual shrink, though. I see myself seated in a slim, leather chair. I'm cool as you can imagine, maybe looking slightly askance at my patient. Nothing they say riles me, no matter how perverted. I'm not the person I am today, who's trying to stanch the river of rage I feel when I think about the tacky flags in the water, or the confusion my mother's letter seeds in me.

What if Thanh walked into my therapist office? I'd be a stranger to him. I'm old with straight gray hair. He needs to unburden himself about a girl—woman?—who he likes a lot, however she's spiny as a sea urchin. I start to counsel him to be patient, then suddenly I change course and ask him why he's hounding someone who isn't remotely interested in his company. He ought to let her be, because she's not the Earth-mother type who lets everyone sit on her lap and makes sure they're warm and comfy. Then I laugh and tell him I'm joking. I'm just trying to get the feel of his relationship with the girl-woman, but my laugh is rather witchy, and he doesn't trust me and can't get out of there fast enough.

I turn onto my stomach and bury my head in my comforter. *What kind of dumb fuck are you?* I hate some of the crap my brain conjures up; the way it ambles down a pleasant road, then takes some truly oddball turn. It's perverse. *I am.* I shake my head as if I could shake out bad thoughts like pepper. I'm getting sleepy and I'm afraid I'm slipping into the land of bad dreams. But I can't stop sleep from overtaking me; I have to hope I get a break in dreamland.

# Chapter 17

It's a hot day and I take Knose to walk in the neighborhood, happily escaping schoolwork and muggy indoor air and everything else that's confining about my life. When we get back, a police car is parked in front, an officer climbing out on each side. I know why they're there, because I made the call with Ivori sitting beside me making I'll-kill-you faces. I take off running toward the house, which Knose thinks is a game. She races after me and grabs for the back of my pants. I can't let Ivori open the door without my being there. I run right up behind them. I wouldn't normally be so forward with police officers, but I have a job to do.

The woman officer knocks on the door as if she's annoyed ahead of time that we've taken too long to answer it. She and the peach-faced young guy officer haven't seen me or Knose, whose neck is stretched to get her nose close to their butts. I'm behind them, but I position myself so Ivori will see me immediately if she comes to the door.

It's Arwyn who answers. When he sees the two officers, he jumps back a little. Arwyn is forever aware of how he appears to others, so it's hard to tell if he's alarmed or has calculated that *shocked* is the proper way to look if you find police officers on your front step. His eyes are on me now, and he bobbles his head like a half-hearted pendulum, trying to get my attention while escaping theirs. I think he's trying to decipher whether I know what's going on.

The woman must notice him focus his eyes behind her because she turns around, and the young man does the same. She frowns sternly. I sense she's unhappy that we snuck up on her despite her policewomanly vigilance. She's taking this a little too seriously. But this might be the most drama she gets on a day in Ann Arbor.

"Can I help you, officers?" Arwyn asks uber-politely.

The woman clearly wears the big boots in this couple. "We've received a complaint," she says. "From an Ivory Ferguson."

I can't help piping up. "*ee-VOR-ee.*" I'm here to safeguard her; I can't let them mangle her name. I have that mother bear thing going, so I'm braver than usual. "I'll get her," I say and go in. I drop Knose's leash, not bothering to unclip it from her collar.

I can hear Arwyn say, "Come in, officers," with utmost politeness as I rat-a-tat on Iv's door.

She's half-awake on her bed in la-la land, which isn't uncommon for either of us when we're alone. "Hey. They're here. The police."

"Shit." She bolts to a sit but doesn't move from the bed.

"C'mon. They're okay. Just ordinary."

She stands up, but she's so nervous that I think she may lose her balance on the stairs and tumble past me. I turn my head a little. "Try to chill. Not a big deal."

"You don't know anything," she mutters. "And this is on you."

The officers are still at the door. I guess they didn't accept Arwyn's gracious offer to enter. Arwyn is standing beside Knose with a hand on her neck, fiddling with her collar.

When they spot Ivori, the officers walk into the living room. "You're Ivory Ferguson?" the woman asks. They must have been prepped that they were looking for someone African American.

Ivori gives a tiny nod and rolls her eyes toward me. I'm not sure if she's highlighting the screw-up of her name or if she's saying, *Fuck, I'll get even with you.* I don't mind because it's just Ivori keeping her courage up.

Now I see Alex has come halfway down the stairs. I'm hoping it's my eyes shooting daggers at him that's stopped him.

"I have a complaint here," the woman says. "Someone is texting you inappropriate messages, Miss Ferguson. You think he may be following you. Is that correct?"

Ivori half-nods. She's tentative about her gestures, as if she doesn't want to incriminate herself through a false step. I see her glance at the unimposing young man and relax a little.

"Why do you think he's following you?" the woman officer asks. I notice her name tag says Officer Lamb. *Not.*

Ivori gives her a look that says *how stupid can you be?* and I try to telemessage her to calm down and not be an asshole to the police. "Men do that kind of thing," she says.

The young man clarifies. "What specifically indicates to you that you're being followed? What evidence?"

"He talks about things I'm wearing," Ivori says.

I take note that she's now wearing flowered fleece pajama bottoms and an oversized sweatshirt, and I'm doubting the creep would get too excited about those. Then I realize Ivori's been wearing this kind of stuff all the time lately, so maybe she's been trying to snuff the guy's flame.

"I see," Officer Lamb says, and she puckers up her entire face for a split second as if a hatred of men just tore through her consciousness at the speed of light. I hope the young guy didn't see it. He's got to spend his whole day with her.

"Would you like to sit down?" Arwyn asks the officers, though there aren't enough chairs for all of us—just two armchairs from the Salvation Army store plunked in the middle of the room. Arwyn hasn't worked his decorating magic on this room yet.

"That's all right," Officer Lamb says, sounding vaguely appreciative.

The young man sees Alex on the stairs and tips his head in Alex's direction to get his partner's attention.

"Who's that?" she asks.

"That's Alexander," Arwyn says. "He's our other housemate." I add *regrettably* in my mind.

"I see," Officer Lamb says.

"He live here long?" the young man asks. I see his name tag now—Officer MacDougall.

"None of us have," says Ivori, rejoining the conversation. "Just this semester."

"Do you know him very well?" MacDougall asks. He seems not to care whether Alex can hear us.

Knose barks sharply, but none of us humans know what to say. For some reason, the question tangles us. "Yes and no," I finally say.

The officers ask a couple more pointless questions. I'm unimpressed with their investigative chops, but I'm glad for Ivori's sake that no one is waving a gun around.

"We're finished here," Lamb says.

MacDougall hands us a business card. "Let us know if anything more happens, or there's an escalation." He looks at Arwyn and turns his back to the staircase where Alex is still lurking. "Keep an eye on that guy," he says quietly to Arwyn.

Arwyn looks surprised, but also ready to assume the cloak of responsibility.

The officer's eyes brighten. "On second thought"—he glances at Officer Lamb for permission, then says, "Young man, come down here."

Alex makes his lazy way down the stairs. He's wearing a cotton bathrobe over some baggy pants, and the robe dusts the floor. "Good afternoon, officers," he says, as if he's welcoming them to a reception.

"Do you know why we're here?" MacDougall asks.

"I believe so," Alex says very mildly.

*Who is this new and circumspect Alex?* MacDougall has an aggressive tone toward him even though Alex is sweetness and light.

Lamb steps in now. "You know anything about who's been dogging this young woman?"

Ivori winces.

Alex shrugs.

"That's not a particularly helpful answer," MacDougall says. "Do you, or don't you?"

Alex's eyes search every corner of the room. He looks at Knose and frowns as if she's blown the whistle on him.

"We're waiting," Lamb says.

Alex stalls then shrugs again. His voice is just audible. "I might."

I'm shocked. Ivori looks worse off than me so I concentrate on sending her calming energy.

"There's your culprit," MacDougall says, wagging his index finger in the air proudly. "I suspected it."

Arwyn has been playing catch-up because Ivori was embarrassed to tell him we called the police. "You?" Arwyn appears ready to slug Alex.

"I was just playing around," Alex mutters. He looks cornered.

"That's no game, young man," MacDougall says. "If there's any threat involved, you're entitled to press charges," he says to Ivori, who is pressing against the wall, as far from Alex as she can get. She is desperate for this whole thing to end. "I'd seriously consider getting this guy out of here, ASAP."

Arwyn looks pained, and I get the feeling he wants the officers gone, as if he needs to be alone with us and our very dirty laundry. He says, "We can handle this internally, officer." I don't know what the hell Arwyn has in mind. I think he's watching too many police procedurals, but he sounds determined, and the officers ready themselves to leave.

"Let us know if you change your mind," MacDougall says, looking a little dubiously at Arwyn, who is wearing fluffy white slippers.

Lamb looks at Alex like she wants to say, *Your mother should have spanked you more.* Or maybe that's me thinking that. We'll soon be alone with Alex. I feel a frantic impulse to call Thanh or my dad. Arwyn is staring at Alex as if he wants to take him out and shoot him. Arwyn's fury settles my fear.

"What's wrong with you?" Arwyn demands. "I think you have to move out of our house." I am guiltily thinking of all the trouble we had finding a fourth body to split the rent. Arwyn and I both look at Ivori. She looks hugely embarrassed.

"He's gone," she says. "Him or me. I'm not living with him spying on me."

Alex is watching Ivori with a plaintive, hungry look I can't fully decipher. I'm not afraid of him and oddly don't hate him that much. I just want Ivori's panic to settle. Whatever will accomplish that, I support.

"You can go live with your mother," I say.

Alex adopts a look of profound misery but doesn't say anything.

"You've got no choice, dude," Arwyn says. "You did this. It's all on you."

"I hate you so much," Ivori says. "You better go, because I might do something to you, you asshole. I'd like to hurt you."

I see Alex's face brighten slightly, and I'm praying he's not going to make an ugly remark. *You can be my dominatrix*, or something of that sort. I have the odd feeling I understand something about Alex: the way he likes to provoke people. I halfway get that part of him, though I'm not going to say we are alike.


Ivori seems a little calmer in the morning, even though Alex spent the night here. I wonder if she's relieved to identify the source of her misery and more reasonably assess the threat. I saw Arwyn go into her room last night. I imagine he talked to her about the male of the species and the asshole things they sometimes do under influence of hormones and social backwardness.

I hear Alex moving around in his room. He must be getting his stuff packed up. Around noon, there's a knock on our front door that triggers from Knose a glass-rupturing *harooom*. I rush down to quiet her. Everything in me is so jangled that I'm half-frantic to maintain peace. It's Mrs. Kuznetsov. I haven't seen her since our long-ago meeting to interview Alex. Her substantial personhood is in a fury and a rush. I don't know if she's angry at us or Alex.

"Get him," she says to me. "I wait here. You get him."

I don't have to get him because he's trudging down the stairs, holding a suitcase and dragging an armload of clothes behind him like a blankie. "Hello, Mother," he says, generally cowed and specifically afraid to look at her. He's reaping the humiliation he more than deserves, but a tiny bit of me sees him as a big dumb kid in need of rescue.

"You fucked things up," I say monotonally to him. Mrs. Kuznetsov is puffing out steam and unwrapping her long scarf then tossing it back over her shoulder like a cast fishing line; then she unwraps and repeats. I don't like her and am glad to say *fucked* in front of her, something I wouldn't normally do with older people.

"Goodbye, Leslie," Alex says. That's it, but I'm struck by his gentle tone.

When he's gone, I knock on Ivori's door, stick my face in, and say, "Hey, he's gone. He's out of here."

Things in the house seem dreary and depressed. It's not that Alex was providing any kind of happiness. God knows he wasn't. I think it's because we've failed. We tried to put together a household—like a happy family—and we didn't pull it off. We got a lurking, reptilian individual who made us uncomfortable and irritated. Then we got rid of him. That's progress, I guess, but you're supposed to be able to fix things when you're an adult. And we failed. We're all knocking around in our bedrooms or the kitchen, disgruntled and off-kilter.

One afternoon, Ivori calls me into her room. She looks kind of grim. "I forgot to tell you," she says. "My mom read your letter. A while ago." She grabs it off her desk and hands it to me. "She just said it was nice, and that she didn't feel comfortable speculating. Because it's delicate or something like that. Personal, I guess. Sorry. No big revelations. You're probably disappointed."

I shrug. Actually, I'm relieved. I think I need to find my own way. I am someone in a dark underwater cave who's following a rope through the cold murk to find the exit. It's scary, but at least I can go at my own speed. I don't need any sea monsters jumping out at me while I'm feeling my way.

# Chapter 18

Thanh, Knose, and I go to our Eden in the morning and flags are everywhere. It would look like a celebration, except it's a wake. Knose dashes from one flag to the next to sniff them, as if she's doing a dot-to-dot puzzle. She can probably smell whoever put them there. I feel panicky. I see Knose's eyes moving among the flags, asking questions, intent on discovering answers. My eyes are wild, too, but I don't know where to walk. I turn to Thanh but have no words.

He shakes his head and tightens his lips. "A developer's been all over the site, mapping wetlands."

"Knose! Knose!" Suddenly, I am terrified she'll run away or get swallowed by the swamp. Arwyn will despise me, and I'll be a mental mess. "Knose!" She is already on her way back. She's a good dog. She's not stubborn like I am. Her legs are caked in muck, but her shoulders and back are clean and sleek, and I don't care about the mud.

"I did some research," Thanh says. He is tentative. Shy. Not sure of me.

"What is it? It's okay. Tell me."

"They want to build fifty houses. A company called Blue Sky."

I feel confused. "Blue Sky? That's a company?"

"Blue Sky Properties. They develop land. They want to call the development Woodlands Preserve. Developers always do that. Like you won't notice they're cutting down the woods, not preserving them."

I weave through the forest, climbing over downed trees, twisted branches, rocks patchy with tiny lettuce-leaves of lichen. I'm getting away from Thanh and his research report, but I run into a flag that catches my pants leg as it bends back. I yank at my pants. They rip a little. The flag snaps upright. I keep going, deeper into the woods. The spicebushes have small green berries now—shiny and perfect. But there are flags here, too. The gaudy pink is all wrong. Plastic trash. I understand that crazy bus guy mooning the world.

Thanh has caught up to Knose and me. He takes my hand. "Look it," he says.

"What?"

"I don't know. Maybe we can do something about this."

"Do?"

"The developer has to get a lot of permits. From the city. Probably the county. Wetlands delineation. Sewage treatment. Traffic studies. Utilities. Density calculations. All of that."

I want to scream but say, "That can help us?"

"Maybe. If they are in violation of a wetlands ordinance or a zoning law or if the neighbors are up in arms. It might."

I look at him like a starving puppy.

"We have to go to meetings, Les. Planning Commission. Zoning Commission. That sort of thing. Find out what's what. What's going on. Maybe make speeches. Public testimony."

"How do you know all this?"

He shrugs. "I read about things. And my dad once had to make a case. At public meetings. He didn't get anywhere, like with most of his projects."

Pain washes over Thanh's face. I don't want to see that. We have enough misery right here. But I ask, "Did your father screw something up?"

Thanh waits, then nods. He looks ashamed.

We find Thanh's car on the street. We're both fucked up and don't know what to do with ourselves. I spread a cloth in back to protect the car from Knose's muddiness. Thanh drives me to my house and in the driveway he takes my hand. He twists around so that I turn my eyes to him in curiosity, and he kisses me. It's not a deep or long kiss. It's a kiss that's a question: *Can I do this?* I don't answer his question, but I don't leave the car either. My face is a blank paper, not wrinkled into the scowl Thanh might expect from me. Now comes a long kiss. He is feeling it. Me, I'm just receiving it. I'm not kissing him, but not pushing him away, either. My body is starting to ring like a church bell, though. He stops and we look at each other. His eyes are loving. I think mine are quiet. I want to kiss him again, and my body melts toward him. I glance at the house and imagine Alex still there, leering out the window. Watching me. That disturbs my peacefulness. "I should go."

He looks wounded, but Thanh is slow to complain. I see him regrouping, thinking of something I might accept from him. "Let's think about the meetings," he says. "Blue Sky is presenting to the Planning Commission on July 28. We should go and listen for the ways their plan doesn't conform to the city's environmental ordinances. Stuff like that. You should tell them about the land

and why it shouldn't be developed." Thanh has more to say, but I'm distracted by fear because he wants me to stand up at these meetings like I'm an attorney and argue a case.

I nod and am grateful he has an idea for plucking those disgusting barbs out of the earth. As I go in, Thanh's kiss and the thought of making speeches both leave me weak in the legs.


I ask Arwyn to go for a walk in the afternoon because Arwyn is my chamomile tea. He calms me and makes me feel safe. Ivori is the opposite: She's my energy drink, but lately she's mad half the time and wildly creating stuff the other half. I think I need to give her space and let her do her thing. Meanwhile, I have Arwyn. I explain to him about the effing Blue Sky company.

He grimaces sympathetically. "Developers always shove their big dicks down the throats of little towns. Force things on people that no one wants. Hey, Les, I have a problem," he segues. He is embarrassed. "I can't afford that extra rent with Alex out. I'll try to figure a way, but right now, I don't have the money." He shows me his empty hands. They are nice hands.

I nod. I could ask my dad but don't love the idea of that. We all feel like deadbeats, leaning on our parents, but no one really wants to go work at McDonald's, either. We're spoiled, but at least have the self-respect to be embarrassed about it.

"I'm looking for a job. My friend Ronnie says they need help at a store downtown. It's queer-centric. Kind of a metro vibe."

I look at Arwyn's socks—one fuzzy with red-and-white stripes and one black with red cats. "You may have to up your game a little." I'm teasing. "But hey, I like the socks. It's a look."

He smiles his meltingly sweet smile. "You think so?" He pauses. "You're not going to beat me up, are you?"

He's lost me, and I'm mildly alarmed. Does he feel the waves of rage rolling off me since I learned about the fifty houses? "What are you talking about, Ar?"

He chases something away with a headshake. "Being insane. Just had a fuzzy clothing memory from when I was a kid." He inhales, slow and deep. "I wore a mohair sweater to school. Two older boys—you know, *proper* boys, unlike me. Ugh." He shakes his head.

"What?" My heart is collapsing over kid-Arwyn's heartache.

"Forget it, Les. Use your imagination." He shakes his head. "The usual. Humiliation."

The word frightens me. "I love your socks. You and Ivori are so creative."

He half-laughs. "I was crazy about a red-haired boy my age, and I wore that gorgeous sweater to catch his eye."

"So, what happened?"

"After class, those dreadful boys came up. Said some awful things to me. Hateful. So mortifying."

"I'm sorry. People are mean." I'm thinking about Mrs. Ferguson. "But me, too. Sometimes you're the only person I actually feel like being nice to."

Arwyn smiles. "Andrew—that was his name—caught up to me. He started talking to me. He said a few words, then he dashed off, like he had too much energy to stand still. I would have let that lovely boy do absolutely anything to me. But the thought of those dreadful boys and their nasty words." Arwyn shivers. "Unbearable."

My mind has slipped sideways to Thanh, to all my uncertainty. "But now, a grown-up, away from those awful people, you wouldn't hesitate? To do anything you want, with Andrew or whoever, I mean."

He nods. "I try to be free. To trust myself."

"I'm not like that. There's just something in me that says it's not cool to let someone be—can I say this?—*inside* me. Privacy. It might be that; or maybe dignity. You've got an inside and an outside, so why should someone come right in? Why would you let them? You might as well hang up a welcome sign." I laugh, embarrassed even with Arwyn; even with myself.

He looks at me as if I am puzzling, or peculiar, but his eyes are kind. "I used to get freaked out about cleanliness. Someone I liked would want me to bottom, but I couldn't. Now I throw those things out, when I can. I literally imagine opening the window and throwing out a big canful of trash. It's got all my self-hating thoughts. It's strange—don't laugh—but sometimes I think about my mom, at the time when I was very little. Still a baby." He laughs and says, "Not gay yet." Then, "Do you know how when you're a baby, it's as if your body belongs to your mom? Total access. You don't have that sense of privacy yet. Any place she'd touch me was just *good* because she was a gentle person, taking care of me and loving me. And it was all fine. All good, right Les?"

I'm getting squirmy. Angry. But I am trying, for once, not to run away. I can't imagine being that close with my mom. But maybe I just can't get back there. I need a time machine. I imagine gentle hands on my skin—my arms and legs, my shoulders. Could that be what I'm looking for? I can see us in the tents we made under the covers, laughing. Maybe she tickled me. I shake my head.

"I don't know. My mom and me. That's another story."

"Your mom died so young, you poor girl."

"Yeah, well."

"Even Alex has his big, bosomy mother." He's trying to make me laugh. He puts his arm around me and I see tears in his eyes. I start to cry and want to shut off my dribbly tears, but I can't, because this is Arwyn. I don't know if I'm crying because my mom died or because Arwyn is teary, and his arm is around me. *Both*, Dr. Dream would say. Arwyn has fuchsia pink nail polish on the hand that's wrapped around me. Those chintzy flags on the property. I won't think about them. Sometimes, my mother would go to a salon and come home with pink nail polish. Or red. She always put out her hands and showed me so I could see how pretty and perfect, how shiny they were. And she'd laugh. I go back to that laugh and look closer. I think the whole paint-your-nails thing seemed silly to her, though she must have liked it enough to go. I think the nail salon was at the edge of her comfort zone because she wasn't that girly, but she shared her nails with me because they were pretty. Pretty but foolish.

I'm trying to tell Arwyn that I like what's happening, what could happen, with me and Thanh, but it's outside my comfort zone. I don't know what's okay for me and what's not. So possibly I'm a little like my mom, though I don't know if that's good or bad in this case.

"What are you smiling about?" he asks.

I want to say, *You. I'm smiling at you.* But I don't say anything.

"I got a text from Alex," he says, and I hear him working to keep his voice level.

"You did?"

"I gather he feels like a shit about what he did."

"He is a shit."

Arwyn nods and hangs his head. We are approaching our house. He looks up at it. "Ivori went to the dentist."

"Fuck. No. Today?"

"Now, I think."

I feel anxious. "I need to see if she's back."

When we get inside, I hear Ivori in her room. I knock, and she tells me to come in. I study her closely to see if she's alright, but I can't tell.

"How was it?" I ask.

"Awful."

"Uh-oh. What happened?" She's sitting on the floor among her art materials, so I sit on the bed. "What did he do? Tell me."

"He fixed my tooth." She bares her tooth so I can sort of see it. "See. It's good as new, like you promised."

"There's more to this story."

"I just hated being there. I couldn't help it. I had those feelings, like I had to get out. Every minute I was there I was trying to pretend to be fine, but I wasn't fine. I was freaked."

"Was it the slavery thing? Or just the creepy man thing?"

"I don't know. Fuck it, Leslie. Now you're making fun of me. I don't need that. Just change the subject."

I don't know if I'm making fun of her or not. I hope not, but possibly a little.

"Arwyn heard from Alex." This is the wrong direction to turn. I'm going from the frying pan into the fire.

"What did the slimeball want?"

"Not sure. Maybe to apologize?"

"I doubt that. What did Arwyn tell him?"

"He didn't exactly share that. Arwyn's worried. He doesn't have enough rent money. He might get a job at some expensive store. Help people pick out outfits. That kind of thing."

Ivori is on her feet now. "He better not be thinking about inviting Alex to move back. I'll move out. I'm not living with that moron. Don't try and make me feel guilty, either."

"No one's thinking of that. Arwyn's just a softie. Always feels sympathetic to everyone's personality deficits."

"Are you saying I'm a hard ass? Fuck it. I don't care."

"I'm not saying that. I'm not saying anything. You have a fixed tooth and don't have to go to the dentist for a long time. Let's just stay with that and forget about Alex, okay? Alex is history."

# Chapter 19

I'm sitting on my bed, my legs straight out in front of me, my back against the wall. I'm not that comfortable in this position, though I spend half my life in it. I pick up the phone and call my dad. I tell him I need to get one of those pillows with side arms. We're just chatting about meaningless things, but I'm thinking about the letter from Mom.

Finally, I say, "I read an old letter I got from Mom. She called me Lessie. That's kind of weird, Dad."

He laughs, too. "It wasn't connotative to her." He gets the point.

"She slipped one time and wrote *Lennie*. Thanh noticed that."

He's quiet. I wonder if it bothers him for me to show Mom's letters to half the universe. I shouldn't have mentioned Thanh.

"Lennie?" he asks.

"Yeah. Two neat little *n*'s instead of *s*'s. Humps instead of curves."

"I think that was a slip, Leslie."

"That's what I said."

"No. I mean a slip that had meaning."

*Meaning?* My anxiety meter jumps. Meaning is what I try to avoid with Dad. My world is about to change again.

"Your mother had a sister who died when she and your mother were little."

"Really?" It's beyond strange that I never knew that.

"Her sister was Lenore. Lennie. She was two years younger than Mom and drowned in a swimming pool when she was four. She stumbled into the water, and no one noticed. Your mom adored her."

"Oh. Shit." This is worse than I could imagine. I am a cartoon character that falls off a cliff and is scrambling their feet in the air. "That's so awful." I was left out of everything important to her. Was I invisible? Forgotten? "She probably was waiting until I was older to tell me. Right, Dad? But that time never came."

"Probably," he says. "She didn't like to talk about it."

That's my cue, because I don't like talking about this either, so I tell Dad I have to get off the phone. I pretend for the dozenth time that I'm hot to get working on that essay.

In fact, I need to figure out how to breathe again. I need another hour of just sitting and thinking, trying to yank the stray pieces of my inner world into some kind of order. Maybe Mom couldn't put what happened into words. Now I have to look at her in a new way, to see through the screen of that drowning little girl. Everything is behind that screen. But I can't tell how it alters the picture. Did Mom feel guilty? Or terrified that she could drown, too, since her sister did? Dad said she adored her. Lenore. *L* like me. *E* like me. What's that about? Mom used to call me *little one*. That came into my mind like a whisper one night when I was with Thanh. It sounds so baby-safe to me. All bundled up and cradled, what Arwyn talked about. Could I tell myself those words when I feel shaky, to make myself feel better? Can you have a talisman made of words strung like pearls?

Thanh noticed the mistake in the letter. I didn't even see it. Now Thanh's in my head kissing me again, so I lie down and let him do that. He's kissing me all over the place and putting his hands anywhere and everywhere. And I understand what Ivori means about Mother Nature having this figured out. Mother Nature clearly is a slut.

He's kissing me and I'm drifting back to the land and the cabin. I love that place, with all its young life. I could go to see Frank, tell him what's going on with Blue Sky, but I'm afraid to see resignation on his face, to hear his dreary words. *We can't do anything.* At least he won't call me by someone else's name. Someone who's dead.

A couple days later, Thanh proposes our next tour-of-parks adventure, though it's nearly a hundred degrees outside. He has us humping hills like soldiers. Luckily, I only have a daypack full of PB&J, carrot sticks, and Doritos to lug. The nature area opens up to a small park adjacent to a grade school, with a swing set and big and small slides. There's an enormous pipe for kids to play on, maybe ten feet long. It's way too tall for me to get my butt on top of it, so I back up a few yards and run at it and throw my body across the top. I'm no Olympic medalist, but that works, and I get astride the pipe. The metal is cool, and I enjoy being up there, so I lay down on my stomach and work at keeping aligned so I don't fall off. After a while, I start to get sleepy from the heat on my back. My attention drifts, and I lose my balance and slip off. Sitting on shredded bark on the ground, I realize that Thanh is gone. I hear dull banging from inside the pipe. Thanh is scrunched inside, with his knees bent and his head pushed forward by the curve of the pipe.

"Come in."

"Nuh-um. Not a possibility."

"It's cooler than outside. Come on."

I sit in the bark, then shift my butt into the pipe and fold the rest of my body into it. I should have gone in so I'd be facing Thanh, not side by side with him. I'm stuck at the end, in the wrong position.

"Come sit by me. It's cooler here in the middle."

I'm skeptical of the thermodynamics, but I scoot over until I'm butt cheek to butt cheek with Thanh. I sit and sweat and try to assess if I'm one degree cooler than before.

"Did you like that preserve?" he asks.

"Good exercise."

"Yeah, but also a nice place, right?"

"We're stuck in here. Now what? Because I might want to get out. It's possible I'm claustrophobic."

Thanh puts his hand on my knee. His eyes are on mine, which I recognize as his way of asking. But it's not enough for him—too many lectures on explicit permission—so he asks, "Okay?" His delicacy annoys me. I shrug. He lets his hand fall halfway down my thigh, on the inside. I think of saying something, but I don't know what I want to say, so I keep quiet.

"What if I lie down?" he asks.

I erupt in chirps. "How are you planning to do that?"

"Back up a little."

"I finally get in here and now you're pushing me out." I'm curious where he's going with this. He squirms around and stretches out on his back.

"Comfortable?" I ask, because there's no way he's comfortable.

"I could be. Try lying down next to me."

Another laugh bubbles up. "There *is* no 'next to you.'"

"On top of me, then."

I'm curious and excited, but my mind hones in on logistics and I don't see how this is going to happen. I like the ridiculous challenge, though, so I start crawling alongside him. I'm giggling now because this is as awkward as you can imagine, and a couple times I fall over onto Thanh and land with my hand here or there. I've almost got my head up near his when he slides his hands under my armpits and hauls me up until my head is at his chest and my body is on top of his. We're lying there like a human hotdog bun.

I'm still laughing, but Thanh is serious now. His earnestness infects me and slows me down so I can feel his body all along the length of mine. He puts both hands on my jeans and slides the waist down a little, manages to get his warm hands onto my cooler butt, which doesn't mind the warmth. Then he lifts his head off the pipe and starts to kiss my mouth. He kisses and kisses, and then he is kissing my neck up by my cheekbone and then the soft skin at the bottom of my earlobe is between his lips. I feel like a rabbit is nibbling my ear and start to laugh. I try to stay with silliness, but his lips are so ungodly soft, and they quiet me until I can feel his heart thumping. We're quiet awhile. Then a pissed-off kid's voice says, "There are people *in* there," and I see a little black-haired face framed at the end of the pipe. I hear the mom, her voice high and startled, say, "You go on the slide instead, darling."

"We should get out," Thanh says, but first he hugs me for a long minute. Now my whole body is complaining that it has to separate from his. And after all that work.

Thanh is laughing as he tries to inch his way out. I squinch myself out one way and he goes the other. He's born out into the world headfirst and I'm born feetfirst.

# Chapter 20

Alex is back with us. It's hard to say how this happened, since Ivori's hatred of Alex remains a bottomless pit. I put it mostly on Arwyn with his soft heart and empty wallet. Arwyn developed a closeted-gay-boy theory about Alex that filled his compassion well and started him making the case for Alex's return. I don't know if I buy Arwyn's gay-boy notion, but I did feel the pressure from Arwyn's empty wallet. Gay, straight, or whatever, he's ours again. Ivori must have taken pity on Arwyn to let this happen. I remember what he was like when he was desperate for Knose to stay, though Knose is an easier sell than Alex.

We're all restless when Alex shows up. He is the first to speak. "You could punish me," he says. I hope this isn't a sadomasochistic thing. It seems more about paying his debt to society—*us*—so he can feel halfway accepted. And he does need punishment, so I'm on board.

"We should put him on trial," Arwyn says.

Suddenly, Alex looks terrified. "You're not going to hurt me, are you?" The bully has become a mouse.

"We should," I say, then notice he is all obedience now and think of his cowering beside his mother. Was he flinching? Arwyn told me something about Alex's mother hitting him. He had a talk with Alex. That's when he developed the repressed-gay-boy notion. I see Alex through new eyes, his obnoxiousness a big fake-out I can halfway understand.

But he needs punishing, at least for Ivori's sake. She's not ready to see him as a victim of Mrs. Kuznetsov or anyone else.

"Just keep away from me," she says. "Stay on that side of the room." To her, he is sparking danger. And contagion.

"Come over here and sit down," Arwyn says to Alex, pointing to a wooden chair. Arwyn looks at me, and I nod for him to proceed with whatever drama he's envisioning. "This is the trial of Alexander Kuznetsov, who has been accused of inappropriate communication with Ivori—Sorry, Ivi, what is your last name again? I don't know what's wrong with me."

"Ferguson." Her voice rides on a wisp of hurt.

"With Ivori Ferguson. If found guilty as charged, sentence will be passed by those assembled. Leslie, come forward and interrogate the witness."

I feel like giggling, but Arwyn seems serious about this so I try to play my part.

"Alexis."

He interrupts me. "Alexei. Alexis is Greek. We are Russian."

"Correction. Alexei. Have you been texting your housemate, Ivori?"

Alex shrugs. "Yes. I did. Not anymore."

"And have your texts been accompanied by inappropriate and unwanted—seriously *gross*—sexual remarks?"

His eyes search for an escape. "Sometimes. In the past."

"Ask him the reason for his horrid behavior," Arwyn interjects.

"Yeah, *why,* asshole?" Ivori hisses.

Alex looks crestfallen. I think he's actually wounded, as if he expected Ivori to have forgiven him by now.

"I told the officer," Alex says obsequiously. "Just fooling around."

"If you ever text me that shit again—don't look at me, okay. I don't want your creepy eyes on me."

"Yeah." I second Ivori. "I'll call your mother and tell her to come get you."

Arwyn glances at me because I'm coldhearted and aiming for Alex's weakness. "We've established guilt," he says. "Beyond a shadow of a doubt, since we have a confession. We need to sentence this defendant."

We are beyond our imaginative resources now and so fall helplessly silent as if we are waiting for a true adult to come to our rescue. Finally, I blurt out, "Housework. Put an apron on him and have him wash the dishes. Every single day." I'm concerned Ivori may not think this is a stiff enough sentence. Also, that emasculation may not suit Arwyn's vision of rehabilitation. I look over to him for guidance.

"Ivori?" he says. "You're the aggrieved party."

"Yeah. Dishes. Whatever."

It seems wrong to me that Alex, who's always in his room, is going to be downstairs in the kitchen, among us. But it's my sentence, so I let it stand. Arwyn ducks out to the kitchen and returns with Alex's new outfit, a beige apron that barely makes it around his bovine circumference.

In time, we get more accustomed to having Alex in the kitchen, though I notice that any time Ivori catches Alex standing too close to her, she wrinkles her face hideously. To remind him of where he stands in her world order.

Several weeks pass, and one morning, before anyone has class or trips to the fitness center, we all end up at the breakfast table together. Arwyn is the only one with something he actually cooked—some eggs, fried I guess, with sautéed veggies. We talk about nothing. The tea kettle whistles, then shrieks.

Arwyn gets up and murmurs, "Mmm, Bengal Spice…so nice." He sits down with his happy tea, waits two beats, and says, "I'm going to the Pride parade Saturday. Does anyone want to go along?"

He looks at me with his eyebrows a smidge lifted, and I gather I'm supposed to say my gay-positive thing, for Alex's benefit, so I say, as if I'm thrilled, "I'll go. I love that parade. Ivori? Coming?" She shrugs. She doesn't know her role in this charade and looks puzzled. She's been glancing at Alex as if she wishes her eyes shot deadly rays.

Usually, Alex is a ghost among us. No one talks to him, though everyone feels his presence. Arwyn covers for Ivori's hesitation, saying, "Hey Alex, want to go with?" Alex looks massively nervous and says nothing.

"Is that a yes or a no, Alex?" I ask, displaying my patience deficit.

"Um. I don't know."

"You should go," Ivori says. "A fun time will be had by all." I can't tell if she's wanting to see Alex squirm or actually is trying to reinforce Arwyn's gay-pride agenda, though that may be an air plant rooted in nothing.

I can see Alex trying to climb up on his high horse. His boot toe is in a stirrup ready to hoist his enormous body. "Parades," he says. "Oh my god, who goes to parades?"

Arwyn looks wounded. He picks up his plate coated with congealed egg yolk and takes it to the sink. I shoot Alex a *you asshole* look and say, "Arwyn and I will have an awesome time without you."

Alex must not like my terseness because he jumps in with, "All right, all right, I'll go, but don't expect me to wave a rainbow flag."

"What a favor to us," I say. "Hooray. Alex is coming with us. What more could I wish for?" I can see Arwyn longs to shut me up, but I can't quiet myself. "Do you think you're doing someone a favor, Alex?"

"Well, it's not exactly the Macy's parade." He smirks. Suddenly, he has escaped his mother's grip. I see how this happens, how he breaks free into asshole territory. I'm starting to get where his lifeline and mine intersect. Normally, I'm happy for eureka moments, but this one doesn't delight me.

"Stop," Arwyn says. "We're going and having a good time, and that's that."

After breakfast, I follow Ivori up to her room and walk in behind her before she can close the door. "What's wrong?" I ask her.

"Seriously?" she asks me, disgusted.

"What? Too much gay pride?"

"How about too much of the guy who sent me repulsive messages, who happens to live down the hall from me, who's now your best friend."

"Arwyn wants me to treat him civilly. He thinks some of his sexual creepiness is because he's gay and repressed by his mother. Who possibly beats him up."

"You two are his gender-comfort support team?"

I shrug. "Just trying to be humane."

"Why is he even in this house?"

"Dunno. We need the money? Arwyn wants us to have compassion for him?"

"Well, good for Arwyn. Pity's not my brand."

"But you agreed to it. Right?"

"I guess."

I am lost now, spinning in space somewhere between Arwyn and Ivori. I retreat to my room. Lie down.

How many hours have I lain here? Thinking. And lost. I'm back at that door, and my mother's not letting me in. *Correction.* It's the kids not letting me in, not her. But she finds it necessary to point out my undesirability, how my company is not wanted by them. Ivori is going to close her door on me. It's halfway shut already. How did that happen? How can she not know I love her and believed we'd be friends forever? She and Arwyn are the only entries in my *forever* file. Other than them, it's empty.

I wake up in the middle of the night. Jesus, what is this dream? Thanh is with me, and he's naked and gorgeous and I'm about to kiss his chest and then who-knows-what, when I see that he's stabbed through with a hundred little metal stakes with pink plastic flags. I'm pulling them out like porcupine quills and crying, but there are so many. Thanh keeps saying, "Don't worry, Leslie," and doesn't seem to be in pain, though I'm panicked and sure he's quietly dying.

I get out of bed and go into the hall to shake off the dream and go to the bathroom. Alex pops out of his room wearing the saddest face imaginable. I'm alarmed because the dream is still carpeting my mind and here's Alex looking ashen, so I ask him, "What's the matter?" He's looking at the floor and shaking his head. I can't help but feel sorry for him. I say, more urgently, "C'mon, are you okay?"

He shrugs. "Maybe not."

"What's the matter?" He glances at me and I'm like, *Oh shit, I hope he's not ready to kill himself.* I can see it's hit him that he's a moron and has no friends, so I say, "You're not that bad."

"*Jerk,* you and Ivori always say."

"Yeah, okay, a little bit jerky but not terrible. You'll grow out of it."

"Are you still going to that parade?"

I'm surprised by his question. "Yeah. For Arwyn."

"You like him a lot."

I nod, but for once I get the message and refrain from gushing about how great Arwyn is.

"Am I still invited?"

"It's not an exclusive event, Alex."

"No, but I mean."

"We can all go together." I pray Ivori's not listening at her door. I take comfort in knowing that's not her style. She'd just barrel out huffing and puffing.

# Chapter 21

Alex is ridiculous. He is the tallest among the thousand or so people smooshed in with us as we cross Main Street at Williams. He's wearing a rainbow tee shirt. I have no idea where he got it. He's also got a flag. His belly is an inflated pool-pillow arcing from his nipples down to his waist. But Alex seems happy—ecstatic even.

"Are you high, Alex?" I ask him. He shakes his head and stops waving his flag. I've made him self-conscious now and I feel bad, so I say, "Hey, just go for it!"

Arwyn keeps glancing over at Alex. He's cheery, too, and suddenly I'm happy and light and amazed that someone we all hated is right here beside us having fun. We all feel like rainbows.

My only worry at the moment is Ivori. Will she accept us putting our arms around him just because he's pulled a Pride shirt over his head? I try to clear my head of Iv and let the river of rainbows carry me. I want to forget about being Leslie for a while. Arwyn has Knose on a lilac-colored embroidered leash he bought her. I think he's proud of having a dog, especially a dog like Knose who behaves nicely. A tall and dignified drag queen is leading our procession. She looks like my mom's peonies in full magenta bloom. She's nodding every which way to the crowd like she's the Queen of England, and the crowd is adoring her.

Alex sweeps his flag back and forth, high and low. In a figure eight. He is giddy, and I have to tell him not to wave it so close to my face. He turns so he can flourish his flag freely, but he can't handle waving one way and walking the other. His inside foot catches on a raised piece of asphalt and he collapses onto his right knee. The people behind us stop. Blood is seeping through Alex's pant leg, which is crusted with dirt and fragments of pavement.

"Oh, shit, Alex!" I yell. He looks down at his bloody knee. His face screeches with alarm.

Arwyn takes a close look, and his grimace says the situation is bad. "We have to go home. If we don't clean it, it's going to get infected." I feel his heart breaking because he loves this parade. But he is so conscientious, so we are leaving. I notice how we're a *we* at the moment and picture us all bent over Alex's knee, picking out the dirt like archaeological finds and gently washing the scraped skin.

When we get home, Arwyn unclips the leash from Knose's harness. I feel Arwyn's grief at that metallic clink that marks the end of our afternoon at the parade. Alex goes to his room and comes back down with his robe properly closed so we can access his knee. Arwyn has piled up cleaning and bandaging supplies on the kitchen table. God knows where he got them, but he is prepared for everything. He pulls a chair away from the table. "Sit here," he says to Alex, who sits and extends his injured leg.

Arwyn dampens the gauze with diluted hydrogen peroxide and runs it lightly over the knee, smoothing off the caked blood and dirt. When he has the debris removed, he wets another piece of gauze with the mixture and holds it against the raw skin. Alex is trying to be brave and not flinch or whine.

I look through the collection of bandages and find a big square one that looks right. Arwyn nods, so I rip one end of the paper envelope and slide out the bandage. I try not to touch anything to the sterile surface. I realize I should have washed my hands and hope Arwyn didn't notice. Alex is in a bliss of being cared for by people who aren't his mother, who might actually become friends. Ivori is crashing around in the living room, not doing anything identifiable. I'm worried but have a job to do. "Flex it halfway," I tell Alex and tap the side of his knee. I smooth on the bandage. "That will stay on for five minutes," I say, but Arwyn is ready with adhesive tape, so my five-minute Band-Aid becomes Arwyn's five-hour dressing.

"Cool," Alex says. He looks as happy as when he was brandishing the rainbow flag. He doesn't even notice when my bandage is wrinkled as a shar-pei as soon as he straightens his leg.

Knose has been lying down watching the proceedings, but now she approaches Alex to sniff his knee. Alex lurches back as if a mountain lion has pounced on him, but soon settles and looks at her. This might be the first time he's truly seeing our dog.

# Chapter 22

It's still July. The land is drier now than in spring. Some of the wetlands are muck, not open water, so Thanh and I get our shoes filthy walking to where the evil flags are. The mud sucks at our feet. I've seen videos of people sinking in quicksand that are probably faked but still terrify me. You are helpless. You're going to go under. It gets to your chin, then your mouth, then your nose, and oh god.

The flags are multiplying, and circles of blue paint mark some of the trees at about shoulder height. I'm cycling between shock and fury. Thanh suspects the Blue Sky delinquents are trying to delineate the wetlands using their drier summer footprint. They can fake that the wetlands are a lot smaller than they really are. I want to yank out those flags. Maybe shove them in upside down, their pink heads in the muck.

Thanh is heading for the cabin. I'm uncertain whether to follow him because I'm awash in emotions. I consider sitting down on one of the fallen trunks but instead I traipse after Thanh like a puppy. He pushes the door. I feel uneasy as it swings inward. I would faint if Frank was sitting on the bed looking up at Thanh and me.

The place is empty. Thanh sits down on the bed where we played botany strip poker. He reaches up and puts his hand on the top button of my shirt. He pauses and looks at me. I say nothing and shift my eyes to the side. Thanh undoes one button, then a second. Again, he stops and studies me. I am silent but stand there like a kid being undressed by her mother. I think he has rehearsed this a thousand times and is trying to stay calm. Doesn't he see what state I'm in about the land? Or is this his remedy? I start to get mad, but his attentive face dissolves my protest. When he's unbuttoned all seven buttons, he stands up and slides the shirt back off my shoulders and reaches between my breasts to unclip my bra before he once more stops and looks. My heart is broken by what's happening to this land, but I'd rather be in Thanh's arms than where my mind wants to take me. I'd rather be with him than anywhere.

He lies down on his side, and in seconds I'm lying next to him, face to face, and I see that Thanh has figured out how to be a man, not a boy, and he wants me close. My body is starting to trill and murmur, and it is here in the present and happy with Thanh and his beautiful skin. It's hard to describe his skin—how lovely it is—and I can't stop stroking it.

We do it right then and there. We have sex, and it is awkward and strange and a little painful but also kind of *wow*, and afterwards I look at him—his face close to mine. Suddenly, I whisper, "Fuck you," and don't know if I'm joking or what. I am joking. Right? It's funny since I did just fuck him. He laughs, but even a dumbo can see that he's hurt, and I feel like a shit. But what am I supposed to do? He peeled away my skin and he wants me to love him for it. Instead, I halfway hate him. My father is calling me to my mother's room again and still I'm not going and still and forever I'm regretting that. Thanh is calling me to his room now and I'm telling him *Fuck you*. I don't want to hurt him and regret it. I tell him, "Don't worry, you're okay."

"Just okay?" he asks, so predictably.

"Better than that." That's all I can squeeze out. "A little better."

"Alright," he says. "I'll settle for that. From you, that's an A++."

Maybe I didn't go in my mother's room because I didn't want to know. You're probably thinking, *You didn't want to know she was dying*. But I knew she was dying. That was obvious. So what then? I hate to say it. But it's *whether she loved me*. Loved me still, even in the middle of her suffering. Loved me and hated to leave me by dying and never seeing me again. That's it. End of discussion.

"Have you gone to la-la land?" Thanh asks me, lifting the hair off my forehead over and over as it falls back down.

"Yes." I lay my head on his chest and his body is like the musclewood trunk he made me touch. Then I'm gone again, lying so far out in Frank's woods that I don't know where I am, alone with Knose, my back balanced along a monstrous fallen tree, trying not to slide off. Why is it so much easier to love the land than to love a human? That's an easy one. A human is always pushing back, countering you, denying you, disappointing you, wanting to open you up and take something from you. And not even bothering to zip you back up so the rest of your insides won't tumble out.

He says, "If I tell you your body is beautiful, you probably will tell me it's none of my business. That's if I'm lucky. If I'm not, you'll tell me to fuck myself. But I'm going to tell you anyway, because it is factually correct."

I can't help laughing at that. "Oh, yeah," I tell him. "You know your facts." And for a second, I start to hate him again, as if I were an egg in the shell and he'd cracked me open and made a god-awful mess of me. My hate is a laser. My shining weapon.

That was yesterday. Today I just want him. Plain and simple. *You want him when he's far away*, I say to myself. I wouldn't have known this before that psychology class. So the class—or maybe life—has taught me something. I remember that the visiting professor told us that people's memories of their early life can be stuffed with meaning. I always return to that same memory: me banging away at the door and my mother frowning, pulling me back. She doesn't understand my determination. She didn't have much fire in her. Or am I remembering her after she got sick? Anyway, she yanked me away, said I should have some pride. What did that mean? If you wanted to get in, why wouldn't you pound on the door? Now, when people invite me in, I don't want to go. I'm not much different from Alex when he scoffed at joining the parade.

Today I'm confused, because I want Thanh to come over and hang out with me. Really, I want him to make love to me and me to him. But I can't decide whether to pick up the phone or hope the feeling passes. He says I'm the most beautiful person in the world. That's so weird to me I can barely stand it, but it's his reality somehow.

I'm still messed up about him being inside my body. I've spent all my remembered life mostly solitary and mostly sort of dignified, so this whole outside-inside thing might make me crazy.

What if I were literally crazy? I close my eyes and start traveling through space and time to find Thanh and all his elements—his skin especially, my favorite part of him.

I want to go to Ivori and say, "Isn't it radical to let someone inside you like that, to become a baying animal for a while?" I want to ask her about dignity, because throughout my life, I've been holding onto that like a kid clutching the silver pole on the merry-go-round. But I don't know how to say any of this to Ivori.

I sit back and sink into my own thoughts again. There could be a tiny Beatrix Potter mouse door at the opening to my body and Thanh has to knock—that's the least he should do. I roll around on my bed for a while. I won't give you all the details. Then I fall asleep thinking I am too weird given all that's in my mind.

For months, I've been catching glimpses of Ivori's leaning towers under construction. Now there are two, like the Twin Towers people talk about when it's close to autumn. Truthfully, Iv's towers are not all that interesting. They're mostly pieced-together cardboard painted in dark, moody colors. I don't get what fascinates her about them. One time, I tried to ask her. I think she picked up that I wasn't getting their allure because she got very prickly very fast. *Where have I heard that before?* she said, mocking me. I had no idea where and I wasn't making any guesses—not under these arctic conditions—so I just shut up.

I'm bummed today and I knock on Ivori's door, but she doesn't answer. I'm sure she's hiding out in there. I'm so annoyed. I just charge in, no permission granted. I don't see her, but I'm possessed by my certainty that she's hiding from me. I squeeze between her messy bed and the clutter of brushes and paint jars and knock over one luckily empty paint jar. I'm pissed it's there and blocking my way.

She's not here. I'm half-disappointed but also relieved that she's not hidden away. I glance at her towers and holy moly—they are different from this viewpoint. Each box is a little prison cell. They're barred but otherwise open to give you a view of the inside space. Tiny dioramas. Some have minuscule beds, even toilets, to show someone's living there. She must have used a magnifying glass to get them right—they are that detailed. There are a couple where she's trying to put a whole scene inside, and one of those looks like a dentist's office inside a prison cell, which rings a bell about her phobia. Some of the cells are bare and basic, but on each one she's hung the bars with all kinds of minuscule treasures that make no sense in prison. Miniature glass animals and hearts. Snowflake cutouts wrapped in silver paper. Stars and moons. Beautiful stuff. The whole creation is weirdly discordant, but it's magical. Way better than the melancholy splotches on the front. The front is a cover-up, a studied dullness so you'll never guess what's going on inside or want to walk around to look. I know I'm abusing her privacy, so I leave even though I want to keep examining her fabulous world.

I'm in bed trying to contemplate the awfulness of incarceration. I think that's where Ivori's going with her art, but I'm keyed on her tiny ornaments and bells, and I'm wandering around in lovely small spaces: the cave my mom and I made under my bed sheets where we'd giggle and play clapping games when I was little, the dorm room Iv and I shared, the cabin with me and Thanh inside, half-bare. I feel guilty that I can't devote even a moment to the misery other people have endured. But then I think, *Fuck it, Ivori hung her jail cells with ornaments, so why can't I.*

Thanh's body is taking possession of my mind. I resent that. Where did he get such smooth, lovely skin, his beautiful wrapping paper? I start giving myself orgasms, trying to have the longest, most fantastic one ever, and I wonder how Thanh would feel about this. I would have to ask him, and that's not going to happen.

The first time I did this was because I read about it. Seriously. I was that kind of nerdy kid. My mother was in the other room, and I was a little freaked out, wondering what she would think if she could see through the wall. It seemed so crude, but magical in its own way. I imagined her saying, *Yes, it's kind of animally.* Would she say *animalistic*? Now I can't even remember how she spoke. *But you know, we're all animals when it comes down to it. C'est la vie.* Maybe even, *Enjoy yourself, honey.* I didn't get any of those words from her in reality. First, because I didn't trust her enough to have a conversation even remotely like that, and second, before I knew it, she was dead and gone. *Sayonara, kid.* Pretty soon I stopped looking around for someone to nod her head and say, *Yeah, relax, live it up.* Because I wasn't going to find her. Couldn't then, can't now. So forget about it.

I get up and go out into the hall and Alex pops out of his room. No instant heebie-jeebies for me because this is benign Alex.

"What's up, Alex?"

"Oh, nothing. My mother called and—a lot of details. She said she wanted to hear and now I'm, I—need a walk."

I suspect his mishmash of mother fragments has deep veins of Dr. Dream meaning, but I'm not going to give him the third degree. He wanders downstairs and I hear the front door whop closed. He stays out a long time, leaving me wondering. Could be a crazy party with psychedelic music and badass drugs. Maybe some place inconceivable and otherworldly like those kids in *The Lion, the Witch, and the Wardrobe* found. I'm not crazy about his walking out on me, even though it's Alex, but I see that his mind is like a deck of cards someone tossed into the air and it landed every which way.

After my mother died, I went looking for her. Maybe someday I'll be able to see her slim figure with its pinched waist—way more delicate than mine—and hear the way she would sigh in exasperation or laugh like a bell, and those pictures will be steady and calm sitting beside me as if we were having tea together. But instead of all that, she's like a dream after you wake in the morning. One minute you're living it and the next it's gone. You're not even certain if it was there to begin with or what it was about. I should have been brave enough to go inside that room where she lay in her yellowed nightgown. A better daughter would have held her mother's hand and pressed a palm against the soft skin of her feverish cheeks. Then I'd be able to feel her skin on my hand now. A better daughter would have said, *I love you.* Maybe my mother would have said back, *I love you, too—I'm so sorry I have to leave you.*

All this imagining is about someone better. It isn't about me, about the daughter I am. When I look for her now, she's been replaced by a flimsy white moth that flies around in the dark. You can't get to know it and you can't say much about it. It flies past from time to time and gets caught in your hair and leaves you frantic to bat it free or scream. Sometimes, I hear a whoosh and I turn toward it, thinking I might see my mother, but instead that awful moth is blindly banging around in the dark.

Many days I don't think about her at all. Sometimes, when I am driving Thanh's car, I hear *The Moth Radio Hour*, where people tell stories of somebody they loved so much and lost. I can't listen for long because I feel like they are delivering a message to me, and it isn't anything nice at all. It is more of a chastisement. I don't need the whole universe telling me I was an awful daughter. What am I supposed to do about it now? It's too late, and the sucky idea that I can never go back and fix it, when truly I need to, clubs me over the head from time to time. A better person, like those Ethiopian monks, would have been guarding their island, but I just let things die. I turn off the radio. The truth is, I couldn't bear to be around her when she was sick and so I stayed away.

# Chapter 23

Thanh and I sit together in the Union, at the Chipotle. "There's a city council," he explains like he's teaching Civics 101. "And commissions. Zoning commission. Planning commission. If you're lucky, an environmental commission. You can speak at a public meeting for any of those. I think Blue Sky has to make its case first at the planning commission."

"What would I say?"

"What would you *want* to say? What do you feel?"

"That all these creatures and cool plants would lose their homes. It's not so easy to find a new home if you're a fox or a snake. Especially not if you're a plant. If you care about things, you have to *take care* of them."

"You could list the species that are out there. Just list them."

"Like reading off the names of the dead after a battle or a bombing. Solemn. That might work."

"I can help you do an inventory of the plants. The animals are harder, but we can look for tracks near the wetlands. Maybe put up a motion-activated camera."

I nix the camera idea. I'd be afraid of the images. Once I have their pictures, the ache will burrow deeper into me.

Thanh tells me I need to stand up in front of people and

give my opinion about the Blue Sky development. That scares me quite a bit, but I plan to do it. Everyone has to be brave at some point in their life, so this will be my time.

"You have to talk at that meeting, too," I tell him.

He shakes his head. "It's for you."

"That makes no sense." I see Thanh winding through the woods, naming everything he sees. I want to prod him about speaking at the meetings. Why is he shining the spotlight on me? But I'm getting a visceral caution flag that shuts me up.

Back home in the evening, I'm bitter that Frank doesn't say a word about fighting for the land. Something in me starts to flare like a cape in the wind. Am I supposed to do this all alone? From my top desk drawer, I grab a blue gel pen like the one Frank used on the treasure map. I write a note to tell him about the meetings. He must have seen the ugly pink flags and figured out what they mean. I end it, *Just thought you might want to know.* I give him the July 28 date for the first planning commission meeting. I probably shouldn't upset him by talking about the land he loves that he's losing again, but *fuck*—isn't it his responsibility to stop them as much as mine? I also give him Thanh's information about all the permits the developer needs. That way, he'll know there's hope for us.

The next day, I leave the note at the cemetery office with a cheerful young secretary who stuffs it in a cubbyhole. After I leave, I feel uneasy. Did I write it in attack mode? My mind flashes to an image of Alex being his nastiest, and I don't love that image. I should have just said, *Hey Frank, do you think you could go to these meetings with me?* But I feel the need to be more convoluted.

The next week, I go back with Knose on her leash because I can't get Frank out of my mind. Not long after we come through the gate, I see his stooped back. His back must ache from all that bending. He is pulling weeds around a grave. I bet someone paid him to keep their plot tidy so they don't have to go there. I never thought before about my dad paying someone to do that for my mom. Some of the graves have blankets over them, as if the dead people need to keep cozy on chilly nights. It's hard to think of anything more pointless, but people do dumb things, I guess, to feel better about the dead. There's no breadcrumb trail you can follow to reach them if you need them, so people pretend they're not far away.

Frank has radar—he senses I'm getting close and turns around. I'm suddenly nervous and don't know what to say. I just blurt out, with a hard face, "Did you get that note I left you?"

He nods. That's it—you'd think he could spare a word or two. Now I'm angry for real and say, "I'm going to the public meeting of the planning commission on July 28. This friend of mine told me about it."

"I got that message, little lady." He glances at Knose's purple collar, the one Arwyn got embroidered with her name.

I nod. "I might bring a list of all the plants and animals on the land." I circle my hand in the air to indicate the whole of the land, as if we're standing there now. "I'm going to read them until they sound the three-minute buzzer and cut me off. I won't be done so they'll get a dot-dot-dot feeling as if my list has no end."

Frank is silent.

"You don't like that idea?"

"I have a list," he says, stepping closer.

"You have one?"

"My father wrote it. He loved everything on that piece of land. Like you do. He was an amateur naturalist. Did I ever tell you that? He knew all the species, every last one, down to the tiniest, most nondescript. Grasses and sedges, saprophytes. Every time he found something new to add to his list, he was joyful. I can see him right this minute."

"And you have the list?" Now I'm tiptoeing.

"I do." Frank isn't jumping to share this list he's so impressed with. His caution frustrates me.

"Are you afraid of something?" I ask him.

He takes his time. "I believe I am, missy."

I ignore the ways he addresses me, which are possibly sexist but kind of sweet. I lift my eyebrows and wait.

"I believe I'm afraid of losing that land, if anyone should learn how precious it is." He shakes his head. "That long list of everything that's there will give it away."

I cock my head.

"But we already lost it, a long time ago," he says with a sad chuckle. "So isn't that silly—to be thinking of losing it when it's already gone."

Now I'm Dr. Dream. "Memories get inside you and mess you up. I'll tell you about my psychology class someday."

"I'd like that. I could use some help." He laughs. "Needing a shrink, at my age!" He looks at Knose tenderly. "Part setter, I'd say. English setter more than likely."

I'll have to tell Arwyn, who is saving up to get Knose's DNA tested. I wonder if Frank's father's handwriting will be as pretty and careful as Frank's. I am impatient to meet his father through the list he made so many years ago. I know it's not the Rosetta Stone. It's just a list of plants, but to me it's a window into another time when someone I never met walked the same land as me and loved it just as much.

The next time Knose and I visit the cemetery, Frank and I wander in a small grove of paper birch trees. I'd want my place of eternal rest to be right here. Frank loops us around through gray and rose-colored granite stones and leads me back toward the cemetery gates. He has me wait while he goes into the office. When he comes out, he hands me the list in a spotless gray folder.

I switch Knose's leash to my other hand so I can open the folder. "The handwriting is just like yours," I say.

"It *is* mine. I copied out my father's list for you. Wasn't planning to give you the original." He laughs as if that idea were absurd or troubling. He's probably had enough of giving his stuff away.

At first, I'm disappointed, but then I realize he could have printed a copy in two seconds, but instead he handwrote it. I like the thought of his kindly doing that for me, noticing each entry as he wrote it.

The list is eight pages long, and each page has at least thirty lines. Most of the plants have a common name and a Latin name. For example, there's mayapple, *Podophyllum peltatum.* That's one of the plants I know, and I get a thrill thinking of Frank's father sitting at a nice wooden desk, writing *mayapple* on his list after he tromped through the same patch I have. Could a plant I look at today be the same one he saw and listed all those years ago? In Botany, we learned about mushrooms with their network of mycelia. That's what I'm seeing now. That network, only it's Frank and his father, me and Thanh.

I'm looking through the list with Frank watching, and I say "wow" a dozen times. Here's another entry I know: skunk cabbage, *Symplocarpus foetidus*. Fetid. Rotten. Smelly. I'm imagining Frank sucking up some groundwater of sadness the way a paper towel draws up water. It flows into Frank and fills every cell. I can tell he's seen some difficult things in his life. I'm not sure I'm ready to hear what they are, and I doubt he's interested in telling me. They're not my business. But for once, I'm going to stand here and not run away, just in case he has anything he wants to say.

Frank pats Knose on the head. I think that's a first. Now that she's not excavating his cemetery, he's taking time to admire her. He lightly touches each of the clumps of black spots by her nose and laughs. "Used to have a nice dog myself. Miss that dog. What do you call this one?"

"Her name is Knose."

Frank chuckles. "You call this dog after her nose?"

I have to explain the whole thing, then, about Doris and Arwyn and the *K* we put in for a little sophistication. Frank is listening, amused and nodding. Looking back and forth between me and Knose. Maybe he's thinking White people are hard to fathom.

Thanh told me how happy his grandfather was when Obama visited Vietnam and gave a speech in Hanoi. He watched on US television, wrote down every word, and kept the speech in his pocket. After a while, he could recount the speech by heart. Now

Thanh knows half of it because of how often his grandfather happily recited it to him. When I come to his door, he sometimes says, "On this visit, my heart has been touched by the kindness for which the Vietnamese people are known." None of this makes much sense, but he is channeling his grandfather. He tells me Obama ate bún chả in Hanoi and drank some Bia Hà Nôi, which is beer. When Thanh talks about his family, he leapfrogs over his father to his grandfather, a subject that puts him in a happier place. There are some potholes in the father part of the family road.

I'm not Obama, and I change my mind about speaking at the planning commission. I'll just go and lurk, even though I'm mad at myself for being a coward. I tell Thanh he should speak since he knows way more about nature than me. He shakes his head but says he'll go along. Two cowards. We're early, and we sit in the third row from the front as other people drift in. They happily chitchat as if everyone here's on the same team. But we're not, because Blue Sky Properties is here, and so am I, and we're definitely not simpatico.

The meeting is opened by an ancient woman with an onion skin complexion and shoulder-length steel-gray hair. She sits at one end of a long table elevated on a small stage at the front of the room. I think she's the commission chairperson, or possibly the ghost of meetings past. She says the first agenda item is approval of the minutes from the previous meeting. Her businesslike tone unsettles me because I'm bubbling with emotion about the bullshit Blue Sky development that's coming up for discussion.

The planning commission members wade through this and that boring conversation about whether someone can build a garage two feet closer to their neighbor's property line than the code allows. I would be off in la-la land, except I'm keyed on the moment they'll bring up the Blue Sky project. I can smell the heat pumping out through the vents.

Finally, it comes. I'm hoping I'm not the only one here who feels like a shaken bottle of pop. Luckily, I'm not speaking, or I might explode and make a god-awful mess. The chairwoman introduces the project director from Blue Sky. She thanks him for attending and refers the other eight people at the table to the plans and permit applications they have in their yellow folders. I lean forward and glance around in search of other faces gnarled up like mine.

The project director stands up. He's a short muscular guy, and his body has that upside-down triangle shape male athletes congratulate themselves on. I picture him grabbing a beautiful fir tree like he's Paul Bunyan and wrestling it to the ground. When he starts to talk, it's obvious he's thinking people will wag their heads at how fantastic his *concept* is and how impressive the *execution* he's promising to deliver will be, but I feel a few waves of skepticism floating through the air. Some other bullshit detectors must be vibrating in sync with mine.

At public comment time, an old Black woman wobbles up to the mike for her three minutes. She's creaky en route and I'm hoping her voice won't be shaky too.

"Any of you all old enough to remember Joni Mitchell?" she asks. I haven't a clue. I look at Thanh, and he shakes his head to show his memory cache is empty, too, but some of the gray-haired people nod. "'You pave paradise and put up a parking lot.' That was Joni's message, and it's my message here." She's halfway singing her little line, but after that she talks in a dignified but impressively pissed-off way about how we're so quick to tear up what's already here because we have our eyes on what *could be*, what we imagine. "You cannot have both. You destroy the one to have the other. This man here, this developer—Mister Blue Sky, and others just the same—shout, *Oh, no, no, no*, and talk of how much they care about the environment and how sensitive they'll be, and they name their development the Woodlands after what's going to disappear. They 'mitigate' the loss of a grand tree by planting a few saplings the deer soon eat." She shakes her head. "No. The integrity of the place is destroyed. Either you value it enough to keep it whole or you don't. You can hold onto a few trees here and there but that's nothing—it's just pretending at wildness, because nature is a community.

"I first visited this land early in my life, back when it belonged to Black folk who treasured it. How they lost it is another story, but right away I knew there was something special there. It's in the air." I wonder who showed her the land. Was it Frank's father? My heart races. Does she know about the list that's in my pocket? Her hair is twisted and fixed behind her head with invisible pins. It's thick and springy, like a fiberfill pillow. The black is laced through with meandering gray hairs.

"I don't know what it is about that place," she says. She's shaking her head one more time as if she can't believe it. "In the springtime, it's the Garden of Eden. 'You don't know what you've got till it's gone.' That's Joni again. You young folks, go listen to her, and you older ones, try to remember the message. She's got something to say."

The buzzer sounds, but she is finished, so they don't cut her short. I'm glad for that and thinking I'll go listen to Joni, and a bit of hope flares that I might even find an essay in what I hear.

I applaud. I'm the only one, so I'm embarrassed, but I do it anyway. Since I'm not brave enough to give a speech, I should at least clap, especially because there's no one here but me to uplift her. Thanh sits next to me, looking peaceful. I imagine him reciting another bit from the Obama speech. "In the many people who have been lining the streets, smiling and waving, I feel the friendship between our peoples." I'm not feeling all that much friendliness here, even though there's some smiling and waving.

The woman sits down in our row, and I see her look over at me. She's probably wondering, *Who is this person who was clapping?* I hope she doesn't think I look like a kid, like somebody's daughter who's here because her mother dragged her.

When the meeting is over, she's slow at slipping things into her purse and getting her sweater pulled on. I dawdle and don't go into the aisle until she does. We end up in different lanes, but we flow together near the door, and I exit right behind her.

Now's my chance, so I say, "Hey, good speech."

She turns around, cocking her head in a friendly-curious way and says, "It's nice to have an ally. Who are you, if you don't mind? Well, I'm Bertha—I should introduce myself first."

"Leslie. I'm Leslie."

"Hello, Leslie. Do you plan to follow this issue and show up for the rest of the meetings?" I have no idea what meetings are coming, but my heart is so churned up, I just say yes. She glances over my head at Thanh's sleek hair, and I think she's reflecting on the fact that he and I aren't the same race. Maybe she likes that and maybe she doesn't. Or maybe she could care less about that kind of thing and just thinks he's cute.

"You speak up, then," she says, with her attention back on me. "The more voices, the better. If it's just one, they won't listen. And me being an old Black lady, that won't help the case, either. With two, and you being young, we're still no army, but two is twice what one is."

I nod and think I don't know what I've gotten myself into, but I'm not regretting anything. The woman drifts away, and for a minute I stand still, strangers flowing around me and Thanh as if we are rocks in a river. I feel a current of gratitude toward Thanh because he told me I could fight and told me I could stand up and do it, which I haven't done yet, but I might.

We go back to Thanh's apartment, and instead of rolling out my regular scowl, I stand up on my toes and kiss him. Not a major kiss, but a real one.

"Wow," he says. "What was that?"

I shrug. I'm glancing back at the new part of me that stood ready to listen to Frank and didn't skedaddle. Frank didn't say a word that was scary or deep, but I was there, just in case. Thanh puts his arms around me and wraps me up so tight I think his arms must be circling me twice. Soon the kisses become spectacular, and I reach that point where I'm just a body that needs his skin as close to mine as possible. And the whole inside-outside thing has flipped so that now I want him outside and inside, too, and don't know anymore which body is his and which one is mine.

I wouldn't be ready to call Thanh my boyfriend if anyone asked, but I'm okay saying that sex is something we do. Not exactly on a regular basis, but it's something that could possibly happen again.

I'm on some email list now, for the city, and I get a newsletter about upcoming meetings. There's another one for the planning commission on August 11. The Woodlands Preserve is on the agenda, but this one's not a public hearing where people are invited to speak. I don't know what any of this means about the future of the land. I comb through any email I get from the city, looking for more information. The depth of my geekiness is astounding.

In a few weeks, I get another highly missable email from the city, but it doesn't slip past me because I'm watching for these things as if they were invitations to the Grammys. There's a link in there to the minutes from the August 11 meeting, which had no testimony, so I didn't attend. I click on the link, not thinking the minutes will be anything, but it says a vote was taken. They voted seven to two to support the Woodlands Preserve and recommend that the full council approve the preliminary site plan.

Someone's socked me in the face. I curl up with my butt in the air and my head next to my knees like when I have the worst cramps. I'm angry and I'm sad and I'm totally guilty because I didn't even open my mouth when I had a chance. I just sat there and fantasized about what I'd do at the *next* meeting when I didn't even know if there would be one. Well, there won't be now, not of the bullshit planning commission, because apparently they don't give a rat's ass about the land, and they think a pretend preserve is a fine idea. I allowed the old woman, Bertha, to stand alone and speak. I gave her a few hand claps, but I wasn't up there letting people look at me and whisper about me like she was. I can hear Ivori saying, *Yeah, of course the Black people always get to be the ones who put their lives on the line while the White people sit back congratulating themselves for their woke opinions. Black people have to fight for what's right or get run over. And then they get run over anyway.* Ivori has stepped farther away from me lately and I don't understand what I did, other than not hating Alex sufficiently. But I know I did something awful to that land by doing nothing at all, just like when my mom was dying and I stayed away. It's not fair but I'm angry with Thanh, too, because he didn't realize this vote was coming when he usually knows these things.

Maybe I will run away and join the Ethiopian monks who protect and tend the tiny sacred forests around their temples and don't let anyone intrude and cut them down or burn them. I would like to see all the scattered islands grow and connect and become one gigantic forest where Thanh and I could wander for as long as we want. The monks are content loving their remnants, but I would not be satisfied with skimpy islands and would always see them as sad remains of what should be. I am hungry. Greedy. I want the whole earth to look like Frank's lovely green place that is going to be ruined now. Ivori has her little prisons that she's trying to turn into a sparkly jewelry store with dozens of rooms. I guess that's her magic, but mine would be to link the little forests into one green wood that never ends.

# Chapter 24

With all that's gone wrong with Blue Sky, my essay doesn't seem important. But it's due at the end of the spring-summer term, and that's in under two weeks, so I need to get going. I sit down to write but nothing comes to me and I can't concentrate. After a while, I take out my nearly-empty motherboard notebook and try to generate some pros and cons about my loving mom thesis, hoping that can become the essay even though it's too personal for comfort. I'm missing something still. Maybe if I talk to my dad more about the past, things will come together. When I look toward her, or look for her, I find thin air. I have bits and pieces. Fog. Nothing whole. Fragments.

Ever since the sexting thing with Alex, my dad has been clingy. He calls me a lot and wants to know what I'm doing, whether I feel safe with "that strange guy." I'll start to get annoyed with him in my usual way, but it's not terrible to have him concerned. I'm also taking pity on him because his dating initiatives aren't going well. I admit I'm at least half-glad about that, because who wants to hear him talk about some woman who's spending time in my mom's house, maybe even her bed.

I go see him on a Monday morning in late August. I let myself in and yell, "Hey, Dad, I'm here." He comes into the living room from the kitchen. "I'm going upstairs for a while," I tell him. I rummage in the attic, probably to put off talking. I check out one of the few boxes I haven't opened. A few items are nicely folded. They've been here forever, just waiting, I suppose, for someone to look at them. The one on top is a pale blue nightgown. I recognize it with a hollow feeling of fear.

I see my mom lying in bed before the time of that awful hospital smell. She's running her hand in a slow circle on the skin of her breast. I've walked in on something private, but she doesn't tell me to get out. She is alone, caring for her own body, feeling how smooth the skin is. Or maybe it's dry and sad because she's starting to be sick but doesn't know it yet. My mom used to rub my feet when I was little. It's funny how I just remembered that. Yesterday I didn't know it and today I do. I liked her to rub my feet when I was falling asleep. It made me feel calm and happy, like being inside a basket jumbled with nice soft clothes, warm from the dryer. I wonder what she was feeling when I was peaceful.

I close the box with the nightgown and see a couple purses hanging from a wire hanger a couple feet down from Mr. Jones's clothes. One is a big squishy tan-colored bag made from soft leather. It's the last purse I remember my mother using. Is it possible I recall her buying it at Lord & Taylor, or am I concocting that out of thin air? I pull open the top of the purse. It's a gaping hole lined in satin—nothing in there at all. There's a small pocket in the inner lining, and I unzip that, just in case. A white card's inside, and I pull it out. It's my mom's social security card. It's so old the paper is soft and frayed at the top edge. I bet she got it when she was still a kid. I put the card in my jeans pocket and make sure it is lying flat. It's too frail to handle any new wrinkles.

I go back downstairs and sit down in the living room until my dad comes in with chips and salsa.

"How's the dating going, Dad?" I ask. It's safe to ask him because I've gotten the vibe that nothing's going on. Plain Jean hasn't reappeared.

Dad shakes his head. "I don't have the touch."

"That's crazy. Just be patient, Dad. You found Mom and stayed married all those years."

He nods.

Dad seems adrift. Suddenly, I spout off as if I'm an expert. "You know, I've been meaning to tell you, you're probably wrong about her being unhappy. I mean, everyone's sad some of the time." I don't know why I'm prosecuting this case. "I think she might have just needed another kid, because practically every family we knew had two kids, at least. Right?" This notion appears in my mind the way a stinkbug appears on your wall in September. You don't see it fly in. You just look up and it's there.

"No, Leslie. That's not the case. I told you that, didn't I?"

"But you might have been wrong. Maybe you didn't understand what she felt, as a woman, I mean."

"That's quite possible, but on this subject—of children—well, she was clear enough."

"I thought she wasn't such a big communicator."

"She wasn't, Leslie."

"So then you don't know, you see."

My dad sighs. A big one. The road ahead should be visible to me by now, but it's heavy mist. "I'll just tell you then, because you keep going. She did get pregnant a second time. She didn't want to," he hesitates, "go through with it."

I feel myself scrambling now, racing down a river toward a waterfall and grabbing for a branch to hold. "Bad timing, Dad. That's true for a lot of women. It wasn't the right time."

"Oh, Leslie. I don't know why you're doing this. Pushing and pushing. Your mother didn't want children. Okay. I'm sorry. She loved you dearly, like any mother. But she didn't want kids. It wasn't in her plan. Something to do with losing the younger sister, I think, though I never really understood. Not everything in life comes clear."

A tide is rushing in but I try to maintain my footing. "I get it, Dad. Not a big deal." My hand is patting my butt for that card in my pocket. I think of other things I could talk about, but they're all awful. The land. Ivori's disgusted attitude toward me. "Did I tell you I have this essay to write? I'm almost done, but I gotta go. Gotta get some work done." I'm one hundred percent lying now.

Back at our house, I grab that motherboard notebook. I'm looking at the pros and cons I've listed, thinking I have the biggest-ever entry for the con list. But I can't write it down. Who can write that their own mother didn't want children? Didn't want you. I start to feel lightheaded and far away from my own body. It's the worst, weirdest feeling. I close the notebook and do a hundred sit-ups in the middle of my floor. Then I call Knose in my emergency voice and get her to come into my room. I get her to jump up on the bed so I can cuddle with her and try to get my mind to come back into my body. I just stroke her forehead and feel the softness at the base of her ears and talk to her about how Frank said she might be an English setter, a nice breed. Nature must want you to pet dogs behind the ears, because the fur stays soft there no matter how rough the rest of a dog's fur gets. I listen for her heartbeat, and it is strong and regular. She puts her head on my forearm and falls asleep. I leave it there and feel her quiet weight.

I'm calmer and think I should go to the undergrad library to try to work on my essay, and probably choose a different topic. There's a chance I could work if I get out of the house, even though I'll have to leave Knose behind. If I can get the essay done, I might feel better. It's a cloudy day but at least the sun's up there somewhere.


I'm examining the desk I've occupied for an hour now. The desktop is full of inked names and scratched hearts and upright penises. It's all so stupid. The linoleum floors are scuffed with a bazillion marks from chairs pulled forward with determination by someone ready to work, then pushed back in despair when they can't work because their mind is a giant balloon unknotted and sputtering air. Between the scuffs are splatters. I'm looking at them, wondering what all this shit is. The whole place is a pit. The walls are dirty up to the height of peoples' heads. I can see students standing around, rolling their oily hair against the wall, trying to decide if they can sneak a hit from their vape pen. No wonder they call this place the UGLI.

My idea that I could concentrate here isn't working, and I'm starting to panic again. I leave my books on the desk and go into a lounge, another zero-charm room where I'm at least allowed to eat from the bag of trail mix I shoved into my purse. A few people are wandering around or sitting on the yellow vinyl chairs. One scraggly-haired guy looks bored or stoned and is rambling around the room. Another guy appears so anxious I think he might faint. In the middle of the room is an older guy who's crazy attractive with the most amazing blue eyes. I'm more interested in asking him if he's wearing blue contacts than in rescuing the anxiety-attack guy. That's how I am. I suppose I'm morally bankrupt—definitely no Florence Nightingale.

Knockout guy's eyes are searching and now—wow—they are on me. There's a vacant seat right next to mine, and I think he's going to sit down there. His hair is long and wavy. Shiny, light brown, pretty like a pony's mane. Fuck, he's definitely coming over. Now he is sitting right next to me and it's clear he's planning to strike up a conversation.

He smiles. His smile is as gorgeous as his eyes. Shit. It keeps deepening until it crinkles his eyes, warm as sunshine. No fair.

"Hey, hi," I say.

"Hey, hi," he says. He might be making fun of me. "Taking a break from studying?"

"Couldn't get anything done."

"I know what that's like. I used to have that problem a lot when I'd come to this place."

"Not anymore?" I ask, because "used to" got my attention. Maybe his blue eyes give him some special powers that will infect me if I stare into them, and then I'll know how to write my essay. "Do you have blue contacts?"

He laughs. "I've been asked that before."

*Fuck. I'm boring.*

"But no, no contacts. And I don't get stuck on my school-work because I'm not a student anymore. I'm a professor."

A professor? Shit. An old person. An actual adult at least. My heart is going to race out of my chest and flee this building. I know what's happening here. I'm just waiting, because it's going to happen. And it does.

There are only so many ways to ask it, so he does it the simplest way. "Come to my house. Do you want to? Come with me to my house?"

And I do want to go there. I know from life with Thanh what my body wants and how my body can relax my mind, which is beyond cluttered tonight. I want to go there. Badly. But I can't say that.

He sees that and stretches out his hand and touches the side of my hand. So light, but a touch. He says, "I'll take you to dinner first, if you want."

That's it. It's only four—not exactly dinner time, and I don't want dinner, but I need that idea—that we'll go to dinner, which is an alright thing to do, even with an older man who's a professor and a stranger. My mind is whirling around, and Ivori, Arwyn, and Thanh—of course, Thanh—are debris picked up by a tornado and spinning inside it.

But dinner...anyone can go to dinner. So I nod and say, "Sure. I'll get my books," and when I'm in the study room picking up my books I think, *I should run out now and leave him standing there.* But what a waste of those beautiful eyes and this excitement.

He shows me where his car is parked. I hadn't imagined a car. Cars have doors and once you're inside, you're inside. You aren't going to jump out along the way, the way you might step away from a walk onto any street you pass, all of them leading home. I close the door and smell the leather of the fawn-colored seats. The car is clean and nice. Thanh and the rest of them are still spiraling inside my funnel cloud of doubt, but it's lifted off the earth and is getting quite far away. Out of sight. And I'm glad for that because I want to be alone with this man, whose name is Michael Vest, who is a professor of European history and wants to go to bed with me. I shake my head just perceptibly when he asks again if I want to go to dinner. I'm trying to get the message across without it being entirely obvious what I *do* want to do. It's a secret between my body and his and I don't want to talk about it.

His apartment is the coolest place. It's very old and has a breakfast nook in the kitchen with built-in walnut benches and an attached table that must be as old as the building itself. My eyes wander the place and light on each thing with admiration. There's a spice rack with every space filled and a red chef's apron with a samurai cat that clenches a giant knife in its grinning teeth as if it's caught a big fish to slice up with that blade. And then there's the bedroom. It's small and has only one little window, but his smile is not apologetic. It directs me to the white ironed sheets with a thousand threads per inch—probably Egyptian cotton, which my mother always said was the best. He's lying next to me on the bed and sliding my blue collared shirt down off my shoulder, which means he has to unbutton one button, then two. And that's enough foreplay to let me know I'm allowing him to lift his body up and lie right on top of me, clothes against clothes, then skin against skin. I see the birthmarks scattered around one dark nipple like a sweet little galaxy. Thanh comes right up beside me telling me I'm hurting him, but I tell myself I'm already such a bad person in a dozen ways that one more offense hardly matters. So I turn away from Thanh and back to Michael Vest, who is taking my body on that roller coaster that creeps you to the top and builds suspense higher and higher.

In a while, we're resting there—me within his bent arm that's wet inside the elbow—and Thanh is suddenly right beside me and isn't an old professor but a young, sweet man whose heart can get broken. I feel sweaty and dirty, so I get up and pull on my jeans. I'm fighting all the mean words lined up to tumble out of my mouth, saying only that I need to go, and I can walk. He offers to drive me because it's getting close to sunset, but I brush him off. At the door, he tries to touch me again and draw me back in, but sees that I have to leave, I just have to, and have to *now*, and so he gives up and says, "I hope you had a good time. I've been so hungry I've felt like an animal. Hunting. Practically desperate. It's embarrassing."

"Okay," I say, and don't look up to offer him any sympathy for his horniness or to see his eyes smile again as I hurry out. I don't want to carry a picture of his lovely eyes with me. I plug my address into Maps. It's two miles to walk, and that's fine with me.

Walking in the cool air that's streaming past my ankles, I'm nowhere and no one, which is what I want. I get home before I want to be there. It's half-dark in the house, and I race up the stairs, desperate to pee. I yank shut the bathroom door. I pee an endless burning stream. Eventually my bladder seems empty, but my muscles won't stop. They are trying to push my insides out. I go into my room and pull out my journal and write some mea culpas. I'm exploding, or maybe I want to explode and get out from inside this skin that won't let me breathe. I see Thanh sitting next to me at that city meeting, and when we leave he makes sure I don't get too far ahead in case we lose touch with each other. If the line between us broke and I wandered away, it would be like it is with my mother, where the cord has broken and there's no way to tie it back. He starts to hug me, but I push him away. *Don't touch me, not anymore. I'm a bad person. You don't know what I did.* There is Thanh quoting his ridiculous Obama speech, and I'm in bed with Michael Vest. No wonder my mother didn't love me, didn't even want me. No wonder. There are no pros and cons.

I go downstairs to try to find some calming tea and leave my notebook on my bed. When I get back, it's flipped shut, but I open it back to the Michael Vest page to pour my heart out a little more. I can see the sun setting from my room and it's melancholy and beautiful; I swear the sky is lavender, a color I've never seen, that's not normal and is probably from climate change but is still beautiful. I want to tell Ivori even though her door is closed, like always. I walk out of my room and there's a square piece of paper on the floor—just hanging out as if it's waiting for me. I brighten for a split second, bend down, and see a written list of names. The words are neat and intentional. My heart takes off at a gallop trying to escape what I'm seeing. Ivori jams through her door into the hall and I thrust out my hand.

"This yours?"

She turns her head away and stares into space. *Don't ask*, she's saying, but I have to.

"Colleges?"

She shrugs.

"You're thinking about leaving? Transferring?"

"Maybe. Nothing's set." She shrugs again.

"You're maybe *transferring*, and you haven't said a word to me?" I feel hysterical. And angry. "Aren't we friends?"

"Yeah. Sure."

Uh-oh. There's a world of hurt in that answer, and I don't even understand what's gone so far off the rails. A hiccup or two around that Pride parade, but still. Now someone is banging a tin pot inside my head.

"You have to talk to me," I say. I take her arm, drag her into my room, and tell her, "Sit down," then I point to the bed while I grab the chair. I'm usually not this brave, but I'm desperate, and adrenaline is helping me. The sun is nearly set. The lilac sky is nothing to me now. Ivori doesn't even notice it. "You're not happy here?" I ask her in a tone that sounds like begging.

She looks this way and that, trying to escape my eyes, and I feel like a jackass because I didn't realize how messed up things were.

"Where would you go?"

"I don't know. HBCU, maybe."

"Oh," I say, but I am silenced. She's on ground that's not for me. "Because of me?" I can't help but ask. "Have I been an a-hole?"

She shakes her head like she's defeated. "It's this place. Everything. I don't fit in."

"It's Alex, right?"

She looks at me, her eyes still. "How can you suck up to him?"

"No. I'm not. Arwyn's not either. I swear. It's just that he's acting more human. So shouldn't we give him a chance?"

She shuts her eyes and keeps them sealed for a second. I think about her pucker, think she's trying to get her balance.

"But I get it if you don't want to. I should have asked you about going to the parade."

"Yeah. You should have. You could have asked about other things, too."

I see the bright arrows pointing to more of my failings. They look like the dreadful pink flags, since everything reminds me of those.

Ivori's gone back to her room. The color is drained from the sky. Everything is ruined. I'm going to lose Ivori. Lose Mrs. Ferguson, too. How am I supposed to bear it all, with more shit coming after this—which is too much already? They will overrun the land with bulldozers, terrify the animals that will have to run for their lives and get hit and squashed by cars on the road. Because they have no home. Every last thing I love has to die. I love that land and the love is so deep it's hard to breathe when I feel it. I love it, and they are going to destroy it so I can feel the weight of death again, which I probably deserve, but still, I don't want it. I don't. And I didn't do anything about it. That's the worst part. I didn't stand up and say a single word.

It would be easy to write that motherboard essay now. To argue, yes, of course, that girl's mother didn't love her because she wasn't a good person who cares for others, she's someone who betrays her friends, even a sweet friend like Thanh, so why would anyone care for her. My mother directs her fake smile at me, and I feel like she doesn't care or give me a thought. But it was me who wouldn't go into her room and look at her face or her bare, lonely feet, so cold from cancer that each one needed twenty socks to stay warm. The thread to her is cut and jagged. It's severed forever. *Forever* is a terrifying word.

I could go away and not see any of this. And not feel it. Just change the channel and have a different show or no show at all. I can die before everything else does. I haven't done anything good—not my essay or helping the land, but that's one thing I can do. I need to not think about my dad or Ivori or anyone when I'm doing it. Not think about Thanh and what I did to hurt him. Not think about Frank or the brave old lady at the meetings. That's another switch I can flip. I can do that, too.

I have a ton of old pills, leftovers that I never threw away because they'd go into the sewer and down to the river and poison the fish there. I go to the little chest on top of my dresser and pull open the drawers where I stashed those orange plastic vials, most of them half-full because I didn't need any more of whatever it was. I dump out all the pills into a giant handful. I leave out the ibuprofen, which ruins your kidneys if you take a lot. I just want to leave this place, black out and not come back, float away somewhere. I don't want to do violence to my organs on the way out, especially my kidneys, which I saw in a bio class video, and they are pretty little things.

*Don't think*, I remind myself. *Don't think. Just swallow and lie down. Do it. It's simple if you don't think.* That's what Ivori told me to get me to go into that awful frat party where I met Arwyn. Oh, Arwyn, who I love. *No. Just swallow and lie down.* I can swallow a dozen pills in one gulp. A girl in our dorm couldn't swallow a single pill and Ivori and I tried to teach her but mostly we tortured her, making her try over and over with M&Ms, making fun of her like she was the dumbest baby. But I can swallow a dozen pills at once. *Just swallow like you've done a million times before. One more swallow.* I freaking do it. Just like that. No more thoughts. Just a swallow. And I don't feel a thing. I swallow a ton of them in two handfuls, and I lie down like normal on my bed, on my back among a tangle of clothes. I close my eyes. I just want to rest, really, not die, just rest deeply for a while, only rest, but I don't have time for a second-round decision because already I am drifting. I think about Knose, who is probably outside the door right now. I should be grieving that I will not see her again, not her spotted sweet nose and soft ears, and that I'm abandoning her and everyone, Thanh, my dad, Ivori. But I am just sliding away, and Knose has Arwyn, always Arwyn, and she and he are floating with me as if I'd lain down in a stream and let the water carry everything. No rocks, just a ribbon of water, and it carries me and that is all. I will be over and done with. I am done.

# Chapter 25

Maybe it's the next day when I start to wake up. I am deep in a mountain of sweaters and blankets. I start reaching for who I am and what has happened. I drift. I sink under and bob to the surface. The pieces begin to assemble. Here I am, prone, feet hanging over the edge, a body on a bed, just where I placed it. I feel my feet flex at the ankles, and I have the image of a body set in a coffin. But I'm not dead, and I bolt up in a panic. There is vomit on the bed beside me. It's awful to see that and think about my poor body vomiting to get rid of poison. Unconscious but vomiting and trying not to die. I am Leslie now and did a terrible thing.

I have to get out of here so I go into the hall, and Ivori comes out and looks so angry that I don't think she notices what a wreck I am. I don't care if she's angry. I need to talk to her.

"What?" I say.

"That fucking teacher. Old White guy piece of shit."

I am half in and half out. Even in this condition I don't want to drop the little thread Ivori is weaving between us. "What did he do?" I hold my breath, thinking even my breathing will disturb the moment. It stinks of medicine and sleep, vomit. But it's good to be breathing. To not be dead.

"I gave him photos of my project…and he said something back, so fuck it." She shakes her head. "*Rude*. Very. I don't know, I don't remember his stupid words. *Frivolous*. That was one of them. *Bejeweled jail cell*. Something obnoxious. He shook his head. So fucking dismissive, just to make me feel like shit."

"Today? He did this today?" *Whatever day this is*, I'm thinking.

Ivori snaps. "Of course not. It's seven a.m. A while ago. I tried to tell you, but you weren't paying attention. But today I have to turn my project in, and I know he'll laugh at it. So I don't even want to show it to him."

"I didn't know about this guy."

"Well, no surprise. You don't notice things that are there right in front of your face. I'd probably have to write it in red in your journal for you to see it."

My journal? I don't understand. I can't process her insults. I don't have any words. No words in my head. It hurts. So I guess we are done because I have nothing to say, and I make noises and faces and go into the bathroom and shut the door and think about it being seven a.m., the beginning of a day I might not want. I shut it softly but in my head it slams. I wish I could vomit now, but I am empty.

I think I fall back to sleep. When I wake up again, I'm panicky. I'm afraid of my mind and where it could take me. I'm afraid of sleeping and not waking up. I call Thanh. I'm scared he'll hear that I'm wasted, but he doesn't ask me if I'm sick or anything. I say I might want to come over and visit him. Probably that suggestion alone is enough for him to think I'm sick, but he's too busy being delighted to make any snide comments. That isn't his specialty anyway. That's me, not Thanh; though not today.

I'm at his apartment and I'm straying from one armchair to another, hanging in space like a spider whose web-weaving has gone awry. Thanh is starting to see that something is not right, so I just blurt it out. "I was so bummed yesterday or whenever about the land and Ivori hating me and going away and other awful stuff, stuff I did, that I took a few pills, just, you know, went to sleep for a while." I say it like it's something funny. Just a sign of how royally crappy the week has been. Ha, ha, ha.

His brow wrinkles. No one can make a worry face like Thanh. "How long a while?"

I shrug. "Maybe twenty-four hours. Not that long."

He looks alarmed. I tell myself it's a performance. He can't be that upset.

"How many pills?"

"Pretty much everything in my medicine chest. Just not the ibuprofen."

"Fuck." He is on his feet and then he is in my face. "What were you thinking?" He practically yells at me. "Why would you do that?" Now he is actually yelling, which I've never heard from Thanh before, and I start to cry. He puts his arms around me like a winter coat and I let him do it. I nod my head into Thanh's shoulder. I think of Michael Vest and I'm tugged between hungering to be back beside his blue eyes and delicate galaxy of beauty marks and feeling terrible because of Thanh, whose body is as beautiful as Michael Vest's and whose black-coffee eyes are lovely too. I think I deserve to be dead after what I did, but I don't want to be dead, I want to be where I am. And all this love and hate is beyond reconciling.

I stay all afternoon. Thanh sees I'm too messed up to talk

much, so he lets me rest. He drives me home in the dark. On the way, he tells me I should see a therapist. I'm slightly offended but can't really argue.

"Otherwise, you need to tell me exactly what happened here, Leslie. *Really* tell me. Not your funny little remarks or half-truths."

"I guess."

"And you need to tell your dad."

"No. I can't."

"Then you're going to talk to me. Tomorrow. You need to come over again and talk. I'm serious."

"Okay." I'm so tired, I just have to sleep now. And I'm not so scared to fall asleep because I have Thanh watching over me. Tomorrow, I'll try to do what Thanh wants. Whatever it is, I'll just try and do it.

"You're okay tonight? You're not going to do anything crazy?"

I shake my head. All my snarkiness is gone. Drained away. Defeated. I keep Thanh close when I fall asleep so my mind won't go anywhere terrifying. I think of that old woman, too. Bertha. The brave woman with the fiberfill hair. I'm not brave, but I'm alive. Trying to be.

I go to see him the next day, like he asked me to. I can't tell him about Michael Vest, not ever, but I tell him about my mother, how she didn't want me and probably didn't love me. "You saw it yourself. You read the letter and said she was trying too hard, that her love was forced." I don't like talking about this. I'm ashamed and embarrassed and can't find words, so I take out my essay folder, which I decided to bring along. Suddenly, I can see what a mess it is. It's a jumble of notes, like my mind. I explain that the assignment was to argue the pros and cons of a thesis, and that thought makes sense, but it takes me forever to pull together a bunch of separate sheets of note paper and receipts with notes scribbled on the back in every color of ink and different sizes and styles of writing.

Eventually, I get things ordered enough to say, "Here is my pro list." I look up from my lap to make sure Thanh is listening. He looks confused but is paying attention. "She bothered to write me lots of letters at camp. She tried to put on a happy face with me, even though it was hard for her because I stuck out my tongue when she tried to take my picture, and later she was sick. We played sometimes—there's a tent game I remember—and sometimes we had a good time and laughed a lot about dumb things. She wanted to see me when she was sick with cancer. She remembered that dumb Momsicle story." I'm remembering now that she might have liked to brush my hair, so I say that and almost start to cry. I glance over at Thanh to make sure there's nothing dreadful crossing his face. I think of something else that's not on my list and add, "She picked a name for me that starts with the same letters as the little sister she lost, who she loved." I look at Thanh again. "Here are the cons, the anti-thesis. It's a long list." Thanh doesn't say a word, so I jump in. "She had a fake smile she often wore that looked like she was pretending to be happy to see me when she wasn't actually. She didn't want kids in the first place, which was a shocker my dad told me. She told me not to knock on a door and try to get in when the kids inside don't want my company. Her letters to me at camp seemed phony. Forced. That one you already know."

Thanh makes throat noises that interrupt me. He looks like

he's going to burst. Then he shakes his head and frowns. "There's something wrong here."

"I know."

"No. With your project."

"Oh." I let my notes drop onto my lap.

"For example, you're making a big point about *fake* versus *forced*. Why does this matter so much? She was trying. Isn't that what counts?"

"I don't know." I feel frozen. Reading these things to Thanh is too much for me. I want to throw them all away, surf TikTok, turn on a sci-fi movie, forget.

"And Leslie, listen. Even if she couldn't love you—or love you very well, very deeply—isn't that about her? Not you?"

"It means I have no foundation."

"How do you mean?"

"It's like being a vase and no one fills you with water and flowers, so you're empty. You're nothing. You don't really know how to be a vase because you're missing what's supposed to be inside you."

Thanh shakes his head, puzzled and disapproving. "I don't get that, Leslie. You're still you. No matter who loved you or didn't love you, or loved you to the best of her ability, which might not have been the greatest. You're still Leslie. Who *I* love. Doesn't that count for something?"

My mouth opens, but I don't have words.

"You better start thinking differently." Thanh is standing up now. He's pacing back and forth in front of me. Gesticulating like a professor explaining the laws of physics. "You're all mixed up. And, by the way, I love you. I'm saying that again. And that should count for something. I wouldn't love you if you were an empty vase. Or a broken one. Or whatever you think you are."

"Are you sure?"

"You're the budding shrink, but I heard that Freud said health was the ability to love and to work. I think you're okay in the love department." I see Thanh trying to wind down his lecture, to lighten things. "You've still got some challenges on the work side. Just joking here, Leslie, but you better get that essay done so I can stop hearing you moan about it."

Thanh gets me to laugh a little and gets himself to laugh, which he needs as much as I do. I'm not exactly whole, but not so rotten. I'd probably feel okay if I could stay cuddled up in his arms forever, but he is going to set a good example for me and study, and I think I should go home and face being in that room, though it still stinks of vomit.

Thanh drops me off at home. I think of calling my dad and mentioning about the pills and all that, but I imagine my dad might crumple. He might die of shock, so I know I won't tell him. I don't even consider telling Arwyn, who for sure would cry. But thinking of it does me some good, because I need reminding that he doesn't hate me for being a jerk with Alex and various other things. And of course there's Ivori, and no, I'm not telling her because I'm afraid she'll just shrug it off, which would be worse than crying. So that only leaves Alex, and telling him would be weird. I play it through in my head nonetheless and see a little tear form at the outside corner of his eye and bumpily make its way down to his badly shaved chin. Despite everything, he likes me.

I don't know why, but a feeling of happiness picks me up like a wave—maybe because I'm alive—and I start twirling around my room, though I know I look ridiculous. I even fall over a couple times because I'm dizzy and that makes me laugh. Ivori should be here tumbling down, too, so I can tease her about her pucker and her shitty balance. That thought ruins my fun, so I fall back onto the mattress and examine the ceiling, as if I might discover Madeline's crack that "had the habit of sometimes looking like a rabbit." That's one of the best lines I've ever read. I hear it in my dad's voice, because he was the one who read me that book. We'd say in unison, full of ferocity, "To the tiger in the zoo, Madeline just said, 'Pooh, pooh.'" Sometimes he substituted Leslie for Madeline, and I liked that, because who wouldn't want to be brave as Madeline, who was fearless but still got appendicitis and nearly died.

That dying thought gets me. It just whacks me. The thought of me half-dead on the bed and my mom dead—not halfway but fully—on her and my dad's bed. I start to think I should get sleepy and escape this feeling, but fading away terrifies me now. Thanh wants to send me to a shrink. After my mom died, my dad did that. I remember walking into her office. Green plants decorated it from floor to ceiling. The place was like an energy drink.

*Hello*, I said. I gave her a smile and she laughed. I got it, because the smile I offered was a smirky one. As if I was making a joke. But what was the joke? Maybe just being there. That was funny enough. Since she got my semi-jokey smile, I conceded she wasn't that dumb.

*How are you doing?* she asked me.

*Ehn*, I grunted. Or maybe it was more like a *moo*.

*Could you spare a few more syllables?* She was smiling still, as if we were having fun. And I suppose we were. In some weird way. I wonder if that doctor is still there, and if her office still looks like a rainforest.

I told Thanh about the pills, but I'm not going to tell him about Michael Vest. Not ever, ever, ever. I let on about Fletcher, and that was bad enough. Bad for both of us, and it angered Ivori toward me, though what doesn't? I hope I don't feel guilty forever, especially when my mind sometimes wanders toward Michael Vest, which it might, because he was gorgeous, and my body thinks it might want to sleep with him again, though it will only be a thought. I promise.

I'm listening to Thanh talking to me in my head. I watch him gesturing like mad because he's trying to reach me and I'm far away, so he's practically using sign language. I hear him though. About the vase and not being broken. Or empty. And I'm keeping hold of that. I'm not going to that vacant place again where nobody's home. Even if she didn't love me altogether. Even if she couldn't, because of Lenore or because of something my dad doesn't understand and maybe I won't either. Ever. I think I need to tell Thanh, *I hear you.* Say it out loud, because he doesn't know. I ought to tell him, I hear you about the vase. I hear you. I can't disappear just because she couldn't appear. That's not right. Not fair to Thanh. Not fair to me, Leslie, and it's possible I count for something. Thanh says so, and I'm listening. Even if I can't write an essay where the pros outweigh the cons, I'll stay here and do the best I can.

# Part III

# Chapter 26

I'm embarrassed to say it, but I didn't get that essay done by the end of the term. My mother thesis was an unraveled cloth after what Dad told me. I had to request an extension, which means I have an incomplete grade in the English class, not a great way to start the fall semester. I feel like I'm doing schoolwork all the time, but my grades still suck and nothing is fun. So many things I have to forget about in order to get to schoolwork. All that's wrong with Ivori and me. All that stuff about my mom. The pills and freaking out Thanh. And the chainsaws lying in wait for the land I love.

On a Sunday in November, Thanh, Knose, and I go to the land, even though it's wintry and the wetlands are a skating pond decorated with clumps of grasses and small tree trunks sprouting through the ice. There are no new flags—the ground is too frozen to sink them in—but the old ones are there. I've considered a dozen times whether to remove them, but I always stop myself; they're evidence of a crime. Though I need no reminding, Thanh tells me that the development will be on the city council agenda just after Thanksgiving, on December 1. The planning commission recommended that the council approve the preliminary site plan—that's the vote I missed—but the council wanted to gather additional information and hasn't acted yet. We have another chance. *I* have another chance. Thanh cheers me on, but I'm the one who has to do the speaking. I'm the one who might fuck this up.

I think of all the people in the audience staring at me and thinking uncharitable thoughts. Maybe they know I'm the person who doesn't know how to take care of anything properly, who's some of the time mean to people who try to love her, so what am I doing standing up there at a microphone pretending I know what this land needs? Maybe the land is longing for a charming housing development with a name to remind you of what once grew there. *You have to have thicker skin*, I tell myself. My skin is like those Belgian lace cookies—holes and bumps.

I want to put all the plants and animals on the land on a massive signboard, then read them off to the council. I could do that more easily if Frank were there, because the list is his too. Where is he? Nowhere. He wants to be a nobody. Arwyn's gone, too. He's floated off in admiration of a new boyfriend. The boyfriend is a fashionista and an engineer at the same time, so what room is there in Arwyn's sweet heart for me? Ivori hasn't said a word to diss me in the last few days, but all I see is her back or her scowly face, sometimes her flatiron expression. She's the one I can hardly handle, but I have to handle things now. Be strong like Bertha, like I promised Thanh.

It's a sunny morning. Thanh is busy, but I borrow his car and grab Knose and a leash and drive to Island Lake Park on the river. The edge of the river is frozen into an astonishingly beautiful shelf of blue ice. A throng of ducks congregate in the water just off the ice. Knose keeps charging them to get them to fly up. You can see she loves this. She is on a power trip. I have an uneasy feeling. I should stop her. But she is having such a good time that I let her go. Her joy is an antidote to everything that's darkening my mind. There must be something delicious to eat beneath the water, because some of the ducks tip their cute butts up in the air and tuck their heads deep into the water. Every time Knose chases them off, they return to continue feasting.

I am distracted thinking about Ivori, how I just can't get things right between us. I notice Knose going out onto the ice. I want to stop her, but my mind drifts again to Ivori.

On her fourth pass, as the ducks lift off, Knose puts on the brakes, but it's too late. She goes into a skid and is in the icy water. I panic as she turns back toward the ice edge and paddles, her fur spread like a cape on top of the water. For a split-second, I think I can breathe because I see that she can swim. But she is struggling—the water has to be freezing. She puts her front paws up on the ice edge and I see immediately that she won't be able to get up. She is frozen and stiff. I can't even think about what she's feeling. A thousand prayers overwhelm my mind; I beg for her to get out. The weak ice edge breaks under her paws over and over. Now I feel her body in that frozen water as if it's my own—getting paralyzed with cold, and so weak. Knose. Knose who I love. She keeps cracking off ice. I hear those cracks like thunder. She cracks off enough to get to a sturdier piece, but she has nothing to latch onto and has no strength. She tries another time and fails. She is getting nowhere. She'll be under the water and drowned in a few more seconds. Without help, she will die, and I'm the only one here to help.

I start to race along the ice. Now my father and a hundred PSAs I've seen are shrieking about thin ice, so I lie down on it and crab my body toward her, telling myself not to stand up, because how many times have I heard all those warnings. But when I get there and grab hold of her collar and the skin of her neck, I feel her weight straining against the ice edge. She has no strength and no leverage and can't pull herself out. I stand up and haul her straight up. With me holding her in the air, her front nails can catch the ice and it holds as I'm yanking her forward. Then we're both on the ice running to the shore, my hand still on her collar, and by some crazy luck or miracle the ice doesn't drop us both into that water. It holds us up.

I'm terrified now she'll die from hypothermia, so I pull my heavy wool coat off, but she's shaking herself out to get rid of that icy water and I can't get her wrapped up. I imagine her body temperature plunging until she's unconscious, and I'm not strong enough to carry her, and no one's here to help. She is running a few feet in one direction, then another, looking back at me like she wants to get back to our walk, which is crazy. Finally, I take off for the car. She follows me at a run and we both barrel into the back seat of the car. I'm yelling, "Knose, Knose, Knose!" and it just sounds like *no, no, no.* No, don't die. No, don't break Arwyn's heart. No, don't break my own already half-broken heart. Together in the back seat, she's looking at me with puzzlement as if she miraculously feels fine now and can't understand why we've cut short our walk and raced each other back to the car. Now it's just me who's drowning and has to hug her and hold her and cry.

After a while, I stop shaking and can drive and get us home. I want Knose to come to my room so I can dry her and make sure she's not going to drop dead from aftershock, but she runs straight to Arwyn's room, and I hear him greet her happily, "Hi Knosey Knose." I should follow after and tend to her. I should watch over her, but I'm too scared to look at Arwyn's face so I don't go after her. I just go to my room and cry into my mattress.

I don't tell Arwyn what happened. I can't. I don't want him suffering with dreadful pictures in his mind. It is bad enough that I can't stop seeing Knose struggling in the freezing water, weak and drowning. During the night, I have a million nightmares. In some, she goes under the water and blows bubbles and drowns, and I am just standing there, desperately watching and breaking into pieces. In some, I am standing frozen myself, looking at her beautiful dead body.

For days I watch her and take time to feel her body over every square inch, as if I might feel something bulging or ripped under the skin. But there is nothing there but her squirmy, loving self. I imagine running my mind through the wash cycle so everything awful that's in it—whatever bad I've done—is washed away, and the water comes out clean. But the washing has to clear away Michael Vest, too, and a hundred other things, and it just can't do the job.

Several days have passed when Arwyn comes to my door in the afternoon. I'm so happy to see him, but his face is somber.

"Can I talk to you?" he asks, which is not an Arwyn way to say hi.

"Yeah. Sure."

Arwyn normally comes in and sits on my bed, but today he stands at the door. I see he's upset. He looks worried, but also mad. I've never seen Arwyn like this before.

"What?" I ask him. My heart is bouncing madly.

"Knose was a total mess when you brought her back the other day."

I nod.

"How can you take her out in the cold for half the day and bring her back like that? She was sopping wet and might have gotten sick. Pneumonia, God forbid."

I nod and try to keep my heart from leaving my body. I try to keep from crying, too, because it wouldn't be fair to wring pity from Arwyn.

"Couldn't you have dried her off, at least? Maybe bathed her? Kept her dry in the first place?"

I'm terrified he's going to ask me exactly what happened, but he's not doing that. I think he's afraid to know. I can't say anything at all. If I tell Arwyn about the river, he'll tell me never to take Knose out again, because I can't be trusted. He'll tell me to move out like Alex and go live in a cave somewhere by myself. I nod and beg him with my eyes not to send me away.

He's still angry. I think he's finding it hard to talk anymore, so he just says, "Okay, Leslie."

I can't stand to hear how he says my name, formally, as if he has to say it so I'll know whose fault this is, but it's not a word he cares for or likes to have in his mouth. He'd rather spit it out.

I already hate myself for paying no attention and letting Knose fall through the ice. I'm such a fuck up.

I call Thanh. When he answers, I don't know what to say, so I just say, "It's me."

He says hi and waits for me, but I have no words. Instead of saying nothing, I say out loud, "Nothing."

"Is something on your mind?"

"Kind of. Yes."

Thanh laughs. I am being ridiculous. But his laughing is a good sign, since you don't laugh on doomsday. It gives me some courage.

"I almost got Knose drowned the other day, and Arwyn hates me."

"What happened? You didn't tell me."

"I let her chase ducks and go through the ice. I should have been paying attention, but my mind was wandering. She would have drowned, but I crawled over the ice and pulled her out. I'm as bad as Alex—messing things up for people."

"I thought you'd decided Alex isn't that terrible. He doesn't deserve capital punishment. Just dishes."

"Kind of."

Thanh sounds stuck, like he is trying to make sense of things, but the pieces won't come together. This isn't a STEM field. The logic is trickier.

"Knose got *herself* in the water," he says after a while. "You got her out."

"I never thought of that."

"Why don't you come visit me. Then I can remind you about some things."

"I remember," I say. "The broken vase and all that. But okay, I'll come." Now I'm thinking about his skin. Of course—what else? Same old Leslie. But I also think about the second when I reached for Knose's collar. Did she understand that I love her, that I wanted to save her, that I was there to help? I hope she did. My poor mom. Losing Lenore when they were just little kids. Given no chance to save her little body. Maybe seeing it lifeless, like me on my bed next to a puddle of vomit. Like Knose in my nightmares. My poor mom.

# Chapter 27

On December 1, I go to a city council meeting with Thanh. It's not yet the one where I'll have to speak; still, my chest is full of butterflies just knowing I'm in the room where next time I'll need to say my thoughts out loud.

A lot of people attend this meeting, and I swear, everyone is dressed in a puffer coat, so Thanh and I are crowded together. I feel like we're inside a pillow. I see him glancing at my hand, which is palm-down on the chair, and I half-wish he'd grab it. I think about Frank and the giant hole of his absence. I'm glad to see Bertha; she's in a nice burgundy wool jacket, not a snowmobile puffer jacket. She's got her head pointed up a bit as if she can only see out of the bottom of her glasses, but there's dignity in her lifted chin, possibly blended with some quiet fury like yours truly.

They've begun discussion of the Woodlands Preserve. Four or five have grumbly faces, and others look so eager to speak about the benefits of the project that they may trample each other rushing to the mic. There's an older woman with a helmet of stiff, sprayed hair dyed golden, who becomes Miss Logic whenever the discussion becomes emotional.

"We may not like the development—I hear it's pretty land—but Blue Sky owns the land, and I can't see any sound basis for denial." *Pretty land.* Like a sweater you see at Lord & Taylor and pick up for a second to feel the soft wool, and then a second later you've forgotten it exists. A couple other people *love* the development. They aren't ambivalent like the helmet-haired person. But at least a few people are shaking their heads disgruntledly.

Afterward, the currents of people exiting the meeting room through two doors bring Bertha and me together again, because I slow-walked a little to get the timing right.

"I'm happy to see you here again, Miss Leslie," she says, and she does seem pleased. She adds, "The next meeting is for public comment, so I hope to hear your voice."

"I'll try," I say. "Though I might be nervous." I giggle. "Shaking, possibly."

She studies me. "You need to let your outrage flow out from your mouth, not disperse itself shaking. Let it pour forth. It can move through the room like a song." She gestures with both hands to show me how my anger should venture into the world. Here comes Mrs. Ferguson singing her arias.

"Don't waste energy hating, either. They're ignorant people. They didn't have what you had to teach you what's there on that land to love. You and I can try to educate them. If that fails, we hog-tie them as best we can." She sighs. "We could use broader ranks though."

"I know someone. I don't know why he's not here. Frank somebody." It's so weird. I don't know Frank's last name. "He works in the cemetery."

She nods. "Frank Yeller. His people owned this land. Years back."

"You know him. Oh, wow. I thought he might come." I'm muttering.

When I get in the car beside Thanh, I think about Bertha saying someone taught me to love the land. I see my mother in her garden and picture the way she gazed at her dahlias and pointed out to me that each petal is its own roll of silk. She wanted me to look. To see it. Did my mother only like perfect flowers with untorn petals, not skinny wild ones all jumbled together? I don't know; that's the truth. Maybe she would have loved my wild place. I'm trying to live with that uncertainty, to remind myself that even my dad has questions he can't answer about my mom.

Thanh and I are in the car outside my house. He looks tense. I think he wants to kiss me. Instead, he clears his throat—a Hollywood ahem—and says, "Leslie, in some ways you don't know me."

*Uh-oh.*

"You think I'm like a sofa. I don't mind that. I like it some of the time."

"A sofa? Like a couch? That's not true."

"It is."

I'm afraid to hear what Thanh wants to tell me. I don't want him not to be who I think he is. I hate that. But I know I have to listen. It's what he would do for me. "Who are you, then?" I press shut my eyelids until I feel the muscles in them.

"Things scare me, too."

"Uh."

"The meetings, for example. I'm scared to get up there and speak in front of people."

"Maybe you don't care about the land like I do. Which sucks, but hey, you be you."

He shakes his head. "I do care. I just get anxious."

"And I don't?"

"I never told you my dad had to testify in court, under oath, when his business partner embezzled from their company. He was so nervous he couldn't get his point across. He lost his cool and blew the testimony."

"And your family needed that money badly, right?" I'm thinking of Frank now, trying to learn to be tuned in to another person's reality.

"Not the money. The self-respect. He couldn't bear people thinking his business went under because he was lousy at it. Piled on that shame was dishonor for trembling like a scared rabbit on the witness stand. He was tongue-tied."

"So at the meetings, you'll just send me up there to humiliate myself?"

Thanh laughs. "You'll do fine. I'll try to speak, too, if I think I can."

"But I have to be the vanguard? Me and Bertha?"

Thanh nods. "Anything wrong with that?"

I like it, actually. "'She was not afraid of mice. She loved winter, snow, and ice.' From a story my dad read me all the time."

I reach for the car door. I guess I'm not getting a kiss tonight, or anything that might follow. Whole-person Leslie only somewhat regrets that, but body Leslie is frustrated. I could reach over and kiss him. I could be the one. But I can't do that. Can't say *I want you* without getting nauseous.

I'm back in my room and a dark cloud is blowing through me because of Thanh's disappointment and because of what will happen if the council okays the dreadful development. The animals gather in my head. I don't think plants know if they are losing their homes. They wouldn't know if they were on the endangered list. I suppose the animals wouldn't know that either. But I know. I am full of knowing.

I wish I knew more about the individual animals though. I don't want to be a fake, complaining of how they'd lose their homes when I can't name more than two without help from Thanh or a guidebook. Thanh, who I don't know properly. That's what he told me. The animals might disappear from the face of the earth because no one sees them, and one of those *no ones* is me. I google *warblers,* and up come life histories and songs, but I start with the images. A+ to Mother Nature for design.

All I have is a plain mechanical pencil and a notepad, but I sketch the black and crimson one called redstart. My mother always doodled when she talked on the phone. She drew women mostly, in nicely tailored suits and high heels, things she seldom wore but I guess were present in her head. I sketch the redstart with the delicate hand my mother brought to her fashion doodles. I do a pretty good job and write the bird's name underneath and cite the northern places where it nests and when it passes through here on its way north or south. I look at it the way Thanh wants me to look at him, seeing all his parts. Not just his pretty skin and big brain but also his scared-to-speak, breath-holding personhood and his mixed bag of happy and broken family stories. There are so many wood warblers, and I have this crazy feeling that if I don't draw each of them and keep them close to me in this notebook—like Frank's father's list—they may *poof*, disappear.

I fall asleep, but I am dreaming about those birds. They're in my pockets—six of them—in the kitchen apron Alex wears, the one Arwyn bought him to dress him up a little when the beige one got too stained. I like having them in my pockets, but I know they are crowded and bumping into each other. One at a time, I take them out and let them go. As each one flies away, it flashes its colors and it is beautiful, which makes my heart stop, and I'm left hoping it will circle around and land again where I can see it, not fly away where I won't ever see it again. But I let them all go and take my chances, and then one does return and alight beside me on a blue railing. It is the redstart I drew, and I am just so happy. It's the kind of magical joy you feel when you're little, but maybe not so much after that—at least that's what I'm afraid of.

I am still in bed with my sheets up to my chin, trying to grab hold of that dream. I don't want the dream itself to take flight. I can see how it's a dream about my mother and the different ways in which I've lost her. But *I'm* in there, too, aren't I? When she admired things, she'd always say, "It's pretty as a picture, Leslie." It's an odd saying, but she used it a lot. And there I was, last night, drawing a picture of a bird that needed to be seen, so that's me, isn't it, trying to be pretty as a picture? And maybe it's Thanh, too, and Ivori and even Frank, though he's old and tired. I love Frank. He told me he'd come and celebrate with us if we can save the land. Put on his suit and tie and look handsome to honor the occasion even though he's old. Everyone is like Tinkerbell, where you have to clap your hands and show you appreciate her, otherwise her light blinks out pitifully. Kids get that. They don't think it's crazy. It makes sense to them how poor Tink would need that encouragement.

I have her in bits and pieces now, my mother. Scraps of her are everywhere. She is a word spoken with a laugh and a word that's a yelp of pain. A picture too dark and dreary to make out. One that's sparkly. I'm in some of the pictures, and in others I'm nowhere and there's no point searching. I have to make do with what I have.

That evening, I get Thanh to take me to buy five sheets of poster board. Back in my room, my purchases litter the floor like Ivori's construction stuff. I tape the boards together across the back with strapping tape, then I stretch the tape around to the front edges. I pull Frank's father's list from my top desk drawer, settle onto the floor with the giant blank board, and unfold the list. He's organized his entries by classifications. Most are plants, but he's got some birds and mammals too, and even a few snakes and frogs. His first category is Grasses and Sedges, but I skip past that one because people won't recognize those names. I go on to Herbaceous Plants. That group is more promising. I start with black-eyed Susan and put the Latin name—*Rudbeckia hirta*—in parentheses, though I doubt I'll read the Latin. Then great blue lobelia (*Lobelia siphilitica*) and cardinal flower (*Lobelia cardinalis*), one of my favorites. I could cover this whole board in herbaceous plants, but I only fill the first panel and part of the second, then move on to the group called Woody Plants, which includes all the shrubs and trees. Spicebush first, then gray dogwood and red twig dogwood, then pawpaw, which Thanh says is uncommon here, and a half dozen other shrubs, also meticulously printed on Frank's list. I go on to the trees. My favorite is the black oak: They are majestic and have heavy black bark that looks like the earth cracked by drought. I want to put my arms around them and press my ear up against them in case they are vibrating with wisdom. Other oaks dot the land. I like them all. I sound like a Dr. Seuss book: Short and tall—I like them all.

I've got the second and third panels crowded with names now, but I haven't begun to exhaust the list. The fourth panel is for animals. First the mammals; that list is short. Then the frogs—bullfrog, leopard frog, western chorus, spring peeper, gray tree frog, wood frog—plus a few turtles, snakes, and salamanders. Finally, a long list of birds, including quite a few I've never seen and can only guess at from their names. I pause to feel mournful about the idea I may never see them because they'll lose their homes and migration stopover points. About twenty are wood warblers, and I barely know them, except I know the redstart a little since I drew it. There's the Cape May, yellow, eastern parula, mourning, myrtle, many more. Too many for my sign. They all go into the dot-dot-dot category. I wonder if I should read more softly at the end to give the idea of fading away. Or I could read more loudly and almost shout, to get across my message and wake everyone up. I'll have to ask Arwyn which effect would have more drama.

I think of my mother. I wish I could see her loving this land. She loved her garden. She called me over to look at this or that flower, see how pretty—how *beautiful*—it was. But I couldn't see what she saw. I probably disappointed her. I wanted her to think *I* was beautiful, not some flower. So I couldn't see her flower. Wouldn't. And I'm sorry for that. One time I intentionally stepped on some of those flowers, flattening them when she wasn't looking. And I waited to hear that sad "oooh" when she saw them and thought it was a monster woodchuck, I suppose.

I just remembered something. A cherry fell off our big cherry tree because the birds missed it and didn't gobble it down. I put my finger deep into the dirt and pushed the cherry down there and shooed away any squirrel I saw go near. And you wouldn't believe it, but it sprouted. My mom squinted and looked close at the leaves on the little plant because she couldn't believe it was the cherry. She thought a weed had sprouted there. But then she laughed and said something like, "My goodness, Leslie," and said it was a cherry tree after all. She told me very seriously how I needed to keep it watered and keep the ground damp all the time when the tree was little so it wouldn't shrivel up and die. I remember she told me, *It's not a tree yet, it's still a seedling, so you need to be careful with it.* But I can't remember the rest and don't know if I watered it or maybe got distracted with playing or other kid stuff and let it die, and then felt bad when I saw what I had let happen. I wish I had the rest of the story, but I'm glad to remember the cherry tree.

# Chapter 28

I already signed up to speak, and I'm trying not to shake. Bertha is sitting behind me, and Arwyn and Alex are to my left with the enormous five-board sign I made. It's loosely rolled, not showing off its content. Thanh is here, of course, and miracle of miracles, Ivori is here, though she parked herself by the door in case she feels a spasm of hating me and needs to depart. I admit it: I broke down and begged her. Thanh is planning to join the sign-holding crew, and I think he's happy about that because he'll be on stage and feel like he's confronting his dad demon just a little.

The only one missing is Frank. He lets me do what I need to do to keep my balance, but I tug at him when he won't follow me. I see the lesson in that, though I'd rather not. I think I love Frank almost as much as I love Arwyn, so I need to be here for his land, even though he can't be. I have to use my voice.

The speeches have been going on for a while; they're about half pro and half con for the development. Bertha pokes me in the back with one finger and says, "Okay, girl. You're next. Go sing your song."

I try to breathe deeply. They call my name. My nervousness carries me up to the front before Alex, Thanh, and Arwyn. I have to climb a couple steps onto the stage, and I feel more awkward than at my junior-high-school graduation, where I nearly tripped over my gown in the high heels they made us wear. I can hear the guys behind me unfurling the big sign, and I know everyone's eyes must be on them, trying to figure out what we're up to. Alex is closest to me and cleaned up decently—I think Arwyn trimmed his beard—and Arwyn is close to the far edge of the stage because our sign is enormous. Thanh is in the middle to keep the whole thing steady.

I say, "Thank you for the opportunity to address the council," like every single speaker, and I give my name and address and introduce Alex, Thanh, and Arwyn as residents of the same address—fudging on Thanh. Now all the busybodies in the audience can wonder what our relationships are. Suddenly I think my presentation is completely ridiculous, and I spark with anger at the friends who let me come up here and make a fool of myself. It's too late to do anything other than what I planned, so I open my mouth, prepare to hear a quivery voice, and say, "I'm against this development. They shouldn't call it a development. They should call it a destruction. And they shouldn't call themselves Blue Sky whatever. They should call themselves Black Hole. And it's not a 'preserve' of any kind, so they have no business naming it that." My voice is skinny and far away. I glance at Bertha, and she gives me a slow deep nod and a sly smile. I'm better now and say, "Black-eyed Susan, *Rudbeckia hirta*—that's a flower that's growing on the land and will be gone, trashed by the bulldozers. And *Liatris,* the blazing star. That one too."

I walk to the edge of the sign so I can read. I just read off the names. No commentary. Just my list. Slow and somber. Attending now to my voice, wanting it solemn. Occasionally, I add the Latin.

Now my plan seems good. *Brilliant.* Alex is shifting from foot to foot and restless as a preschooler, but I don't care if he looks silly. He's my friend, and he's here to support what I'm doing. I'm starting to feel like I own this voice. I go through all the herbaceous plants and start in on the woody ones, and the buzzer sounds to tell me my time is up, but I keep going with my voice a little louder like Arwyn suggested, so I can insist on black oak and burr oak and the redstart. Then in the air I space out the dot-dot-dot with my index finger and hope that people get that. I'm done.

Arwyn leads the way down the stairs with the sign twisting among the three of them. They don't roll it up but walk it down the aisle and out the door like we planned. Alex is grinning, and I picture even Ivori being amused by him, though that is pushing it. I go back to my seat, and Bertha tickles her finger on my back and whispers behind my ear, "You go, girl," and I'm proud and happy, though I don't know if we influenced a single person. Arwyn, Thanh, and Alex come sneaking back up the aisle as the next speaker goes to the mic. They slide in beside me. They must have stashed the sign somewhere in the lobby, and they are giggling a little.

The next speaker thinks the development will be a boon to the community, but he makes a shitty case. He doesn't say anything that would counter my great list. I assume the speaker is an investor. I start to get riled up and want to put a plug in his mouth, but I remind myself that I don't run the zoo. Running it sounds nice, but if you're in charge of everything, all the things that go wrong are your fault too, and I've got enough blamed on me already. I glance around toward the door and see that Ivori is gone. My chest hollows, but okay, she stayed for our list, so that's cool.

They don't vote on anything tonight. The helmet-haired woman says they need to see a traffic study first and a plan on wetlands mitigation. That sounds to me like another name for replacing grand trees with baby ones, like Bertha said, but at least there's nothing to rock my world other than the prospect of more meetings and more chances to get terrified about public speaking.

People crowd the exit and try to get their mittens and hats on before they're pushed out into the cold. I complain to Thanh that I may fail geology at the rate I'm going and not get the English essay done if I keep having to come to these meetings and worry about all this, though I think I'm being a little drama-queenish on that score. I see Bertha smiling, looking at us all, and I hope she hasn't heard my whining, which would probably sound beyond childish to her.

In the parking lot, Bertha finds me and says, "Leslie dear, how about you and I have lunch?" She hands me a printed business card that identifies her as a librarian. "Retired now, but still have a drawer full of these," she says. "There's the phone number you can call to reach me. Or send a text if you like that way better." She gives me a confident smile that says, *I expect you to do this now, so don't go and forget.* I know I'll do it because she's counting on me. The only thing that goes badly the rest of the night is that Ivori doesn't come out of her room to say one single thing about my speech.

# Chapter 29

The next afternoon, Mrs. Ferguson comes over. I'm not flying quite so high, because I'm remembering the shock I got when the planning commission voted yes for Blue Sky. That could happen with the council, too. I hear Mrs. Ferguson come in and linger in the living room, talking to Arwyn. I can tell from their voices that they are charming each other. I am excited she's here, but afraid. When she comes up the stairs, I'm hanging around in the hall, and Ivori is in her room. Surprise, surprise, her door is shut.

"Oh, dear Leslie," Mrs. Ferguson says to me. Her hug squeezes the breath out of me, and at the same time fills me with warm slush. Simultaneous with the hug, she's tap-tapping on Ivori's door with her plum-colored fingernails. It's cold out, and she is wearing a wool coat that feels like cashmere.

"Yeah. Come in," Ivori calls out, her irritability flying out ahead of her like a Frisbee.

Mrs. Ferguson shrugs, says to me, "Come visit us in a bit," then opens the door. Even though she doesn't need my pity, I feel sorry for her. I resist the urge to stay near the door and listen.

I watch the clock and try to calculate the right time to visit, but I have no idea. I wish Mrs. Ferguson would come tow me in, since I feel like a stranded boat. In half an hour, I knock lightly, thinking the sound is soft enough that Iv can ignore me if she wants.

I hear Mrs. F. say, "Oh, Leslie," in her lilting voice. Then she opens the door. "Leslie, Leslie, do come in. Ivori and I were just talking about her future plans, but my god, you girls are just sophomores, so there's no hurry."

"There might be," Ivori says mysteriously from her seat on her bed, and I know she's hinting at HBCUs. She's turned in her project, but she's already started on something new, and her construction stuff is strewn all over. She has moved most of the materials toward the back wall so that her mother can sit down, and apparently I'm allowed too, since she nods toward her other chair.

Mrs. Ferguson must see me sitting upright as a candle flame because she says to Ivori, "We could buy you some more comfortable chairs, child." She adds in a whisper, "How are things with your housemate?" referring to Alex. I'm thinking Ivori might want to complain about the housemate sitting right next to her too. I look at Ivori's face and think I must look pitiful, as if I'm pleading.

"Sit. Sit," Mrs. Ferguson says to me. I am already sitting, so I think she means, make yourself more comfortable, which I try somehow to do. Then something comes over me and I can't help it, I just blurt it out. "Ivori's mad at me."

Mrs. Ferguson looks at Ivori with distressed puzzlement and says, "You're angry with Leslie? You two are such good friends."

Ivori gives a one-shouldered shrug.

Mrs. Ferguson says, "No, no, none of that," as if she's experienced her daughter's cryptic gesturing before. "Just say it out loud if you have a problem. No guessing games."

"She pisses me off royally," Ivori practically shouts, and I cringe.

"It's about Alex," I say. I feel less vulnerable if I say it myself.

"It is not," Ivori says, and shakes her head hard. "I'm over that. You can be his best friend for all I care." Another cringe.

"What is it, then, Vori?" Mrs. Ferguson asks. "You know how I dislike it when you are evasive."

Ivori's eyes flare open and fixate. "You wouldn't believe how she's fucking around with this nice guy who adores her. Sleeping with other guys whenever his back is turned."

I'm beyond mortified, but also shocked, my eyes circling to escape. I didn't tell anyone about Michael Vest. Then I remember that night, leaving my journal on my bed. When I came back from getting tea, the journal was shut. She sneaked a look. Just like I would have done.

"That's true, Leslie?" Mrs. Ferguson asks, somewhat sternly. "Though you need not talk about it if you prefer not to."

It's my turn for shrugging. "There's a little truth there. Not every guy I meet, though. That's way overboard. Just one guy, one time."

"What about that guy Fletcher, who wasn't half as cute as Thanh?"

"Yeah, but that was just kissing though and a little—y'know— other stuff." He was, too, cute, I'm thinking.

"What's the difference? That's still betrayal."

Maybe I can defend myself here. "I was barely with Thanh then. We were just friends."

"And you teased him about it. Tortured the poor guy."

I scrunch up my face. Again, I have no words. I think of Thanh yelling about the pills and being a sofa. All of my bad behavior. Piling too high.

"I'm going to speak out of turn," Mrs. Ferguson says. She looks very intentionally at Ivori. "You can hush me up if you want to." She turns back to me and says, "Ivori's father—my husband—has been unfaithful. Habitually. It infuriates her. Me as well, mind you, but Ivori and I handle it differently."

"That's right," Ivori hollers.

"I didn't know," I say lamely.

"Yeah, well knowledge of my family is not relevant to your behavior."

"Well now, I'm not certain I agree with that," Mrs. Ferguson says, loud and clear. "Leslie isn't married to this young man you're feeling sorry for, is she? Can't you let her sort things out?"

Alex went on trial for his revolting behavior. It's my turn to plead guilty.

"I fucked up," I say, and wonder if I can say those words in front of Mrs. F. Probably. She already knows worse things about me than some bad language. "She's right. One day I met this spectacularly gorgeous older professor guy and he—well, I was messed up about some other things that day and I did go to his apartment. For a while. One time. I'm not always the best human. But I'm trying to be better. Making progress. A little."

When Mrs. Ferguson is ready to go, she wraps herself in her soft wool and takes a good look at Ivori, then at me, and says, "You young ladies had better work this thing out. Don't let it fester." She hugs each one of us and leaves.

"So that's what you're so angry about?" I say to Ivori after her mom's gone. "The thing about guys? That older guy?"

"You make it seem dumb, but it's not. It means something."

"That I'm a dick?"

"You're *unfaithful*. Ever heard that word? People who love you can't depend on you."

I am shrinking into a dried pea. "Am I the worst person in the world?"

Ivori grudgingly laughs, as if I've said something sufficiently over-the-top to smirk at.

"Second worst," I say. "Maybe after Alex."

She laughs again. "That's about right."

"Do you want me to scrub floors?"

"Our house is going to be very clean. Arwyn will be delighted."

"I love Arwyn," bubbles out of me. It calms me to center my thoughts on him.

"I guess he better watch out, then."

Cringe.

"And I have work to do," she adds, stiff again. She is kicking me out of her room. I just leave. I can't think of one thing more to say.


Later that night, a note slips under my door. It's an old-fashioned piece of flowered stationery and handwritten words from Ivori: *And there are other things. I told you about the asshole professor who deigned to comment on my art project proposal and thought it was an expression of "childish sentiment" or something of that sort. You might have asked what happened after I turned it in for real.*

That's all she says, and it's not too terrible, especially when I consider that I had just about offed myself the day she finally told me about the professor. I hope that's the whole list.

My gut is sore from all the blows, and I'm visualizing a cracked vase full of nothing but dregs from dirty water. I am trying to patch it in my head and fill it with clean water and at least a wilted daisy or two. I've been trying to hold onto the things Thanh wanted me to see: that he loves me, that you can have a mother who can't do a whole lot of filling, or just gives you dribs and drabs, and still you are okay or at least have a chance to be. Unfortunately, Ivori is telling me I'm not okay. Mother or no mother, I could be a terrific person—that's within the scope of possibility—but in fact I'm not. That's her opinion, and it hurts me.

Lots of what I find when I visit the land is small and unfinished. Or imperfect. It's spindly trees with eight leaves and four of them have ragged holes chewed by insects, or trees that are massive but they are weighed down by fungi or strangling vines, and in storms they drop a limb or two. Nothing's perfect there, but I still love it. That's how Thanh loves me. My dad loved my mom and misses her even though she left him with some regrets and some mysteries.

I go out into the hall and Ivori wanders out too. I feel embarrassed. "So what *did* happen?" I ask, my voice soft. I don't bother to apologize for not being who she wants me to be, because what's the point. And I don't want to shine additional light on my glaring defects.

She shrugs. "Nothing much. He was kind of neutral. Commented on design characteristics and that sort of thing."

I think of all the work she poured into her project and contrast that with my dithering around my essay. Sympathy floods through me. "I'm sorry. You worked so hard on it, and it's so cool."

I'm restless that night, so I get up from bed and without thinking I pull out the box with Mom's letters. Maybe my mom's secrets will be in this letter in the baby-blue envelope. Here she's telling me all the ordinary stuff I'm missing at home. Tomatoes ripening in the garden, though those horror-movie hornworms got some of them. Jehovah's witnesses stopping by to talk her onto their righteous path, just as she was getting out of the shower. I'm skimming all the insignificant newsy parts of the letter, impatient for the end where she might say how much she misses me. Will she say she's counting the days until I get home? I was tallying them, even though I was supposed to be a happy camper. But she doesn't say anything mushy like that. She just signs off, "Bye for now, dear. Have a good week. Love, Mom." Her mind is elsewhere and mine is a ship going down.

There's nothing in the letter, but there must be something in this box I can find. A bit of her and me together. I pull out the photo I found a while back. We're both looking straight ahead at the camera, but she's holding my hand, even though I look too old for that, maybe eight. She's probably just holding it to keep me still for the photo.

I have only a smattering of memories of that age. Most are school. Mrs. Bennett is teaching us how to blow our noses properly, but her technique doesn't work for me. She wants us to blow out of both nostrils at once and not squeeze either one closed. She gives a dire warning about nose slime backing up into your brain. A scrap of my mother sails by now. I close my eyes and grab it by the corner, pull it back. I tell her Mrs. Bennett's warning. *This is what happened in school today.* But I'm fishing: I want her to tell me the danger isn't real. She won't pay attention. Her back is turned. Maybe she's ironing or folding clothes, but I see her giggling now. Giggling like me. And I see her turning around—facing me—and we're both laughing and thinking Mrs. Bennett's idea is ridiculous. Here is the mother I've been looking for. The other mother is here as well. Sometimes I think that neither one is real, that both are illusions. But tonight, I see both as real. They are the pieces of her, and, because the memories belong to me, they are pieces of me.

# Chapter 30

I should call Bertha, but instead I go in search of Frank. It's almost dusk and snowing lightly, but it's so pretty that I need to be outdoors. I head to the cemetery. My footprints are clear against the bare sidewalk. I'm excited but afraid that Frank won't be there. I feel oddly scared that something happened to him, a heart attack maybe. I might find him dead in the snow, curled up like a frozen snail. I start to panic. The coming darkness must be doing this to me. Later, I'll be walking home in the pitch dark. I should have brought Knose, but Arwyn was having a goofy conversation with her.

I see a blurred shadow far off in the cemetery. Anyone sane would run the other way, but I relax because it can only be Frank. He's here, like he always is, hanging out with Tabitha and the others. I can breathe again. When I get close enough for him to distinguish me from the shadows, he's happy to see me. I tell him about the giant sign, the friends who held it up, all the plants sprawling across it. I'm a kid at show-and-tell and recite the names from memory as well as I can, in Latin no less. "*Liatris, Lobelia cardinalis, Rudbeckia hirta*." I tell him that *hirta* means *hairy*. Two gross hairs have been sprouting from my neck. They're kind of revolting, but interesting too, because they're out of place. I halfway like them because they are so impressively odd. And you know me, I like that kind of thing. Maybe they stand for my own general weirdness, which I'm trying to get on better terms with.

He prompts me, "What about the vines?"

"*Celastrus scandens* and another *Celastrus*, both the native one and the invasive."

"Now what else? What about the woody ones? Those were Daddy's favorites. Those and the sedges with the sharp edges you can feel with the side of your finger. Don't forget about the sedges."

"You should come to the meetings." I try again. Why can't I leave him alone? "Sit beside Bertha. She needs someone her age. I'm like a kid to her. Boring."

He shakes his head. "I don't know that I can work on saving the land for some other folks, though I can see that might sound selfish."

Frank wants to be left behind. Everyone else is marching along in a ragged procession, but he's stepped to the side to let the parade pass. We have to straggle on without him. I need to let that be, though I hate it.

I drag myself out to the grad library to try and get back on track with school. When I get home around ten, Arwyn, Alex, and Ivori are sitting at the kitchen table drinking Alex's black Russian tea. I smell its bitterness. The kitchen is decrepit but sparkling. I suspect ours is the cleanest student house on campus. I am happy to see the three of them gathered there.

"Sit down, sweetie," Arwyn says. He pushes a chair away from the table for me, and I straddle it backward and wrap my arms around it. I want to cry. I'm afraid I might. Why does Arwyn have to be so nice to me?

"I decided I'm going to forgive you," Ivori says.

"Because your mother told you to?"

"What are you forgiving her for?" Alex asks. I suspect he's glad that someone else is in trouble for once, not him.

"A lot of things," Ivori says. I hope she isn't planning to enumerate them for the whole world. They're definitely not endangered species. She keeps it vague and says, "Deficits in sensitivity."

"Tea," Arwyn says. "We all need another round of tea. Herbal this time. Chamomile?"

Ivori gives him a spiked eye. She doesn't like him trying to shut her down in his anxious, fiddly way. "I don't need more tea."

Arwyn nods. The seat of his chair grabs his bottom like a magnet and yanks him down. Apparently, he doesn't want any tea, either. He looks enormously sad and defeated and says to Ivori, "You're not leaving us, are you?"

"I doubt it. You're all too deep under my skin."

*Like chiggers*, I think. Though Thanh told me they don't burrow; the skin grows up around them and traps them, which is equally horrifying.

"Even me?" Alex asks with visible excitement.

"I'll have to think about that."

"You can tell them," I say. "If you want. All my offenses."

"That's all right," she says.

I'm still working on forgiving myself, especially when I think about Michael Vest, but I feel lighter knowing that Ivori's forgiven me, at least halfway, and just maybe she's going to stay.

I meet Bertha at Pizza House on Church Street, which she says is her favorite restaurant. She tells me she wants to treat me to lunch, and I'm to get what I want and don't be shy about ordering. I'm nervous being here with her, but I'm hungry too, so I get the Deal of the Day. Buffalo chicken sliders.

"I wanted to talk to you," she says, studying me in a way that is careful but doesn't make me feel as if she's staring at the two gargantuan hairs. "I've been seeing you at these meetings. And I heard you get up there and tell all those folks what's precious about that land you and I both love. And I feel how much you care about it, just like I do."

I nod.

"I also overheard you tell your friend you're behind on your schoolwork and have an essay that needs writing. I hope you don't mind my listening in."

I'm embarrassed now about my whining and start to jump in and say I was being a baby and shouldn't have complained, but she waves me off and shakes her head vigorously and says, "That's nothing." Then she says, like Mrs. Ferguson might, "Your schoolwork is important, and I'm sure someone's working hard to pay that tuition bill. An essay takes concentration. You can't be distracted, your mind going every which way. You need to settle down and give it your attention."

I can't figure out where she's going now. Am I in trouble here?

"What I'm trying to say, Leslie, is that it's okay to take a break from worrying about the land and let me carry that load for a while. You've done your part for now, and you have some other things that need your attention. You can let the old folks haul it down the next leg of the road. I'm retired. I have the time. And I might drum up some others to lift their voices. Maybe even your friend Frank."

I shake my head. "He won't. He's too tired."

Bertha laughs. "We'll see about that. Old ladies have some special powers. And we're not above twisting arms. Anyway, Frank Yeller and I have roots in the same soil; those roots are tangled together. Frank used to be the first to speak out, you know. Got himself in some trouble, though, one time. Actually got himself arrested. Maybe I shouldn't tell on him, but it's been a long time now. They called him a vandal. I guess he quieted down after that. But it might be time now for him to use that big voice again. We'll see. But don't you do the worrying, Leslie. For now, get where you need to go with your schoolwork. That's your number one job. You understand?"

I'm confused and thinking for a minute Bertha doesn't want me to be part of things. I start to ask, "Did I not do a good enough job?" and she rushes in with a campaign of head shaking.

"No, no, no, that's not my point at all. You and your friends did a very fine job." She gets a serious look. "That's why you can take a rest and let me carry it. You come back to it when you get your schoolwork done."

After that conversation, I am determined to take Bertha's advice and finally write my essay. I give up on the motherboard. It's too private. Too unsettled still. Instead, I argue the pros and cons of sustainable development. Is that a real thing or an oxymoron? Right away, the paper comes together. The essay is only one part of my problem with school, but it's a start.

# Chapter 31

Cause for celebration! I got an A- on my essay. I'm happy with that, and relieved because I'll get that "incomplete," which I never liked the sound of, off my transcript. It is late January, and we are spending a lot of time in our drafty old house discovering the ways in which it's not very comfortable. Arwyn marches around the house staring into a corner or running his eyes across a wall, contemplating what he can do to make the spot more appealing. On a Saturday morning, after football season traffic insanity is over, Ivori asks me,

"Do you want to go to Treasure Mart and look for some better chairs?"

I don't know the place she's talking about, but I'd go with her even if it were the city dump. I offer up a casual "sure," but my heart is surging with the memory of our trips to Detroit.

The place is three stories of an old house and full of every kind of junk and treasure you could think of, as if it's an attic to the entire country. Too many things are piled up on every surface for us to look at everything, so we scan for armchairs among the historical gadgets and memorabilia. I imagine the chairs relaxing and enjoying their unique surroundings. When one of us spots one that has potential, we take turns sitting down to give it a test.

I am in a jet stream of happiness.

Ivori and I go down to explore the basement. The shabbier stuff is down here, but some good things, too. Up against a wall is a wheeled metal rack of clothes. Most are vintage, and they remind me I haven't been back to help my dad take care of the rest of my mom's clothes. I spot a long bathrobe of beautifully patterned turquoise and burgundy silk paisley, all the swoosh marks twined around each other. My mom would have liked it. I'm overtaken by the knowledge that I'll never have a chance to buy it for her. I'll never see her model it or see her again at all. The feeling comes to me as if I never experienced it before, as if I never knew it.

After she started chemo, her hair started falling out—first in patches, then finally she just shaved the rest, which didn't look entirely awful. I'd seen a lot of people with shaved heads, and she had a pretty good head shape, so hers had some fashion potential. One day, I saw a silk scarf from Cambodia on sale at Ten Thousand Villages downtown and bought it for her. *What the heck.*

"Scarves look good with a shaved head," I told her.

She said, "That's so kind, Sweetie." I felt like a five-year-old when she called me that, but it was okay. I felt a little softer toward her that day. I could see she was sick. Her skin looked like ancient, yellowed lace that falls apart when you touch it.

When the wave of sadness breaks, I return to Ivori. "I found a robe my mom would have loved."

She looks several long seconds at me. I can see she's in heavy cogitation mode. "You don't mention her much." She pauses. "She was your mom, after all."

I search every corner of the huge basement to find Ivori something she'll love. There's one chair in a side room that is a little

ridiculous—purple and gold brocade, huge cushions, and pol-
ished, curving arms. *Mahogany,* the tag says. When I sit in it, it's so
down-pillow comfy that you could possibly forgive its appearance.
I call Ivori over and she seems to like the historical way it looks. It's
exotic. It could grow on you, like opera. When she sits in it, her eyes
spring up to meet mine and she doesn't have to say the *wow* out
loud. We both know this chair is what her mom calls a *keeper*. She
looks at the tag and it's only seventy dollars, so that's that. We pay
and arrange for them to deliver it to our house. I can't wait to show
Arwyn, even Alex. It's supposed to be for Ivori's room, but Arwyn
might finagle it for the living room. If so, we'll just come back here
again and find another treasure for Ivori. I want to show the chair
to Mrs. Ferguson, too. I imagine her big laugh.


A Council meeting is coming up, and I haven't decided whether
to go. I wonder if Bertha called Frank after our talk. Frank's thing
is to stand by the side of the road and wave at the marchers, and
I should let him, but the picture still gives me a gloomy feeling.
I haven't thought of the monarchs for a while. I am afraid they
are losing their battle. It's death again. I don't want that, and I
want Frank to step forward and stand with Bertha and have them
knit a net for me in case I lose my balance shouting out about
the land or just trying to do stats homework. Maybe Bertha can
spark his spirit. Luckily, I have Thanh at my side, and my dad is
there waiting if I ever want him. I think about my mom, how all I
have is her social security card at the back of my wallet, probably
even thinner and more fragile than the day I put it there, and her
driver's license, with a picture too lovely for a Secretary of State

to capture.

I keep having that dream where you need to go to your statistics exam and you realize you haven't attended a single class or done one minute of homework. You are beyond unprepared and certain to fail. If you're lucky, you wake up just as you're walking into the exam room to face your academic demise. The problem for me is that I can't wake from that dream because I have, in reality, blown off my statistics for the last two weeks. The stat boat sailed off without me while I was lost in thought. I should have gone to my TA's office hours like a responsible student. I didn't. I started copying onto my laptop every single thing that was written on the board as if I were a scribe. My plan, to the extent there was one, was to learn during pre-exam study days all of what I'd copied down. Do I need to tell you that I was fooling myself, or is that painfully obvious?

I guess a lot of people struggle with statistics because they have this exam retake option. So now I'm set to take that exam again. My dad isn't happy about me and school. I hope he doesn't feel a need to share his pain with the latest girlfriend. I can handle his look of distress but don't want to imagine some woman friend thinking I am a loser. Luckily, he isn't crabbing at me too insufferably because he knows I at least got my essay done and erased the "incomplete."

It's Sunday afternoon, and Thanh calls me, excited about something coming up astrologically with Jupiter. It sounds cool, but I should be working, not hanging onto the phone bathing in his delight bubbles. It turns out Alex of all people is solid on statistics. Soon I'm sitting on a chair beside his desk. I'm actually inside his inner sanctum looking at the latest revival of pizza box tower wondering if I should joke about calculating the probability that cockroach A crosses paths with cockroach B en route from the lower to the upper tier of the tower. But I need statistics help badly enough to shut my mouth and not say out loud any of my nervous dumb comments.

Alex is a patient, methodical teacher. It's hard for me but I'm giving him credit. He walks me through analysis of variance until it makes sense. It's easy-peasy. How can that be? After an hour I go back to my room. I'm not looking in the mirror but it's possible I'm glowing with relief because I understand this stuff and should be able to answer questions on an exam. I could even teach another kid what Alex taught me and become Leslie, stat instructor extraordinaire. Okay, overshooting there.

After my Monday classes, I figure I need to work on statistics again, since analysis of variance isn't the only show in town this week. Ideally, I'll get more help from Alex.

"Come in and sit down," he says after I knock. I am on the line between nervous yelping and considering this a normal room, not the den of a beast. My mind flashes to an image of the old lady murdered in *Crime and Punishment,* who could be me; or Alex, done in by rabid Leslie. I need Alex to talk me through confidence intervals. Ha, ha, because I have no faith in this situation. But he is taking his job seriously and makes sure I understand before he moves on, and I can't help but appreciate that. He is so careful that I think he is interviewing for some kind of job and almost laugh aloud remembering his awkward interview for housemate. I think he's trying out for "friend" now, and that's kind of touching.

"I've got it," I tell him. "It's not hard when it's properly explained." I give him that kudo because he deserves it. He smiles like a kid who's gotten an enormous gold star from the teacher. "You ought to be an instructor," I say, taking this whole lovefest one step further.

"I'm surprised you didn't ask Ivori," he says. "Arwyn says she's a wizard at math. Or ask your Chinese guy."

I twist my mouth about Ivori and let the stupidity about Thanh pass.

"Well, thanks for the help," I say.

"You can visit me again when you get to inference about a population proportion."

"Can't wait."

I go downstairs for a coke and Arwyn is reading at the kitchen table.

"Hey," he says, and I see the pleased curiosity in his eyes as he studies me, then nods. I know where his mind is. It's Arwyn the eternal peacemaker, delighted with me and Alex being civil.

"Yeah, well, he's helping," I say. "Statistics." I change the subject and ask, "How's it going with that new guy? Anderson, right?" Arwyn blushes a little. I don't like that he's feeling awkward. "It's *me*," I say. "You can talk."

Arwyn wipes his index finger across his lower lips three times in some kind of weird sign language. Something is coming.

"You know, next year." He pauses. "There's a house getting together, getting organized. Of queer people. All guys, I think. Not sure."

Oh, no. "You want to live there? Leave?"

He hangs his head and looks up at me. "Maybe. I'm just considering."

I feel stunned and angry. I want to say something mean, lumping him together with Ivori flying off to an HBCU, but I can't think of the words.

"Oh, honey," Arwyn says, and puts his hands out on the table where mine are. He takes one of mine in each of his. "You can visit all the time—if I do it, that is."

Visiting isn't the same. Not nearly. Now it's my turn to drop my head and try to hide my dribbly tears.

"It's alright," Arwyn says. "Really. It's all alright."

I run off to my room, but I can't run from my feelings. I feel myself spiraling down. I'm going down the road to being unloved and hopeless and furious. Unloved because there's something wrong with me, so of course it's my fault that people leave. But angry, too. Somehow, I manage to pause. To stop the river. To understand that I can't do this blaming and self-blaming anymore. I have to let Arwyn live his life and grow in whatever direction he needs. It sucks. I will hate, hate, hate it if he leaves. But no more temper tantrums. I just have to learn statistics and geology and the rest of it so I can have a future as a scientist or something like that. I can't hang around with Arwyn and my gang of dorks forever unless I want to wave goodbye to them one by one while I'm standing, like Frank, by the side of the road. I could pack up and leave right this minute and be the first one through the door. Instead, I get my stat book and review confidence intervals, which are so simple now that I can't understand why they once looked to me like Niagara Falls to the guy peering over it from inside his barrel. I won't need to beg Alex for help anymore. That will disappoint him, so maybe I'll just go into that creepy room and have a conversation with him from time to time so he doesn't get depressed. It's bad enough having one depressed person in the house, which is me, if I let myself think about Arwyn.

I've actually been thinking some about Alex, and not in the usual way. He wants to help me and I'm letting him do that. I could shut him out forever. Just hang a "jerk" sign on him that identifies him as permanently useless, a sign that never fades. But I'm letting him become someone a little better than that. Okay, it's true that I needed his help with statistics, so there was something in it for me. I haven't forgotten that part, but still. If I can do that for Alex, I should do it for myself. Let myself be a person who can go from being sort of a jerk and not the best friend or student to someone who's a better friend and decent student who knows how to love people who are sometimes fucked up but do their best.

One evening, Thanh comes by without calling. He knocks on the front door. While my eyebrows are still pinned to my forehead in surprise, Thanh takes my arm and drags me out into the pitch-dark street. I think he wants some kisses, but he points into the dark sky and says,

"Look, Les. It's Jupiter."

"That star? Wow. So brilliant." It looks like a shining pearl you could reach up and grab out of the sky to hold in your hand.

"That's right. You could stand anywhere on this earth. It's the same beauty. And you get to have it, no matter whether your essay is incomplete or who your mother was. It's there, just the same, for everyone."

I want to correct him about my essay. That's ancient history. But I get what he's saying, and I love that it was important enough for him to get in his car and run over here to share his idea and his planet with me. I give him a million kisses and leave it at that.

I pass the statistics exam with a solid C+. Not winning awards here, but good enough, and I have a transcript free of incompletes and have untangled some of those life complications I've been struggling with. Figuring out my mother is still pending. I still don't know about that freckle on the breast—whether she had one or not. If she'd left the door open and let me wander in and out, I might have known that. And other things I could have known. She shut the door though. I'm left with its blank whiteness, and I'm longing to know what is on the other side. I wonder if my dad spotted the marks my mom's body had—not the marks of sickness, but those of being herself. *Molly.* That was her name.

When she was sick and I had no choice but to look at her, I'd concentrate on detecting whether there was less of her that day than the day before. The answer was always yes. Soon she'd disappear like water evaporating off the pavement, leaving you to study the dry spot, to lay your hand there and see if you could still detect a bit of moisture. I felt guilty about the way I studied her, as if she were a biochemistry experiment. That cold part of me that gets excited by information was running the show. The rest of me was too freaked out to show up.

Ivori thinks I'm a dick sometimes but still can be my friend, and we can have dumb adventures with each other, maybe even love each other. I still want her in my life forever. She told me she's going again to that dentist. I told her I'd go with and pray for her in the waiting room. She wasn't sure God listens to fake Christians like me but seemed to appreciate the sentiment. Arwyn is on my list of worries because the boys he falls for break his heart, which is a very tender one, and now he wants to live with them. Alex, though, is coming along. He's a long-term project that needs a lot of work, but there's hope.

And Thanh. Shit. What do I say about him? He keeps trying to wrap himself tighter and tighter into the gears of my life. I push him back a little, except sometimes when we are having sex and I am all skin and flowy energy and I can't help but love him one hundred percent and kiss him a ridiculous number of times all over the place. Lately, one or two of those kisses have been creeping out of the sex-drunk universe, and I feel like quietly kissing him on the shoulder or the foot when we are sitting on the hideous brown sofa. Mostly I don't do it, but occasionally I do, and he gives me a surprised, beyond happy look.

I wonder now whether my mom is floating somewhere inside me when that feeling comes over me to kiss his sweet foot. Maybe a part of me is holding a memory of her being lovely-dovey with me like moms are with little kids, kissing every part of them, especially their tender little toes. I'd be happy to have those memories, though they'd mess me up even more about Thanh. Because what if I love him and let him be flowery with me and then he goes on a fishing boat like his relatives and the boat capsizes and he's nothing but bubbles? I don't want to think of Thanh in some faraway after-land flying around with my mom, neither one of them where I can reach them.

I'm going to keep thinking about this stuff and see if it changes me. I think the jerky parts of me are calming down a little. Happiness-wise, I'm pretty good now, but who knows, maybe I'll be happier still. Maybe for a change I'll know what I want to become and be able to tell my dad I have a major. Right now though, in this moment, I'm wondering how I got fortunate enough to have Thanh love me. And Arwyn. Maybe even Ivori, on good days. Sometimes you just luck out in life, and you don't have to pay a thing for it. It's like Jupiter. Yours for the taking. Mine.

# Acknowlegements

T hank you to all the friends and family who have helped bring this book to completion by reading and discussing portions of it, sharing thoughts about cover art and titles, and giving me pep talks when my confidence flagged. Special thanks to my small but mighty writing group, Julia Davies and Dan Greenberg, and to Nancy and Irv Leon who each took the time for a cover-to-cover read-through and discussion. Working with the Boyle & Dalton team on a second book was a great pleasure. Thank you to the publisher, Emily Hitchcock, who brings intelligence, clarity, and enthusiasm to every project, to editor extraordinaire, Heather Shaw, and to Clair Fink, who ties up all the loose ends and picks up every dropped stitch.

# About the Author

Susan Beth Miller lives in Ann Arbor, Michigan where she works as a clinical psychologist. She is the author of three novels, including Indigo Rose and A Beautiful Land, and five psychology books, including When Parents Have Problems, Shame in Context, and Emotions of Menace and Enchantment. She loves the natural world, surprising ideas, art, democracy, science, inspiriting friends, and dogs of all shapes and sizes.